Praise for *M*

"Clarke brilliantly weaves a riveting, action-packed, grisly murder mystery with a heartwarming story of loss, deliverance, and love. An inspiring tale of a man who embarks on a journey to save lives—even his own."

—Jane Edberg, author of *The Fine Art of Grieving*

"If you want something compelling to read, you have found it. Clarke transports the reader to the magic of the Appalachian Trail in this beautifully written page-turner of a tale infused with memorable characters, including a remarkable dog you will love."

—Debra Decker, Senior Adviser, Stimson Center
author of *Before the First Bomb Goes Off*
and *Advancing Accountability in Cyberspace*

"The opening scene on a university campus is almost predictable, until it introduces a criminal law professor and, by the end of the first paragraph, a double homicide. From there, Duncan Clarke weaves a tapestry of vivid detail and riveting pace, threaded with human frailty, leaving his readers breathless and unwilling to turn off the light without reaching resolution. *Murder on the Appalachian Trail* was crafted by a scholar, an outdoorsman, and a sleuth."

—Lisa Crawford Watson, author of
What We Wished For: An Adoption Story

MURDER
ON THE
APPALACHIAN
TRAIL

MURDER ON THE APPALACHIAN TRAIL

DUNCAN L. CLARKE

BELLE ISLE BOOKS
www.belleislebooks.com

Copyright © 2025 by Duncan L. Clarke

No part of this book may be reproduced in any form or by any electronic or mechanical means, or the facilitation thereof, including information storage and retrieval systems, without permission in writing from the publisher, except in the case of brief quotations published in articles and reviews. Any educational institution wishing to photocopy part or all of the work for classroom use, or individual researchers who would like to obtain permission to reprint the work for educational purposes, should contact the publisher.

ISBN (Paperback): 978-1-962416-80-1
ISBN (Hardcover): 978-1-962416-92-4
ISBN (eBook): 978-1-962416-81-8
Library of Congress Control Number: 2024924414

Designed by Sami Langston
Project managed by Robert Pruett

Published by
Belle Isle Books (an imprint of Brandylane Publishers, Inc.)
5 S. 1st Street
Richmond, Virginia 23219

BELLE ISLE BOOKS
www.belleislebooks.com

belleislebooks.com | brandylanepublishers.com

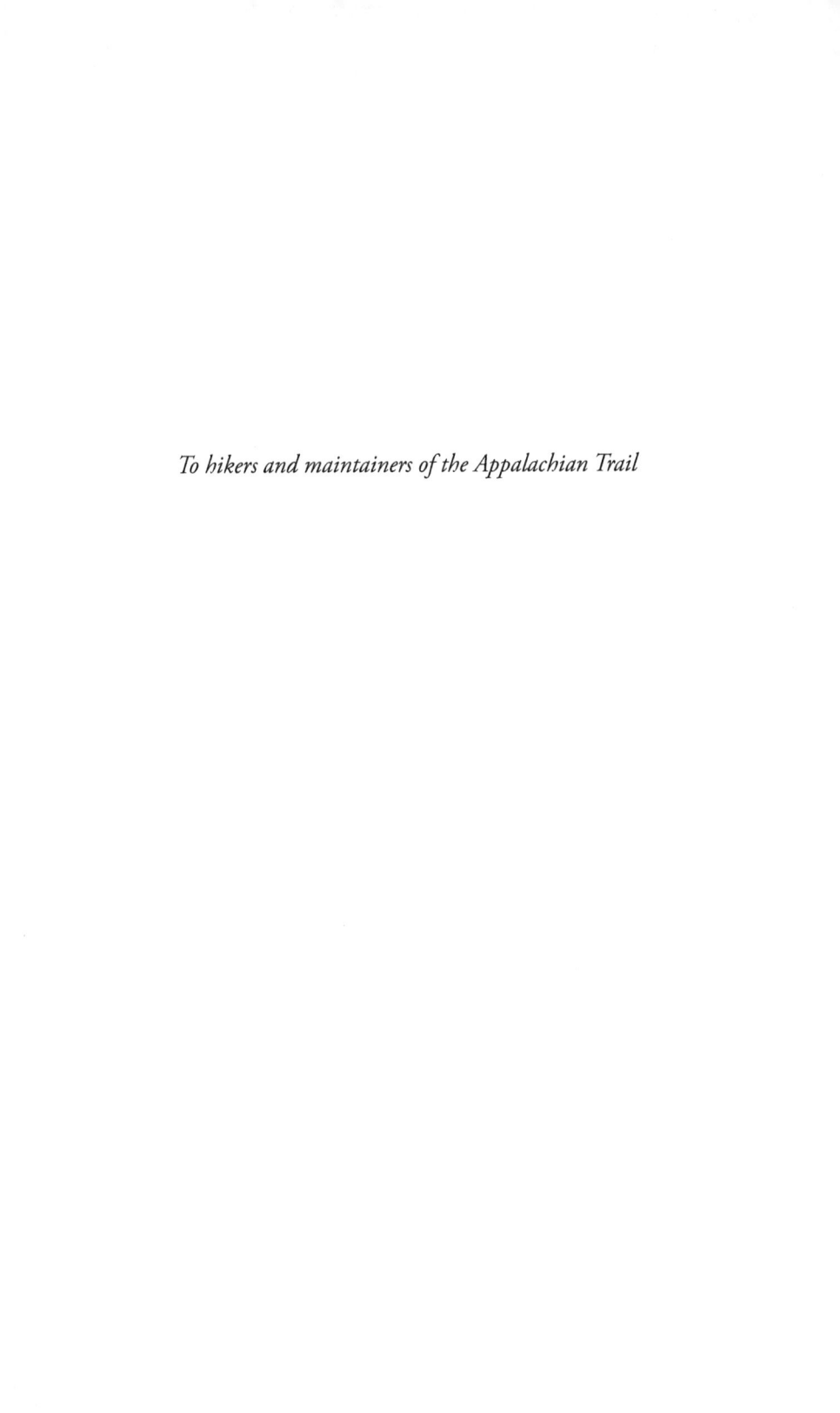

To hikers and maintainers of the Appalachian Trail

Contents

Disclaimer	1
Acknowledgements	3
Chapter 1: Another Couple Murdered	5
Chapter 2: Harpers Ferry	10
Chapter 3: Duncannon	17
Chapter 4: Clary Shelter	23
Chapter 5: Willow	29
Chapter 6: Twosome	35
Chapter 7: Walking with Willow — Day 1	40
Chapter 8: Affinity	51
Chapter 9: Train	55
Chapter 10: Port Clinton	61
Chapter 11: Log Messages	70
Chapter 12: Snakes	77
Chapter 13: Dust-Up	81
Chapter 14: Holy Spirit Moments	89
Chapter 15: Parting	92
Chapter 16: Lev Komaroff	99
Chapter 17: Grace	104
Chapter 18: Moving On	112
Chapter 19: Love Again	120
Chapter 20: The Calls	128
Chapter 21: The Meeting	134
Chapter 22: Henry Dubois	145
Chapter 23: Monson	151
Chapter 24: Wilderness	161
Chapter 25: Mountains	171
Chapter 26: Intelligence	181
Chapter 27: White Cap	186
Chapter 28: Attacked	194
Chapter 29: Closing In	201
Chapter 30: Swamp Search	207
Chapter 31: Found	211
Chapter 32: The Cliff	220
Chapter 33: Dearly Beloved	225
About the Author	229

Any references to real people, living or dead, locations, entities, or events are either the products of the author's imagination or are used fictitiously. This book is presented as a work of fiction.

ACKNOWLEDGEMENTS

Special thanks to three strong and talented women. My lovely wife, law professor Ann H. Clarke, read every line. Jane Edberg's sharp eye and careful editing is evident throughout. The insights of Heather Lazare proved invaluable.

I am indebted to Jerry Elprin, A. Gustav Konheim, Tom de Marco, Todd Masse, Gordon May, Bill Rosolowsky, and an anonymous reader for their critical commentaries and professional expertise.

CHAPTER 1
ANOTHER COUPLE MURDERED

Dell Peterson had just adjourned his morning criminal law class when a student, an avid hiker, rushed toward him holding a copy of the *Washington Post*. The student pointed to a headline and read it out loud: "Another Couple Murdered on Appalachian Trail."

"Professor Peterson, have you seen this story in today's *Post*?"

Dell reached down to retrieve his briefcase and stepped away from the podium.

"No." He scanned the story—"Pennsylvania state police officer Stanley McGraw said, 'the homicides were the most brutal I've seen in thirty years on the force.'" Dazed and nauseated, Dell handed the newspaper back to the student and hurried from the lecture room into the hallway, tripped over his feet, and sent his briefcase spinning across the floor. Another student scooped it up and handed it to him.

"You okay, professor?"

"Yes, yes. Thank you," he replied.

Dell took a deep breath and rushed to the faculty mailroom to collect his mail before leaving campus. A pink memo from the dean's office was taped over his box: "Professor Peterson—Call Brad Hornbeck. URGENT." Instead of heading home, Dell sprinted upstairs to his office to return the call.

Brad had contacted him last summer about a rare and vicious murder of a couple on the Appalachian Trail (known to hikers as the A.T.) in Virginia's Mount Rogers National Recreation Area. Back then, Brad wanted Dell's active involvement in that unsolved case. But Dell begged off as he was caring for his wife, Patricia, who had end stage ovarian cancer. She died three months later.

"Apologize old buddy, for calling you at the university," Brad said. "This past year has been hard on you." He paused, sighed. "It's been a while since we talked. I hate—really hate—to tell you this, but there's been another murder."

Dell had been close friends with Bradley Livingston Hornbeck since they were in fifth grade. Brad headed the organization that oversaw and coordinated the maintenance of the A.T., the Appalachian Trail Conference. Largely because of Brad's support, but also because of Dell's pro bono legal work for the ATC and his firsthand knowledge of the trail, Dell was a member of the Conference's advisory board.

"Yeah, I saw today's *Post*," Dell said. "It sickens me."

Brad said, "Pennsylvania state police called. It happened at the Clary Shelter outside of Duncannon on a ridge a few miles east of the Susquehanna. Young couple. Horrific. Police said the woman was so brutalized that . . . Well, it was appalling."

With these two recent Pennsylvania homicides and the two in Virginia last August, four hikers had died violently on the A.T. in less than a year. Brad was alarmed. Hiker safety was his top priority. Dell knew how extraordinary these murders were because hikers rightly saw the trail as a safe haven from a sometimes-violent world. A.T. hikers were more likely to encounter the Easter Bunny than a murderer.

"I'd like to see you up here in Harper's Ferry tomorrow," Brad said. "Both Pennsylvania State Police and the FBI will be here. Your trail savvy and legal expertise will be helpful to them and invaluable to me."

Dell's heart told him that Patricia wanted him back on the trail. The A.T. had always been their refuge, but he hadn't hiked on the trail since she passed. He could almost hear her say, "Now, sweetheart, do it! The trail is calling." Dell rubbed his eyes. He would not refuse Brad.

"I can be there by noon," he said, leaning back in his chair.

"I knew I could count on you. To be honest, people will avoid the trail if they think it's unsafe," Brad said. "I'm scared shitless."

"Brad, you know better than anyone that the A.T. *is* my family, especially now with Patricia gone and my daughters grown. I'd love to get the bastard who did this. See you tomorrow."

Dell hung up the phone. He wondered whether a fifty-two-

CHAPTER 1: ANOTHER COUPLE MURDERED

year-old could still handle the rigors of the trail, but quickly dismissed the thought. Reaching for his briefcase, he heard a knock on the door, and it opened.

A smiling woman leaned in the doorway. She swept hair from her face, revealing her springtime-green eyes. "Well, hi there, stranger."

Dell gave her a sheepish smile.

"I was doing some research in the law library today and thought I'd stop by to see if you might be in." She wagged a finger at Dell. "You haven't returned my calls."

Respected family law attorney Grace Lombardi had been Dell's former law student before she graduated about thirteen years ago. She had since married and divorced. Grace and Patricia were best friends. Dell knew her well. He stood up and gave her a hug.

"I plead guilty as charged, your honor. Sorry. Afraid I haven't been adjusting too well."

"I've got to run downtown for a pre-trial hearing," Grace said. "But you're forgiven only if you promise to call me tonight."

"Deal."

Grace kissed him on the cheek, turned, and dashed out of his office.

Hmmm. Dell touched his cheek, grinned, and rubbed his chin.

* * *

That evening, Dell sat alone at his dining room table as he had for every one of the one hundred and seventy-seven nights since Patricia's death. It was the same walnut table on which an eight-year-old Dell had once carved his initials—an act that earned him a sound thrashing. The same table where his children sat for meals and homework. The one he shared with his wife all twenty-five years of their marriage.

Most of the bulbs in the overhead chandelier had burned out since Patricia's death, but Dell hadn't bothered to replace them. The smell of half-eaten, charred hamburger hung in the air. He lingered in the faint light, rocking back and forth on a wobbly, oft-repaired mahogany chair with a glass of Jim Beam and staring at a small cedar box on the table. Not a fancy bronze urn. It was rough cut and unfinished, like life without Patricia. His future with her reduced to ashes in a box.

Through a window, Dell noticed daffodils blooming in his backyard, but until today, he'd had only a vague awareness that spring had dislodged winter. Tara, his five-year-old German shepherd, eased her head onto his lap. Her brown eyes met his, and he stroked her head. "Yes girl, you miss her, too." He wondered why dogs always seemed to know when their people were hurting.

Dell downed what remained of the bourbon, got up slowly from the table, and walked into the bathroom. He felt disconnected from the guy in the mirror brushing his teeth who stared back at him. Salt and pepper hair covered his ears but not the receding hairline. The bridge of his nose jogged to the right, which called up a memory of his four years of college wrestling. He was a long way from that level of fitness, but he was in reasonably good shape, despite the love handles. A shade over six feet, still pretty lean and muscular. Dell shook his head and said, "Not so bad." He glanced at the clock. *Too late to call Grace tonight. Maybe tomorrow morning.*

Tara trotted behind Dell as he made his way into the bedroom. He lifted the framed photograph of Patricia off the nightstand and sat on the edge of the bed staring at it. Dell recalled the blizzard of pink and white rhododendron blossoms the day they were married outdoors at Maryland's Old South Mountain Inn, just steps away from the A.T. He thought of their honeymoon and remembered how a downpour in a thunderstorm had almost washed them off the trail as they began backpacking north from the southern terminus of the A.T. on Springer Mountain, Georgia. And for the thousandth time, he swallowed hard remembering their victory kiss atop the summit of Mt. Katahdin, Maine, a 2,200-mile trek that took five months.

Sleep had not come easy these past seven months without Patricia beside him. The bourbon probably didn't help either. After Patricia died, the dean of the law school told Dell to take whatever time off he needed. But Dell continued to teach his usual courses in criminal law and criminal procedure in the spring semester. He knew the time would pass quickly and, beginning with the summer break, he'd be on sabbatical for the academic year—1991-1992. The possibility of getting back on the A.T. offered a glimmer of excitement. For the first time since Patricia's death, and despite the risk, Dell looked forward to his time off to do something meaningful.

CHAPTER 1: ANOTHER COUPLE MURDERED

He crawled into bed and slept more soundly than he had in months. The next morning, Dell woke to the foul smell of dog breath, Tara's muzzle in his face. He pushed the dog away, let her out, and fed her. Popping an English muffin into the toaster, and leaning his elbows on the counter, he dialed Grace's number.

"Hi there," Dell said. "Glad you stopped by the office yesterday. It's been a while."

"Good to hear your voice, *finally*," Grace said.

"Guess I've been pretty negligent. Sorry about that, but just minutes before you stopped by my office I received some news, and you might be the only one I can confide in."

Grace went quiet for a few seconds, mulling this over, before she replied, "What a nice thing to say. You can always confide in me. So, professor, what's the important news?"

Dell drew in a long breath and said, "The ATC has asked for my assistance concerning the recent murders on the Pennsylvania A.T. I'm leaving for Harpers Ferry in a couple of hours."

"Good grief. I saw the article in the *Post* about those murders. Scary. Hope you're not getting too involved."

"It's only a meeting."

"Dell, listen. Why don't you keep off the damn trail for now? Leave that to the cops. We've lost Patricia. I don't want to lose you, too."

She cares about me. "Right," he said, as he tossed a treat to Tara.

"Be sure to call me after the meeting," Grace said, making it sound like an order.

"Sure," Dell replied.

Then Patricia came to mind. For some reason, he recalled how her fingers would caress his neck when they kissed.

But maybe not, he thought to himself.

CHAPTER 2

HARPERS FERRY

Dell arrived a few minutes after noon at the ATC headquarters, a white, two-story building on Washington Street in Harpers Ferry, West Virginia. He was met at the front door by Brad's chief of staff, Cherie Nardone. "Everyone's here, Dell. We've been waiting for you," she said with a welcoming smile.

Cherie was in her late thirties with shoulder-length blonde hair. Her hands were on everything of consequence to the organization—fundraising, trail maintenance, membership, publications, and Brad.

Dell kissed her lightly on the cheek and followed her across a large room to the pine-paneled office he had been in many times. Brad—about Dell's height but jowly and heavier—glanced at his watch. "You're late, man," Brad said, then laughed and waved Dell into his office.

Brad stood next to a gray-haired state police officer in a pressed uniform and a thirty-something guy with a crew cut and a tight-fitting blue suit. The police officer gave Dell a penetrating but cordial look. "Sergeant Clayton Ward, sir. Pennsylvania state police. Drove down from Harrisburg this morning. Mr. Hornbeck tells me you walk on water, that nobody knows the trail better than Dell Peterson."

Dell cleared his throat and glanced at Brad. "Since we were kids, Hornbeck has had a habit of exaggerating things, whether it's the number of bass he caught in the Potomac, his IQ, or the size of his pecker."

This earned Dell a not so playful punch in the shoulder from the ATC president who probably felt that their tone should be one of greater solemnity. Rightly admonished, Dell kept his mouth shut as Brad, hands on his hips, said, "Look, I'm not exaggerating at all. Peterson and his late wife, Patricia, completed the entire trail from Springer to Katahdin for a third time three years ago in less than four months. Not bad for a couple in their forties."

Sgt. Ward nodded. "Impressive."

Blue suit flashed his badge and spoke up. "Mr. Peterson, I'm Tony Scaperelli, FBI. Mr. Hornbeck here's been chewing my ear off on how you're the master of this trail."

"Master is right," Brad said. "Dell and Patricia also section-hiked it with two young daughters and their dog, Tara, a highly trained search-and-rescue dog who knows the trail better than he does. Smartest dog I've ever seen."

Scaperelli grimaced, moved closer, pointed his finger into Dell's face, and said, "I'm pretty sure I remember you. Didn't you represent that cop killer, Morrison, a few years back."

Surprised, Dell wrinkled his forehead. *What's this all about?* He'd never met Scaperelli or heard anything about him. All of Dell's prior interactions with the Bureau had been cordial, or at least professional, and several of his former students were FBI agents. Dell had defended Johnnie Morrison in 1986 in the D.C. Superior Court. The jury found him not guilty, and rightly so. Dell's immediate instinct was to tell Scaperelli to fuck off but, instead, Dell stared at him with a satisfied smile and replied, "Yes."

Brad saw the friction, and his face tightened. "Everyone please take a seat."

Cherie closed the door and the five of them sat down around an oak table. On the wall was an A.T. poster of the Great Smoky Mountains with the words, "The journey is the destination."

Still puzzled by Scaperelli's confrontational behavior, Dell sat up in his seat and continued to look directly at him before speaking—"I'm not surprised the feds are involved. The Virginia incident was on federal land; it could well be an interstate crime. And doesn't the Bureau often pursue suspected serial killers?"

Scaperelli looked up. "Well, we're . . ."

Brad interrupted him and waved his arm toward Dell. "Professor Peterson's here because he's an experienced criminal lawyer who serves on our advisory board."

"Yeah," Scaperelli scoffed, glancing at his watch.

Brad's eyebrows shot up as if launched from his forehead. They descended slowly as his eyes narrowed. "And, because Dell Peterson knows *every* inch of the trail."

Scaperelli shrugged and rolled his eyes.

Brad clasped his hands together so tightly that Dell could see his knuckles had gone white. He turned toward Scaperelli. "Tony, you have a problem?"

Scaperelli again twisted his mouth into a grimace. "Maybe." He pointed a finger at Dell. "I haven't forgotten about that bastard, Morrison."

Brad glanced at Sgt. Ward, drummed his fingernails on the table, and looked over at Dell. He paused, then stared at Scaperelli. With a forced smile, he said, "Let's get back on track. Dell and his dog have conducted successful searches for lost hikers and missing people." Brad paused for a moment. "Tara's nose doesn't miss much." And, he added with a grin—still looking at Scaperelli—"she's an infallible judge of character."

Scaperelli's expression softened. "Interesting. What kind of a dog?"

"German shepherd," Dell replied.

Scaperelli said, "I have one, too." He leaned back in his chair and gave out a muffled harrumph. "Okay. Mr. Hornbeck signed a confidentiality agreement earlier this morning." Scaperelli pointed at Dell and Cherie. "You two also must agree in writing not to divulge any information we might provide. What's been reported in the press is incomplete and inaccurate."

"Of course." Cherie said, signing the form Scaperelli handed to her.

Dell had seen many nondisclosure forms, but he took a few minutes to read this one before signing.

Scaperelli turned to Dell again. "What we're about to reveal explains why the FBI is involved and, yes, the Bureau is often active when there is a suspected interstate serial killer."

In both the Pennsylvania and Virginia cases, Scaperelli and Sgt. Ward explained, the victims were couples sleeping at night in one of the many three-sided shelters found along the length of the A.T. No other hikers were apparently present at either of the shelters. They speculated that the murderer almost certainly arrived after the couples were asleep. The weapon used in each case was a knife. The men were killed first, stabbed multiple times.

Because the women's bodies were found eighty or ninety feet from the shelter and, in both instances, there were clear signs of a struggle, the female victims probably either ran or were dragged from the shelters before they died.

Brad held up his hand. "Wait a minute, Tony." He leaned over to Cherie who was sitting beside him and said, "Are you *sure* you want to hear this. It is unspeakably grotesque."

She looked at him. "I'm good."

Brad's ears reddened as he rested his hand on the table and sighed. "What happened to these two women was bestial."

"No need to shelter me. Facts are facts," Cherie said.

Brad clenched his jaw. "Go ahead, Tony."

Scaperelli glanced at Cherie and Brad and shifted uneasily in his chair before continuing. "The women's bodies were desecrated, hatefully so. Faces and scalps were slashed to the bone, and in each instance one breast was sliced off entirely."

Cherie gasped. "Jeez."

"Good God," Dell said.

"No semen was present," Scaperelli said. "We have a psychopath on our hands, someone who hates women and takes pleasure in killing them."

"There are other commonalities between the Virginia and Pennsylvania cases," Brad said. He emphasized how both shelters were close to roads, which made them accessible to anyone. "So, the murderer may or may not have been a hiker. In fact, almost all of the very few homicides on the A.T. since its completion in 1937 have been committed by non-hikers."

Dell nodded in agreement.

"Also," Scaperelli said, crossing his arms across his chest, "the murderer cut off the left ear of each of the male victims. It's the *same* sonofabitch in both instances."

"Certainly looks that way," Dell said.

"And," Sgt. Ward chimed in, "Virginia authorities told us something else about their male victim. His ear was found on the shelter's floor near a scrap of brown paper with 'PA' scribbled on it in blood. We think this might refer to Pennsylvania." He placed his hands on the table, palms down.

Dell bent forward, glanced at Sgt. Ward and Scaperelli, and said, "I'm impressed with what you've learned so far."

Ward smiled. Scaperelli gave Dell a blank stare as he leaned back in his chair, hands clasped behind his head. Top dog status had been established, at least in Scaperelli's mind.

Dell asked, "Blood types? Fingerprints? Any scrawled notes from the Pennsylvania shelter? Other evidence?"

"All blood samples appear to be from the two couples," said Sgt. Ward. "No useful fingerprints in Virginia. Results from my state are thus far inconclusive. We haven't found any other evidence."

The Pennsylvania murders had widespread coverage in the press, and the ATC had alerted all of its chapters about the homicides. Beyond this, Brad and Dell knew that the informal and astonishingly rapid word-of-mouth communications system among A.T. hikers—Paul Reveres in boots—had likely already spread word of the murders throughout the Pennsylvania section of the trail.

The four men agreed Tony Scaperelli would be the group's principal contact person for the exchange of information. Sgt. Ward was the key liaison in the Keystone State.

Scaperelli revealed that an FBI profiler had already surmised that the killer was shrewd enough to know that everyone would be looking for him on the A.T., and everyone around the table agreed he was likely off the trail, possibly headed for the northeast.

"After the August 1990 murders," Scaperelli said, furrowing his brow, "Virginia police concluded that he'd left the trail immediately. This guy is cautious and calculating."

"There's a more compelling reason why he'd leave the trail," Dell said, glancing at Scaperelli and Brad. "My guess is that the murderer *knew* that most of the Pennsylvania section of the A.T. north of the Susquehanna follows exposed rocky ridgelines without much dense forest into which to flee. If so, he would have known that it was unsafe to remain on the trail because most of these ridges could be surveilled by air."

Scaperelli slapped his hand on the table. "Good point!"

Everyone had already exchanged contact information and Scaperelli soon left the building to return to D.C.

Sgt. Ward came up to Dell and said, "If you decide to visit the Clary Shelter, and I sure hope you will, please bring your dog. She could be helpful. I'll let them know you may be coming. The forensics guys should be finished in a day or two. The shelter is off-limits to the public, but I'll see that you have access."

CHAPTER 2: HARPERS FERRY

"Thanks, Sergeant," Dell said. "Where I go, Tara goes."

"What about carrying?" Sgt. Ward asked. "I can make it happen."

Before Dell was married, he had done some duck hunting and target shooting, but Patricia was emphatic, *"Bring a gun into our house and I leave."* Out went his shotgun and pistol.

"No thanks, Sergeant." Dell replied, "If I do go to Pennsylvania, don't think I'll be carrying."

"Hope you're making the right decision, Mr. Peterson. Let me know if you change your mind." With that, Sgt. Ward went out the door and left for Harrisburg.

Brad, who'd been standing next to Dell listening to his conversation with Ward, patted Dell's shoulder and cleared his throat. "I hate, really hate to ask you this. You've been through so much . . ."

"What's up?" Dell asked.

"I really would appreciate it if you could take a look around the Clary Shelter. We'll be tearing it down soon. You know the area, and it's an easy day's drive from your house in D.C. An experienced hiker might see things the cops missed."

"Sure thing," Dell said as he put his hand on Brad's back. "You pay me so much, how could I refuse?"

Brad chuckled.

Dell reassured Brad. "I'll be in Duncannon in forty-eight hours."

* * *

Spring semester at the university had ended and Dell was now officially on sabbatical leave. Daughter Amanda was married and living outside of Boston. His other daughter, Joanna, was nearby, but she had her own life. *I'm free! Getting back on the A.T. sure beats sitting alone sipping bourbon, and Tara will love the adventure.*

Before getting into his Jeep to return to Washington, Dell looked back and stared at the ATC building. *How fitting to be here.* He knew that long-distance hikers considered Harpers Ferry, located at the confluence of the Shenandoah and Potomac Rivers, to be the "psychological midpoint" of the A.T.—a clear geographical demarcation between southern and mid-Atlantic states. What some younger hikers might not have known was that the town also symbolized a historical demarcation between north and south because the ATC headquarters sat on the exact spot where federal troops, led by Colonel Robert E. Lee, subdued the fiery abolitionist John Brown in 1859, seventeen months before the outbreak of the Civil War.

The midafternoon sun glinted off the river as Dell drove his Jeep over the Potomac River Highway Bridge into Maryland. He was at ease and contented, sensations he hadn't felt since Patricia's death. He was thrilled to pursue what he believed was the core mission of the ATC—to preserve and protect the sanctity of the trail. *The A.T. is hallowed ground.* The trail was Dell's place of worship. For him, the scent of Virginia's wild azaleas was incense, the rush of wind through New Hampshire's tall pines was an organ prelude, the quiet of Maine's deep forests was prayer, and the restorative power of a Carolina mountain spring was communion with God.

CHAPTER 3
DUNCANNON

Nobody likes to thru-hike the A.T. from the Susquehanna River north to the New Jersey line. This 144-mile stretch of winding rocky ridges destroys knees and sprains ankles. Boots go here to die, and rattlesnakes are more common than reliable water sources.

For the past two and a half years, the demands of full-time teaching and caring for Patricia, followed by the trauma of her death, had ruled out serious hiking for Dell. He knew he was rusty. But Dell was anxious to get out on the trail to help catch the SOB who killed those hikers in Virginia and Pennsylvania. Most of all, he wanted to live again, to regain a sense of purpose.

Unsure of how long he might remain on the trail after visiting the murder site at the Clary Shelter, Dell inventoried his hiking gear and spread it across his living room floor and sofa: the boots Patricia had given him for this birthday, four pairs of wool socks and clothing, toiletries, his tent and fly which had a whiff of mold, his sleeping bag which he sniffed and fluffed, slightly torn ground mat, rain coat, rain hat and baseball cap, frayed Pennsylvania A.T. trail maps, hiking sticks, mini stove, aluminum cooking pot and Sierra cup, a fuel canister which he shook, bug repellant, and head lamp and flash light with extra batteries. He crammed all of this, plus rations for Tara and ten-days of freeze-dried food and snacks into his backpack. Knowing the Pennsylvania trail well, Dell added plenty of moleskins for blisters and a third canteen as insurance against infrequent and unreliable sources of water. His pack weighed in at just under forty pounds, a shade heavier than usual.

Dell didn't want to alarm his daughters or the dean, so he lied. "I'll be hiking for a while in North Carolina," he told them. Dell knew Brad would cover for him, so he gave them Hornbeck's number at ATC headquarters if they needed to contact him.

The A.T. passed through only a few towns, and Duncannon, Pennsylvania, was one of them—what hikers called a trail town. Duncannon was small-town America located at the base of the Appalachians on the west bank of the Susquehanna River. The simple two- and three-story frame buildings lining both sides of North Market Street looked almost as tired as the hikers who trudged between them. Some had peeling paint, and most flew American flags in anticipation of Memorial Day.

The working-class community of 1,600 residents generally embraced the A.T. as good for business. The owner of the laundromat was especially welcoming, with every hiker hauling a pack full of damp smelly clothes. The cobbler repaired tattered boots and worn-out soles, and the pastors of five churches stood ready and willing to repair hikers' souls. Duncannon's hospitality was treasured by every hiker who sought a respite from the trials of the trail.

Dell noticed that nothing had changed since his last visit three years ago. After driving three and a half hours from Washington, D.C., to Duncannon, Dell pulled his dented, rust-spotted Jeep in front of The Doyle Hotel. Outside, he inhaled the spring breeze coming off the river as he admired the four-story brick building, with its wrap-around second-story wood porch. The early nineteenth century structure, well-known and well-loved by hikers, became The Doyle in 1944 when a young Jamie Doyle purchased it, reportedly after winning $444,444.44 in the Irish lottery. He made it his place of business as well as his home.

Like the town, the hotel looked as though it had seen better times. Its wide-board oak floors were worn smooth by the thousands of hikers who had passed through its doors, which were often left open as a welcome. The porch sagged, and it was anyone's guess when the building had last been painted. But it was a life-well-lived kind of aging. The place pulsed with an aura of the reciprocal gratitude by the hikers for the comforts of the hotel, and by The Doyle itself for the streams of hikers whose patronage kept it alive.

Bare bones. No concierge service here—or blow dryers, plastic shampoo bottles, or daintily wrapped chocolates on the pillows.

CHAPTER 3: DUNCANNON

And that's how hikers liked it. With its time-worn dark wood panels and classic, well-stocked Irish pub, The Doyle was where hikers schmoozed with one another and reveled in the hot showers, cold beer, comfort food, and clean sheets, all at a reasonable price.

Inside, Dell made his way to the reception desk. Jamie Doyle, who spoke perfect American English but would sometimes lapse unconsciously into an Irish accent, was pushing eighty. Jaime brushed aside his untamed mane of white hair and, grinning from ear-to-ear, greeted Dell with his usual exuberance. He put down his gnarled Celtic cane, "me shillelagh," he called it, and grabbed both of Dell's hands so firmly that Dell's knuckles cracked.

"Your grip hasn't weakened in the slightest," Dell said.

"Where's that dog of yours?" Jamie asked. "Go get her. Tara's always welcome here. She smells a helluva lot better than most long-distance hikers."

Dell whistled, and Tara bounded out of the Jeep's rolled down rear window, bolted through the hotel's open double doors, and immediately found Jamie. One sniff and she was all wiggles and wags.

"I missed you, too, sweetheart," Jamie said.

Jaime walked over to the bar and reached under the counter for a piece of beef jerky. Tara snatched it from his hand and swallowed it whole. He bent down to pet her and was slathered with dog kisses.

"Bet it's the Clary Shelter that brings you to Duncannon."

Dell nodded. "Yup."

"A state trooper was here yesterday. Another cop came this morning," Jaime said as he retrieved a couple of frosty beer mugs from the fridge and motioned to Dell to sit down with him on one the pub's sticky bar stools. "Why don't you have a pint of Guinness with me?"

Jamie couldn't recall the names of the two officers, but he gave a pretty accurate description of Tony Scaperelli and Sgt. Ward. "The cops went through my sign-in book and asked what I remembered about the guests."

"Did the police indicate a particular interest in any of them?"

"No. They only asked questions. The guy in a tight-fitting blue suit treated me like a suspect. Pissed me off. The state trooper was nicer."

"That sounds about right. *I* sure don't want to piss off an old friend, but would you mind if I asked some questions?"

"Not at all. Those guys don't know shit about the trail. You do. Oh, I . . . heard about your Patricia. She was so charming. Still remember that peach pie she baked for me in the kitchen last time you two were here. I'm really sorry." Jamie hung his head and said, "I lit a candle for her at St. Bernadette's."

"That's very kind of you." Dell went silent, looked away, then chugged down half his beer. He was brought back to earth when Tara pressed against his legs. "Do you remember a man who might have seemed a bit out of place?" Dell asked. "Someone who didn't resemble a typical hiker?"

Jamie inhaled deeply, then tossed Tara another piece of jerky. "You've turned on your lawyer face."

Dell smiled. "He probably would have been alone and kept some distance from others."

"Well, let's see . . ." Another, longer, pause as Jaime took a swig of beer.

"I wonder if this guy paid in cash and was hesitant to show any type of identification?"

Jamie swigged more beer. His fingers burrowed into the wilderness that was his hair.

"Well, you know, I get lots of folks in here who aren't hikers. Kayakers, photographers, birders, whatever."

"Sure."

"There was one fella I told the cops about." Jaime squeezed his chin. "Clearly not a hiker. Quiet guy. Polite. Older than the usual teens and twenty-somethings I always see. Forty-five, fifty, or so."

"What about him?"

Jamie squinted and scratched his jaw. "Can't really recall what he looked like, except that he was more than a tad overweight. He had a small day pack. He wore a pair of mud-caked L.L. Bean boots, the kind with leather tops rising about ten inches above the rubber bottoms. That's why I remember him; no serious hiker would hit the trail in those Bean boots."

"Certainly not in Pennsylvania." Dell pulled a pen and small notepad from his pocket, jotted down some notes.

"Said he was going to run on the trail, but those were no running shoes." Jamie huffed and put his mug of Guinness down on the bar. "Didn't look like a runner neither, too heavy. And most runners avoid the rocky ridges around here." He drained the last drop. "Oh, he did ask me about parking by the trailhead on the east side of the river."

"Well, that's interesting," Dell said, as he scribbled more notes. He looked back at Jaime. "Anything else?"

Before Jamie could answer, Dell turned toward the hotel's lobby. He'd smelled them before he saw them. A couple in their early twenties had walked in and dropped their packs and hiking sticks on the floor. Obviously enamored with one another, they sidled over to where Dell and Jamie were sitting and waited for Jamie to notice them. The young man held his partner's hand while conveying a sense of urgency. He cleared his throat.

"Uh, uh, Mr. Doyle?"

Jamie gripped his cane and slid off the bar stool. "That's me, my friend. What can I do for you?"

"We need a bed, I mean room. With a shower," the young man said.

Jamie checked them in. They grabbed their packs, vanished around a corner, and we heard them clomp up the stairs giggling.

Jamie flashed a toothy smile and sat back down on his bar stool. "Get couples like that all the time. Now, where were we?"

"That quiet, polite guy with the Bean boots."

"Oh, yes. He did, in fact, sit by himself and, as I told the police, there was something else. He ordered a beer, and when I asked for his ID, as I always do, he hesitated. He showed me a Maine driver's license but insisted on holding it in his hand. I could read the birth date, which I can't recall, but he made every effort to cover his name and address with his thumb."

Dell bent toward Jamie, hands on his knees. "And?"

"He signed in only as 'Mark Paulson, Virginia,' which didn't jibe with the Maine driver's license. He paid in cash." Jaime pursed his lips.

"Ha!" Dell said. "The guy paid in cash, refused to show identification, and asked about parking at the trailhead. Eureka!" Dell held his hand up for a high five and he and Jaime slapped hands with a loud smack. Tara saw this and rolled onto her back, all four legs flailing in the air, tongue lolling out.

"You can stay here with me anytime," Jamie said, and rubbed her belly.

"Mark Paulson, probably a pseudonym, wouldn't have spent much time on the trail with only a day pack," Dell said, squeezing his hands together, prayer-like, and resting his chin on his fingertips. He stared up at the pressed tin ceiling. "But he could have parked at the trailhead, walked up to the nearby Clary Shelter, killed the couple, and returned to his car." *His car! Hikers with cars who stay at The Doyle usually leave them at or near the hotel to avoid the vandalism that is common at the trailhead.* "Did he leave his car at the hotel?"

"No. I don't recall ever seeing either his car or him in a car."

Dell was pretty sure someone who had just committed a horrific crime would want his getaway car to be right at the trailhead. No murderer would expose himself by walking about a mile from the trailhead along well-traveled roads to return to the hotel parking lot.

"One more question, Jamie. Did you tell all of this to the police officers?"

"Maybe not. You ask better questions and know more about hiking. And I feel a lot more comfortable chatting with you than with the fuzz."

Dell walked up the stairs to his room, took off his shirt, and pulled back the bedsheets. He thought about calling Grace. After all, she had asked him to call. *She's bright and beautiful, divorced, we get along, and it wouldn't hurt to just chat about what I learned from Jamie.* But he recalled the night he and Patricia had spent at The Doyle, their joy of being together. Dell chickened out.

Instead, he called Brad to relay what Jamie had told him. Brad said he hadn't heard anything from either Sgt. Ward or Scaperelli, but he assured Dell that he'd call them right away with this new information. Brad added, "I'm putting our Maine A.T. chapter on high alert. Sure hope the killer is not up there. Too many places to hide."

"You're right," Dell said. "Tara and I will push off in the morning. We should get to the Clary Shelter in a couple of hours. I'll be out of touch for a while."

"Be careful, buddy. Glad Tara's with you."

CHAPTER 4
CLARY SHELTER

Despite the risk, Dell was itching to get back on the trail after a long absence. The Doyle Hotel was less than four miles from the Clary Shelter, so he anticipated an easy tune-up hike. After breakfast, he left his Jeep at the hotel, strapped on his well-worn Gregory pack, and walked with Tara through town, past the Assembly of God church with its "Hiker's Welcome" sign, and onto a pedestrian sidewalk that took him over Clark's Ferry Bridge. The busy four-lane bridge spanned a shallow, almost three-hundred-foot wide, Susquehanna River which was very near the geographic midpoint of the A.T. Once over the bridge on this overcast day, Tara and Dell followed the A.T.'s familiar blazes—white painted vertical rectangles—across railroad tracks to the trailhead, where two unoccupied vehicles were parked—a Pennsylvania state police van and a squad car from the Dauphin County sheriff's department.

Yellow CRIME SCENE tape stretched across the A.T. and flapped four feet off the ground. Posted in the dead center of the trail was a three-foot-by-three-foot white sign with bold black lettering that no one could miss.

WARNING! CRIME SCENE

The Clary Shelter is closed and off-limits to the public. Violators will be prosecuted. Hikers are strongly advised NOT to hike between this point and the Delaware River. Proceed beyond this point at your own risk. To report concerns or suspicious people, and for current information call 717-783-5500.

Pennsylvania State Police
Pennsylvania Game Commission
ATC Mid-Atlantic Office

While hoping to deter hikers, the ATC and police were well-aware that they could not seal off the A.T. in any meaningful sense. Many younger long-distance hikers who'd struggled for a thousand miles all the way from Georgia would disregard any attempted closure of the trail. And numerous side trails, highways, and old lumber and mining roads afforded easy access for hikers, hunters, and others, including murderers. The sign served only as a warning.

Dell and Tara ducked under the tape and hiked up a modest incline through a mixed hardwood forest. Below, he could see the roiling moss-green Susquehanna, the rooftops of Duncannon's houses, and the spires of its churches. The sky was gray and turning grayer. Distant thunder rolled through the mountains and Dell smelled rain. Within an hour, he and Tara reached the rocky outcroppings of a 1,200-foot-high ridge leading to the Clary Shelter.

They followed the A.T. along a narrow winding rock ledge with scrub trees and car-sized boulders. Tara halted. She plopped down on the trail, with ears erect, a clear sign that someone or something was nearby and probably approaching. Tara let out a low growl, the hair on her back rose. Dell stopped. He hoped it was law enforcement, but he gripped his hiking stick tightly and thought, *maybe I should've taken Sgt. Ward's advice to carry a gun.*

The tension was broken by what sounded like a muffled groan and the crunch of gravel.

Dell and Tara watched as a police officer navigated around a boulder about fifty yards in front of them. The officer stopped and stared in their direction. Even at fifty yards, Dell noticed his bulging paunch. The officer toddled toward them, his eyes fixed on Tara.

"Stay!" Dell commanded. Tara didn't budge.

The red-faced officer reached them, breathing heavily with sweat dripping off his bulbous nose. "Good dog, I hope," he said, before warily extending his hand to Tara.

"The dog's okay," Dell said. "I'm Dell Peterson."

Tara sniffed the officer's hand and remained in place.

"Why are you on the trail?" he huffed, pointing his finger at Dell. "Wasn't our warning sign clear enough for you?"

"I'm with the Appalachian Trail Conference. Sgt. Clayton Ward should have contacted Pennsylvania authorities about my visit to the murder site."

"Oh, that's right. George did mention your name." The officer took off his hat and wiped away perspiration with the back of his hand. "Frank Mead, Dauphin County sheriff's office. Sorry to have been so abrupt, Mr. Peterson. At least half the hikers ignore our warning."

As they shook hands, Dell asked, "George?"

"George Oliver, state police. He's wrapping things up at the shelter."

With that, Mead put his hat back on and patted Tara on the head. "Good dog." He waved goodbye and continued weaving his way down the A.T.

Dell and Tara continued on the rocky trail lined with gnarled oaks. Within a few minutes, they came to a side trail that was blocked off with more yellow CRIME SCENE tape. A small plastic sign with red letters was nailed to an oak tree: KEEP OUT. CLARY SHELTER CLOSED. Like most side trails off the A.T., this one was blazed with vertical blue rectangles painted on trees or rocks. Dell and Tara skirted the tape and walked about two hundred feet down the trail to the shelter.

As soon as it came into view Dell realized that he and Patricia had once spent a night there. *It could have been us.* With the notable exception of a fresh gash across the top of the bloodstained picnic table and an overturned bench, the shelter, also called a "lean-to," was typical of scores of others on the A.T. that are commonly designed to accommodate six or more people. Like many, this one was made of pine, with a floor, three brown-colored walls, and a roof overhanging an open front.

Dell knew that the bodies had been removed shortly after the event, but he saw a heavy black tarp covering the floor as he approached. Seconds later, his nose was assaulted by a sickly-sweet metallic smell mixed with decay and the unmistakable odor of urine and feces. No need to speculate about what the tarp concealed.

Tara's ears shot up. Dell saw the hair on her back rise. For an instant, he imagined himself being hunted and butchered like that couple. *Son of a bitch.* Dell heard the crackle of leaves, scuffs on dirt. He stepped behind the picnic table and clutched his hiking stick. Tara snarled and barked, then lunged forward. Dell grabbed her collar.

"Down! Stay!"

A short wiry man clad in dirty canvas coveralls and carrying a backpack stepped out from behind the shelter. Rimless eyeglasses gave him a scholarly appearance. He wore latex gloves, dragged two large plastic bags that appeared to be filled mostly with leaves and soil, and approached the picnic table where Dell and Tara were standing. "You must be Dell Peterson," he said, smiling. "Been expecting you."

"I sure hope you're George Oliver," Dell said, laughing nervously.

Officer Oliver chuckled and stuffed the plastic bags into his backpack. He glanced over his shoulder at Dell. "Just about finished," he said. "Don't think I found much of value today. Maybe the lab will come up with something."

Tara crouched low and slinked over to Oliver. Her nose worked over his coveralls and backpack, but he ignored her. She twitched her tail a couple of times and trotted back to Dell, a sign that she approved of the officer.

Dell took off his backpack to help Oliver hoist his heavy pack.

"That's it," Oliver said. "We're through here. Feel free to look around, but leave the yellow tape up. There's a good spring down the hill behind the shelter, but don't camp too close to here tonight. It's probably safe, but the stench is unsettling, not to mention the flies. A decent tenting site is located up where this blue-blazed trail intersects with the A.T."

"Yes, I saw it. I'll poke around a bit here before we're washed out. Rain is coming. Gotta get my tent set up."

Oliver cinched his shoulder straps and tightened his waist belt. "By the way, Clayton Ward thinks highly of you. Told me you and some FBI agent didn't hit it off." Oliver spat on the ground. "The damned FBI. Those guys think they're kings of the hill."

Dell grinned. "Yes. They're take-charge types."

With that, Oliver waved and trudged up the blue-blazed trail and out of sight.

CHAPTER 4: CLARY SHELTER

Tara had disappeared, but Dell heard snuffling in the underbrush.

"Tara, come!"

She zipped up to him from somewhere behind the shelter, sat, and looked up as if to say—*What do you want? So much to smell, so little time to smell it.*

"Okay, girl," Dell said.

Tara returned to the back of the shelter as Dell wandered about, unsure of where to look or what to look for. He peered under the shelter and kicked over rocks and dead branches. Dell scoured the area for two hours but found nothing.

A strong breeze came up as he sat on a rock near the picnic table, watched fast-moving gray clouds, and ate some cheese and his version of gorp—mostly M&Ms, peanuts, and raisins.

He walked down to the spring to top off his canteen and tossed Tara a dog biscuit. They hiked back up the blue-blazed trail to the A.T. and the tenting site, a small patch of flattened weeds about sixty feet off the trail wedged between two large lichen-covered boulders. The breeze grew stronger and dark clouds gathered as Dell erected his tent. Tara wandered about sniffing every twig, leaf, bottle cap, and God knows what. She again disappeared from sight, but Dell could hear rustling in the woods. He stopped, listened, and hoped that was her rustling. After attaching the rain-cover fly to his tent, he took a few steps into the bushes to pee.

"Hey, what's this?" he said out loud.

A frayed baseball cap hung from a nearby branch, two feet off the ground. It was dry and appeared to have been there for a relatively short time. A solitary carpenter ant meandered along its brim, but the cap seemed otherwise uncontaminated by the weather or local fauna. Dell bent over to have a closer look and saw the words "Moosehead Lake." The A.T. came within a few miles of Maine's largest lake.

Tara came up behind him and brushed his leg.

"Sit!" Dell shouted, before taking her collar and leading her out of the bushes, away from the hat. "Stay!"

Dell retrieved one of the plastic bags he had stashed in his pack, turned it inside out, and used it to carefully pick up the cap without touching it with his fingers. He tore paper coverings from two gauze pads without handling them with his bare hands, dropped the pads into the plastic bag with the cap, and sealed it. He'd learned this procedure for preserving scents from hundreds of hours of search-and-rescue training with Tara and had employed it in searches for lost hikers.

By 3:30 p.m., Dell detected a more pungent smell of rain. He knew it was imperative to get the cap into Jamie Doyle's freezer to preserve whatever odor it might retain. If this was the killer's cap, it had been there for about four days. Two days would have been better, but it might still retain a scent.

"Tara," Dell said, "did we get lucky?" She tilted her head.

When the first raindrops hit his face, Dell threw on his raincoat and hat. Everything else went into the tent except for his hiking stick and the bagged cap. Dell figured he and Tara would arrive at The Doyle in a little over an hour if they really trucked along. Tara leaped playfully over and around wet rocks as they sped downhill in the rain, but Dell's eyes were locked on the ground and his feet so as not to slip and fall on the slick stony path. As the A.T. veered off the ridge and descended toward the Susquehanna, Dell and Tara, slipping and sliding on the muddy trail, ran into—almost ran over—a lone female hiker.

CHAPTER 5

WILLOW

"Yikes!" Dell shouted. He dug in his heels trying to avoid colliding into what looked like a teenage girl whose head protruded from a green garbage bag, a makeshift raincoat. Dell skidded on rain-slick leaves and slid off the muddy trail into some brambles, Tara right behind him.

The girl gasped and stumbled backward, almost losing her balance.

Dell pushed himself upright with his hiking stick and brushed wet leaves off his dank, earthy-smelling pants.

"So sorry," he said.

Tara scampered over to sniff the girl who was barely five feet tall. Dell saw that she had no hat, no boots, only shoddy sneakers. Her simple canvas pack, which looked like a school kid's book bag, was soaked through. And the garbage bag, for all he knew, might have once lined a public trash can.

"Wasn't expecting anyone. Thought the police were the only ones on the trail," said Dell.

She flinched, her shoulder-length black hair drenched with rain. "Police?" she asked, as water dripped off her chin.

"You must have seen the warning sign. Cops were collecting evidence at the Clary Shelter. They left several hours ago. You okay?"

"So, they're gone?" she asked, trembling.

"Yes."

Her eyes narrowed. "Are you sure?"

"Yes."

The girl seemed to exhale. She flashed a faint smile. That's when Dell noticed an ugly bruise on her cheek and a jagged two-inch scar over one eye.

"I'm Dell Peterson, working with the Appalachian Trail Conference," he said. "And this is Tara. What's your name?"

She hesitated and stepped back.

Dell guessed she was quite young. *Good God, she's just a kid. She shouldn't be out here. But I've got to get this cap into Jamie's freezer.* "Hmmm," he said, rubbing his forehead. Dell tipped his hat. "I'm sorry miss. I only wanted to be polite. No need to tell me your name."

She muttered softly, almost inaudibly, "Willow." Her lips were purplish. She hugged herself and shivered.

Tara nuzzled up against her. She backed away. Tara persisted, wagging her tail, until Willow relented and gently stroked Tara's wet coat from head to tail. The rain picked up and Willow's garbage bag raincoat whipped in the wind.

"Are you hiking with anyone?" Dell asked, glancing at her sneakers.

She shook her head and looked away. "I'm . . . okay."

Dell took off his rain hat and handed it to her. "Here."

Willow stared down at the muddy trail.

"My raincoat has a hood," Dell said, pulling the hood over his head. "I don't need this hat. Take it."

She reached out, snatched the hat from his hand and placed it on her head. The hat's rim fell below her eyebrows.

"Perfect fit," Dell said.

This brought a reluctant smile.

"Look, I'm in a hurry, and you're cold. I'm bringing something down to The Doyle Hotel in Duncannon. The owner is an old friend. Why don't you come along? Jamie Doyle will give you a hot meal and some dry clothes."

"No!" She raised both hands and backed further away. "I'm *not* getting off the trail."

Dell leaned forward on his hiking stick. "Willow, listen to me. Hiking alone in a rainstorm when you're cold and wet is hazardous. I have two daughters. I sure wouldn't want them to be out alone in this weather if they were as ill-equipped as you. Tara and I have rescued many hikers who were in trouble. Believe me, another hour out here and you, too, will be in trouble. Jamie and I could contact people who would keep you safe."

"No way!" She turned and bolted away from him.

"Wait!"

CHAPTER 5: WILLOW

After running a few yards up the trail, she stopped and turned around. Her eyes narrowed and fixed on Dell. "Safe! What crap!" she yelled, tugging stringy wet hair from her face. Tara ran over to her. She reached to pet Tara. "Those *people* at Child Protective Services tied me up, slapped me . . ." Willow was shaking. "Go away!"

"Jeez, I'm so sorry," Dell said. "But look, you *are* in real danger. Two hikers were murdered right up here at the Clary Shelter just a few days ago; the killer has not been caught. I can't leave you up here by yourself, but I sure as hell can't drag you down to Duncannon."

Dell stepped toward her. Willow tensed, poised to run. She glared at him and muttered, "Uh-huh."

"I'm camped just off the trail, about a quarter mile from here. There might be room for another tent, but I'm betting you don't have one?"

"Nope." She looked away, teeth chattering.

"Do you know what hypothermia is?"

"What's that?"

"It's when your body temperature drops dangerously below normal. You could die."

Willow yanked the rain hat down to almost eye-level and mumbled, "Uh-huh."

"Listen to me. *You, Willow*, can get hypothermia and die. It happens fast."

She said nothing. Dell walked up to her, pulled his wallet out of his rain jacket, and showed Willow his American Rescue Dog Association card. "Tara and I are a team.
I know what I'm talking about."

Tara sat down beside Willow in the cold rain, pressed against her leg, and gazed up at her. Willow, pale and shivering, gently petted her head.

What to do? Dell remembered that the consensus opinion at the Harpers Ferry meeting was that the murderer would likely be off the Pennsylvania section of the trail. That was speculation, of course, but a few hours ago Officer George Oliver seemed unconcerned about Dell setting up camp only feet from the A.T.—"it's probably safe," Oliver said.

"Tell you what," Dell said. "Why don't we go up the trail to my tent? My backpack is inside. You can change into some of my dry clothes. They'll be much too big, but the wool sweater and polar fleece will keep you warm. Tara will stay in the tent with you. She really likes you, and no stranger will dare mess with my German shepherd."

Willow gazed down at Tara and stroked her head again. "Maybe. I guess," she mumbled.

With that, Willow followed Dell and Tara the short distance to Dell's campsite. The rain had let up a little when he unzipped the front of the tent and pointed to his pack.

"Clothes are in there. Help yourself. Leave your muddy sneakers and wet pack out here under the horizontal tent cover."

Willow nodded.

"Gotta go. Be back before dark." Dell tapped a tent pole with his hiking stick and snapped his fingers. "Tara, come."

She hesitated, but shook water off her coat, crept into the tent, and flopped down on the ground mat.

"Tara, stay," he said.

She whined. Dell scratched her head, waved goodbye to Willow, and rushed down the trail confident that Tara would not leave her young charge but very uncertain about whether he was doing the right thing.

* * *

Jamie Doyle sat at the bar watching a Phillies game. He was surprised to see Dell again but readily agreed to store the bagged hat in his freezer.

Without removing his raincoat, Dell asked Jamie, "Can I use your phone for two quick calls?"

"Of course." Jaime reached behind the bar, handed Dell the phone, and asked, "Where's Tara?"

"She's at the tent site guarding my stuff and keeping another hiker company." Dell leaned his hiking stick against the bar.

"Another hiker?"

"Yes. A young girl who's in bad shape. No decent rain gear. Refused to come down here with me. Runaway, I'd guess. Said she'd had some kind of horrible experience with Child Protective Services. I told her she could stay in my tent with Tara."

Jamie put his hand on Dell's shoulder. "You've always had a soft, trusting streak, my boy. That young lass couldn't be in better hands, I mean paws, what with a murderer on the loose."

CHAPTER 5: WILLOW

It was after 4:30 p.m. when Dell called Brad Hornbeck. "I'm at The Doyle Hotel. I have to leave right away to get back to my tent. Call Sgt. Ward and Scaperelli. Tell them there's a bagged baseball-style cap in the hotel's freezer. It might be the murderer's."

"Wow. Where'd you find it?" Brad asked.

"Just off the A.T., near the Clary Shelter. Tell the cops they need to keep the cap at below freezing temperatures at all times or it will lose whatever scent it still might have."

Dell's second call was to Grace Lombardi at her D.C. law firm. When she'd been Dell's student, she was the editor of the law review and graduated first in her class. Several years later, she became the first female partner of the old-line firm of Cloverdale, Thayer & Weiss in Washington, D.C. She'd stayed in touch with Dell and had often consulted him when her family law practice touched on criminal matters. Patricia and Dell had enjoyed their frequent dinners and theater outings with Grace and her former husband. The two women became close friends.

Grace was an accomplished and enthusiastic hiker. After her divorce, she often joined Dell and Patricia on weekend hikes in Maryland and Virginia. She had called Dell several times after Patricia's death but, although he'd always enjoyed her company, he had not returned her calls. Indeed, until Grace's surprise visit to his office, they hadn't even seen each other since Patricia's memorial service several months earlier. Funny thing though, he never stopped thinking about her.

"Hi, Grace. Dell."

"Why didn't you call? I tried calling you. Where are you?"

"Duncannon, Pennsylvania, but I'm camped a few miles from here on the A.T. I need a good family lawyer."

"Oh? Everything all right? Sounds like you're in a hurry."

"Afraid so."

"I've been thinking about you," Grace said. "A lot."

"Well, I've been thinking of you, too."

Jamie brushed past Dell on the way to the kitchen as Dell sat on a bar stool with the phone and summarized the matter of Willow to Grace.

"She's a totally unprepared, nearly hypothermic teenager I just encountered on the A.T. She's probably a runaway, and she vehemently refused my pleas to come to Duncannon and safety.

Claimed she'd been abused by CPS." Dell sighed heavily. "I believe her. So, I can't in good conscience bring myself to call the authorities and have her hauled away."

"Not calling them could be problematic under Pennsylvania law."

"That's right," Dell said.

"Where is she now?" Grace asked.

"In my tent with Tara. That's why I'm in a hurry. It's pouring rain and getting late."

"How old is she?"

"Don't know, young. Maybe fourteen or fifteen. I know it's risky for me to harbor an underage female runaway, but she could have died. I need your opinion."

Jamie emerged from the kitchen and handed Dell a hot Irish coffee with whipped cream. Dell gave him a thumb's up in thanks.

"You probably did save her life," Grace said. "I'm confident you're doing the right thing, morally, but risky is the right word. Be careful. She could accuse you of anything."

Dell sipped the coffee. "That's my concern. I know nothing about her."

"Not to mention there's a murderer out there somewhere," Grace said with an edge in her voice.

"Don't worry; we think he's off the trail and somewhere in Maine." Dell took another sip and said, "Thanks for your reassurance. That's what I needed. I'll call you when I get home, maybe before then."

"Please do. I *am* concerned about you, and, of course, Willow. Promise you'll call.

"This time, I will keep my promise."

Dell tasted a generous splash of Irish whiskey as he downed the last gulp of coffee. He grabbed his hiking stick and said, "Thanks, Jamie. I'm off."

Jaime stood behind the bar washing beer glasses. "Wait!" He disappeared, but soon returned with a ham and cheese sub the size of a mailbox, wrapped tightly in wax paper. "Take it."

Dell punched him playfully in the shoulder and tucked the sub under his raincoat. "You're one-of-a-kind."

"Take good care of my dog," Jamie shouted, as Dell rushed out the door.

CHAPTER 6
TWOSOME

Pummeled by heavy rain, Dell angled into wind gusts that blew him sideways as he crossed Clark's Ferry Bridge over the swirling Susquehanna. After passing the warning sign at the trailhead, he ascended a trail that was now a rushing stream. He slipped on moss-covered rocks and tripped over wet roots but made it back to his tent before nightfall. A dead tree branch had fallen nearby, and the dried-out, gray lichen-covered boulders by the tent had turned a succulent green.

Dell unzipped the tent's front flap, peeked in, and got a nose full of Tara's farts and the ripe odor of wet dog. Asleep on his ground mat, Willow had her arm around her new malodorous companion and guardian. Dell chuckled when he saw her in his fleece sweater, which stretched to her knees. She'd used his wool shirt and a threadbare shawl she must have picked up somewhere to cover herself. Her wet clothes were piled in a corner.

Curled up nose to butt on Dell's sleeping bag, Tara raised her head. She gave him a German shepherd happy smile, flicked her tail, and bounded outside to greet him. Dell reached in, quietly removed some dog kibble from his pack, closed the flap, and sat outside with Tara under the sagging horizontal cover that protruded from the front of the tent. He ate half of Jamie's sub and saved half for Willow, wondering when she'd last had anything to eat.

The rain was cold and steady. He took off his raincoat and boots, covered the boots with the raincoat, positioned them flush against the tent, and whispered to Tara, "Down. Stay." She dropped to the ground next to him and he gave her the kibble. Tara whined to get back inside with Willow, but there was no way Dell was letting a damp, vile-smelling dog back into his tent.

Sleeping in the same tent with someone he didn't know—especially a teenage girl—unnerved him. Dell considered waking Willow to ask permission to sleep there, but he quickly dismissed the thought. *She's flat out, I'm dead tired, it's my tent, and she has nothing to fear from me.* He opened the flap, gently nudged her to one side, and scooted in. After stripping off his shirt and socks, he slipped into his sleeping bag, removed his pants and pushed them to the bottom of the bag so they'd be mostly dry in the morning, and fell asleep.

Rain pelted the tent throughout the night, but eased up in the early morning, and stopped altogether shortly before sunrise. Glints of sunshine peeped through the tent.

Willow stirred and lifted herself onto her elbows, rubbed her eyes, and gave Dell a puzzled stare. "What's your name again?"

"Dell. Remember?"

"Oh, that's right." She sat up and threw off the shawl and wool shirt. "I'll be right back."

"Where are you going?"

No answer.

Dell rolled over and closed his eyes as Willow wriggled past him. When she unzipped the tent flap to exit the tent, Tara shuffled out of her way. Seconds later, a sound like Niagara Falls.

After Willow returned, she chided Dell—"Why was Tara left outside?"

"Oh poor dog," Dell grunted. *Of course, she remembered the dog's name.* "She stinks!"

Willow started to pull the fleece sweater over her head, revealing her bare midriff. "Don't look," she said.

"Hold on!" said Dell, "I'll go outside." He put his pants on, climbed out of his sleeping bag, and left the tent to Willow. Outside, barefooted and shirtless, he stretched his arms up toward a robin's egg blue sky in the brisk early morning air. Birch, stunted ash, and scrub oak lined both sides of the trail, their wet leaves rustling in the breeze.

"Okay. I'm dressed now," Willow said.

When Dell reentered the tent, he assumed his most parental voice, gentle but stern—"Willow, listen up. I am not your father or brother. I'm a goddamn stranger. Don't ever dress or undress around strange men. It's dangerous."

CHAPTER 6: TWOSOME

Willow pressed her hands against her cheeks. "Um . . . sure. Guess you're right." She blinked several times, ran a hand through her hair, and asked, "Do you have something I can tie my hair back with?"

Dell fumbled around inside the dank, cramped tent littered with wet clothes. Without Tara's stink to mask it, it smelled like a men's locker room. He reached into an exterior pocket of his pack, extracted a red bandana, and handed it to her.

"Thanks," she said, smiling. She tied her hair back and stepped out of the tent. Willow threw a stick down the trail for Tara, who chased after it.

Dell grabbed a shirt, followed her out, and finished dressing in the bright sunlight.

"Sun's up," Willow said, pointing to the sky. "No more goosebumps."

"What'd you eat last night?" Dell asked.

"The big Hershey bar I found in your pack," she confessed with an impish grin.

Dell laughed, reached into the pocket of his raincoat, and handed her the other half of the ham and cheese sub. "Wow," Willow said. She sat on a rock, tore off a piece for Tara, and wolfed down the rest. Dell fixed himself some granola with powdered milk.

"How'd you get that scar over your left eye?" Dell asked, immediately regretting his question.

Willow flinched and lowered her head.

"I shouldn't have mentioned it," Dell said. "I apologize."

Willow clenched her jaw. "Karl hit me with an axe handle."

"Karl, who's Karl? Some sonofabitch; battering a young girl." Dell stopped eating, picked up a stone and hurled it into the bushes. Willow stared at the ground. He wanted to know more about Karl but refrained from pursuing it.

"I'm sorry that happened to you. How old are you? Fifteen, I bet."

"Good guess. And you?"

"Fifty-two."

"Jeez. That's much older than my father."

"Where's he?"

"Dead." Willow looked down.

"I'm sorry." Dell thought it best to postpone this conversation for another time. "You have no boots, tent, sleeping bag, rain gear, or decent pack," Dell said. "What *do* you have?"

She shrugged, then laughed. "A couple of Snicker's bars."

Dell shook his head, mumbled "shit," and pointed his hiking stick at a white A.T. blaze on a nearby oak tree. "Where are you headed?"

Willow gave a blank stare. "I dunno. Anywhere north."

"Let me take a wild guess. You're running away from something."

She leaned over, ran her fingertips through Tara's fur, and muttered, "Uh-huh."

"I'm going all the way to the Delaware River. As I said yesterday, I'd really like to take you someplace where you'd be safe."

She kicked a sodden stump. "No way!" With teary eyes and clenched fists, Willow glared at Dell. "I am not going back, *ever!*"

"You won't survive up here unprepared and alone. Where is your mother?"

Tara paced back and forth between Willow and Dell, her anxious eyes flitting from one to the other. Willow looked up at the treetops. Tears trickled down her cheeks.

Something horrible happened to her, worse than being smacked by an axe handle.

"Can't I come with you?" she asked, then turned away, shoved her hands into her pants pockets, and scuffed her feet in the dirt.

Tara stopped pacing and ran to Dell. She plopped down squarely on his foot, looked up at him, and licked his hand. He sighed, rolled his eyes. Dell imagined his daughters as teenagers.

He looked at Willow with a serious face. "You have chutzpah I like that."

"Please," she said, eyes wide, face flushed.

"Well, if you stay out here alone it could be a death sentence. If you can keep up, guess you'd better come along. *Que será, será.*"

Willow's face lit up. "Don't know who Kay Sarah is, but I can keep up with you, grandpa."

Dell laughed, removed some moleskins from his pack, and handed them to her.

"I saw your feet. You need these for those blisters. Do you know what moleskins are?"

CHAPTER 6: TWOSOME

She snatched them from his hand. "Yeah, I've had blisters before."

"We'll share my food supply," Dell said. "If we reach the Delaware Water Gap in a week or less, it should hold up."

"Cool. Thanks." She began to remove a moleskin from the packet.

Dell tossed a tube of antibiotic ointment to Willow. "Apply this before putting those moleskins on your heels and toes. Don't take them off."

Willow frowned. "Can't you say *please* put on the moleskins?"

Tara was chomping on kibble and Dell started to pack. After rolling up the tent, he turned toward Willow. "Please put on the damn moleskins. And please, Your Royal Highness, don't wear cotton on future hikes. Hikers have an expression: when cotton gets wet, it gets cold. When it gets cold, cotton kills."

Willow saluted. "Yes, Gramps."

Dell shook his head and smiled. *She's feisty. We'll get along.*

They broke camp and hoisted their packs. With Tara in the lead, they headed out on the trail.

"We'll have to truck along," Dell said, tightening his waist belt. "At least twenty miles today."

"Let's go," said Willow, pumping her fist in the air.

CHAPTER 7
WALKING WITH WILLOW - DAY ONE

Dell squinted into the sunlight as he, Willow, and Tara started out on the trail. No wind, clear sky. The smell of pine filled the air. The day promised to be warm, probably hot. Dell had hiked this section of the Appalachian Trail three times before and was well-aware of the paucity of springs and other good water sources. That's why he'd packed an extra canteen. All three of his liter canteens were full, as was Willow's smaller one. Dell knew they would spend most of the day hiking along an exposed, rocky, fourteen-hundred-foot-high ridge with little shade. Indeed, most of the Pennsylvania trail between the Susquehanna and Delaware Rivers consisted of rocks, rocks, and more rocks.

Kruck, kruck, kruck. Overhead, a large raven was perched on the swaying bough of a pine tree. The bird cried out again as if to say, *look at me, look at me.*

"Wow," Willow said, pointing at the raven, "that big black bird has only one good eye! The other's all white."

"Maybe poor eyesight explains why it landed so close to us. Did you know that many people believe ravens signal danger, even death?" Dell winked. "But sometimes they're seen as good omens."

Willow stretched out her arms and bowed toward the bird. "Be nice, Mr. Raven."

Dell was well-aware that this section of the A.T. was not wilderness. The trail was compromised by powerlines, pipelines, abandoned coal mines, and highway crossings. His hope was that they might make it all the way to the Rausch Gap Shelter, twenty-six-miles to the northeast. Dell didn't share this aspiration with Willow. Even fifteen miles would be a heroic achievement for a fifteen-year-old with battered sneakers and blistered feet.

CHAPTER 7: WALKING WITH WILLOW – DAY ONE

The map indicated they'd have only one significant ascent and descent during the entire day, which was unusual for a two-thousand-mile-long trail of continuous ups and downs. Because of this, Dell guessed they might make good time.

And indeed, they reached the first transmission tower, a steel-lattice structure, in an hour and a half, covering almost four miles.

"You're really flying. How are those sneakers holding up?" Dell asked, looking at Willow's feet.

"Pretty well, Gramps," Willow said with a red face, "but I'm thirsty."

They stopped to drink from their canteens. Dell poured water into an aluminum Sierra cup for Tara. At 8:29 a.m., the plastic thermometer on his pack read eighty degrees.

A couple more hours of hiking brought them to a rusty iron footbridge which spanned Pennsylvania Route 225. Cars, pickup trucks, and eighteen wheelers roared under the bridge as they crossed. They'd more than doubled their mileage, and took another, longer, water break on a bench near the bridge.

By noon, Dell and Willow reached the blue-blazed Whitetail Trail where it intersected with the A.T. They sat down amid a circular pile of stones at the trails' intersection. Perspiration ran down their faces. This, and sweat-soaked clothes soon attracted deer flies that dove, kamikaze-like, onto Tara's ears and into Willow's hair. Tara flicked her ears again and again, and Dell bloodied his fingers crushing several of the fiends feasting on her. When they landed on Willow's head, she'd flip strands of her thick hair over the large bug-eyed flies, trapping them. Then, she'd zap each one between her fingers with an audible "pop." She was so skilled at killing deer flies that she'd cleared the air for lunch.

Dell had gorp, and Willow devoured her two melted Snickers bars and several handfuls of gorp. They'd come twelve miles. Willow had finished her small canteen and one of Dell's long ago. Much more alarming, she'd accidentally knocked over another of Dell's canteens while swatting flies, spilling all of its contents.

"I'm really concerned about our water supply." Dell said, wrinkling his brow and handing his remaining water to Willow. "Here, drink what's left."

"I'm sorry," Willow said, looking down.

Dell looked her in the eye. "Drink it."

She grabbed his canteen, drained it in one gulp, and handed the empty canteen back to him. Wiping her eyes, she said, "It's all my fault."

"Could've happened to anyone," Dell said. "We'll deal with it . . . somehow. But dehydration can be more lethal than some screwball who jumps out of the woods and rushes you clutching a bloody knife." Dell sighed, wiped his sweaty forehead on his shirtsleeve, and asked, "Where'd you get on the A.T.?"

Looking away and licking chocolate off her fingers, she said, "I-81."

"How'd you get to the interstate?"

She stuck out her thumb. "Hitched."

Dell raised an eyebrow and shook his head. "Murderers pick up hitchhikers."

Willow shrugged, said nothing.

"That's not too far south of Duncannon. Did you stay at The Doyle Hotel?"

"You must be kidding. I don't have a dime. I slept on a park bench by the river."

"Hmm . . ." Dell shook his head again.

Dell's thermometer read eighty-seven degrees. Willow got up and reclined against a scraggly oak protruding from a fractured slab of rock. She had Tara's head in her lap, and her hand rested on the panting dog. Dell sat a few feet away in the scant shade of a boulder.

After a short catnap, they hiked two miles to Shikellamy Rocks, an exposed scree slope of rocks and boulders running down the mountainside. The thermometer registered ninety-two degrees and they were out of water. No shade anywhere. Dell knew that the next reliable water source was at Rausch Gap Shelter twelve miles away—another six hours of hiking.

Along the narrow path, a tall, lanky man with bushy sideburns and a goat-like beard approached from the north. Dell assessed the man's fluid steps and the rhythmic clicks of his hiking sticks as signs of an experienced backpacker. Dell tensed when he saw a sheathed hunting knife on the stranger's belt. Tara growled and crouched protectively next to Willow.

"Hi, I'm Dell." Dell extended his hand, eyes glued on the stranger.

The hiker, clad in a faded, pin-striped, New York Yankees

CHAPTER 7: WALKING WITH WILLOW – DAY ONE

T-shirt and ragged shorts, gave Dell a firm handshake. "Bump's my trail name. Is Dell your trail name?"

Willow squished her eyebrows together. "What's a trail name?"

"Distance hikers," Dell explained, "often adopt a unique name while on the trail, like Bump, Blue Belle, Feathers, Dog Breath, or whatever."

"Cool," Willow said.

"We could call you Fly Swatter," Dell said. "You were really good at zapping those deer flies."

Bump laughed.

Waving her arms in the air, she said, "Great! Fly Swatter it is."

Dell turned to Bump and said, "Dell's my real name. For years, my trail name was Odysseus, but it might be Gramps now."

Willow grinned. "Gramps. Perfect!"

Bump pointed his hiking stick at Willow. "This your granddaughter or daughter, Gramps?"

Dell hesitated, unsure of how to respond. Willow piped up. "He's my grandpa." She elbowed Dell and grinned.

Bump removed his pack. "About time for a water break. Hotter than blazes."

"Sure is," Dell agreed. "We spilled one of our canteens earlier. We're completely out of water. Kind of desperate."

"Good grief!" Bump said, handing his canteen to Willow. "Here, have some of mine." Willow and Dell both took deep gulps and thanked him profusely.

"About three miles from here in the direction you are headed," Bump said in a monotone voice, "after you've descended a quarter mile or so into Clark's Valley, there's an unmarked side trail on the right by a large V-shaped rock. Keep your eyes peeled because it's overgrown with brush and easy to miss. Leads to a spring that's not quite dried up."

Dell took off his sweaty hat, flicked perspiration off his brow with his fingertips, and said, "Man, that's great news. Thought I knew every spring on this section of the trail. We passed a couple, but they were dry."

"Game warden told me about it when I met him in the parking lot off Route 325," Bump said.

Dell noticed that Bump avoided direct eye contact and unconsciously scratched his arm. He appeared distracted, maybe lonely, and wanting to talk. Bump's hand brushed his hunting knife as he tightened his belt.

Tara snarled and Dell took a quick step backward, raising his hiking stick.

Bump seemed confused. He rubbed his beard. "Did I do something?"

"Sorry," Dell said. "I'm a little paranoid, what with the recent knife murders."

Bump shook his head. "Yes, how awful. Don't worry about me. I'm a cream puff."

"You seem a little down Bump," Dell said. "Are you concerned about something?"

Taking a deep breath and still avoiding eye contact, Bump said, "Well, got on the A.T. in Connecticut, near Cornwall." He leaned forward on both of his hiking sticks and gazed off in the distance. "My wife left me four months ago. She took our two kids with her. I needed time to think, to recover." He peered down at his hands with a vacant stare. "I can take the physical demands of the trail, even the pain. Something always hurts out here on the A.T., but that's fine. Pain takes my mind off things."

Dell's mind was focused on water, but he kept nodding supportively as Bump spoke. Willow listened attentively.

Tears streamed down Bump's face when he glanced at Willow. "You're 'bout my daughter's age, love. Sure do miss her."

Willow rubbed her nose with the back of her hand, hung her head, and turned away. Dell went over and put his hand on her shoulder. "You've got me, Fly Swatter," he whispered.

"God, hope I didn't say anything wrong," Bump said.

Dell looked at Bump. "Not at all. Grief affects all of us. My wife left me, too. Patricia died last November."

"Oh. I'm terribly sorry." Bump's chin dropped to his chest.

Willow turned back toward Bump, wiped away tears, and half-smiled. Bump went quiet, his eyes watered.

A father without his daughter and a daughter without her father.

When Dell shook Bump's hand, he held it for a while. "You're a good man, Bump. We wish you Godspeed."

Bump looked directly at Willow, then Dell. He stroked Tara—who'd never left Willow's side, lifted his pack, and headed south down the trail.

CHAPTER 7: WALKING WITH WILLOW – DAY ONE

Dell and Willow resumed their hike north toward the Rausch Gap Shelter.

"You were great back there," Dell said to Willow. "I didn't know what to say when Bump asked if you were my granddaughter or daughter."

"Wish you were my grandpa."

Dell's heart did a back flip. He peered over at Willow. She gave him a quick glance and said with a flushed face, "I'm thirsty. Wish I hadn't spilled that canteen."

"Stuff happens. If you feel dizzy, faint, or disoriented tell me right away. We should get to Bump's spring in about an hour."

"Okay," Willow said, maintaining her pace. Touching Dell's arm with her fingertip, she asked, "People seem to be on the trail for all kinds of reasons. Why are you on the trail?"

"I know the A.T. very well," Dell said, keeping pace with Willow. "The Appalachian Trail Conference asked me to help the police investigate the recent homicides."

"Yeah, those murders are scary," Willow said.

"I take them personally."

As they began to descend into Clark's Valley the only sound was the crunch of footsteps as their boots dug into the trail. Two turkey vultures circled overhead in the clear sky and, far below, they saw the multicolored patchwork of Pennsylvania farms, a mosaic of greens, browns, and yellows.

"Why personally?" Willow asked.

Tara was panting heavily, lagging behind.

Dell's mind was on his and Willow's dehydration but he replied, "The second time I did the A.T. was with my two daughters and late wife. The four of us section-hiked the entire trail over a period of several years. Our kids grew up hiking on it. I think of the A.T. as my family."

Willow went silent, pensive. They continued to descend on the dusty trail in the late afternoon's oppressive heat.

A full minute passed before she said, "I'm sorry your wife died."

A lone tear ran down Dell's cheek before he said, "Her death is why I decided to hike all the way to the Delaware after examining the murder site at the Clary Shelter. I found something there that might be helpful to the cops. That's why I had to leave right after we ran into each other." Dell swung his hiking stick, mowing down a few of the many nettles that lined the trail. "The A.T. is my tonic. Keeps my mind off traumatic stuff, off Patricia's passing. Sort of like what Bump said, I suppose."

They continued hiking without saying anything until Willow broke the silence—"You're okay, Gramps."

Dell looked back. *Where's Tara?* He dropped his pack. "Stay here, Willow. Don't move." Dell rushed back to search for Tara. He found her collapsed by the side of the trail, tongue hanging out, severely dehydrated. Kneeling on one knee, he lifted her head. "We're close to water, girl."

Dell strained and, with a deep grunt, lifted the eighty-pound dog onto his other knee. He bent low, slipped both arms under her, and stood, slinging Tara onto his shoulders.

"Stay with me girl."

He staggered downhill holding Tara in a fireman's carry. Dell gagged when he smelled a foul odor, then felt warm diarrhea dribble down his chest. His boot caught on a tree root and he and Tara tumbled to the ground.

When Willow saw this, she ran to them, yelling, "Gramps!"

Dell got up slowly, rubbed a skinned knee, and said, "Watch Tara. The spring must be close. I won't be long." He retrieved an empty canteen and water filter from his pack and sprinted down the trail, almost over-shooting the V-shaped rock that Bump had mentioned. A thickly overgrown side path led three hundred feet off the A.T. to what could only charitably be called a spring. Sediment-filled brown water coated with a layer of dead black flies seeped from under a moss-covered stone into a shallow mud hole the width of Dell's palm. Another few days and the water would be gone. It took several minutes to pump the gruel-like liquid through his mini-filter into the canteen. He ran up the hill with the precious liquid.

Tara lapped water from Dell's Sierra cup, gulp after gulp, until the liter canteen was empty. Dazed, she struggled to get up, but finally stood, wobbled, and managed a full-body shake. She dropped back down to lick her rear end.

"I feel like I'm gonna puke." Willow gagged from the smell and turned away. "Yuck! Can't tell Gramps and Tara apart."

"You're so unkind, my dear," Dell quipped. "I'm going back to the spring to fill up all our canteens. We came close to losing Tara."

CHAPTER 7: WALKING WITH WILLOW – DAY ONE

Dell stripped off his shit-smeared shirt and shoved it under a rotten log with his hiking stick. "We're going to have to wait till we reach the shelter to wash," he said. "Flies are already on her, they'll deposit eggs. If Tara's rear isn't cleaned soon, maggots will penetrate her anus and she could die."

"Oh my God. That's so awful, and so gross." Willow held her nose with one hand and stroked Tara's head with the other. "Poor Tara."

When Dell returned, they all drank their fill of the rank-smelling, funky-looking, but filtered water, hoping it was reasonably safe. Hydrated and feeling better, they resumed their trek toward the shelter. Tara was back in the lead.

Crossing busy Pennsylvania Route 325, they dodged cars, walked through a State Game Lands parking lot, and began a gradual ascent up the north slope of Clark's Valley. They passed several abandoned mines where orange, acrid smelling fluid oozed from iron-gated mouths. On their way to the top of Stony Mountain, Dell angrily denounced that section of the trail as "desecration of God's good earth." At the summit, they climbed a deserted fire tower and were rewarded with a sweeping, forest-carpeted view down rolling green hills into Fort Indiantown Gap.

From this point, it was a straight and level shot along a ridge to the Rausch Gap Shelter. As they approached the blue-blazed side trail to the shelter, they looked east to what Dell had always considered the most appalling sight on the entire A.T., a vast, toxic wasteland left by an abandoned open-cut mine. Nothing whatsoever grew on this scourged land that reminded him of wartime photos of Verdun or Hiroshima. Utter devastation.

The sun was beginning to set as they arrived at the Rausch Gap Shelter which was located off the ridge in a small grove of birch trees. It was 7:30 p.m., but still light. A couple and their snoring black lab had appropriated three-quarters of the floor space of this open-front, log and stone shelter designed to accommodate eight people. When Dell and Willow dropped their packs in the unoccupied portion, a man's head popped out of a sleeping bag.

"Welcome."

That was all they heard from them. Dell shrugged and looked at Willow, who had taken off her torn sneakers. She sat barefoot on the edge of the shelter, swinging her legs.

"My dear Ms. Willow," he said, "Could you please spread out the mat and sleeping bag while Tara and I search for water to wash ourselves? And why don't you take my mat tonight? You'll sleep better."

Willow hopped to the ground. "Sure thing. Thanks, Gramps."

"Oh, and fish out the stove and two freeze-dried dinner pouches from my pack." Dell paused. "Please."

"Okay."

The trickle from the shelter's nearby spring was slow, but reliable. Two small creeks flowed close by. Sulfurous smelling Rausch Creek was contaminated with mine runoff, but Haystack Creek ran clear and cold. After Dell bushwhacked some distance downstream on Haystack, he stripped off his clothes, coaxed Tara into a pool, and scrubbed her tail and behind with soap. While she shook herself off on the bank, he gazed up through overhanging branches at the fading indigo blue sky. He waded deeper into the pool, quickly ducked under, and washed himself in the icy water.

After Tara had rear-gunned him with diarrhea that afternoon, Dell had been content to hike bare-chested. But this dip in the stream and the cool evening air chilled him. Back at the shelter, he put on a clean shirt and was delighted to see his small aluminum pot filled with spring water and boiling on the mini stove. Willow had placed the stove on a heavily stained pine plank table located about twenty feet from the shelter, its surface covered with carved hearts and Tom-Loves-Betty-like adornments. Dell's teenage companion was perched cross-legged on a bench by the table holding a spoon in one hand and two open packets of dried chili con carne in the other.

"You and Tara arrived at the right time," Willow said, as she turned off the stove and poured hot water into both packets.

"You found the matches, but how'd you figure out the stove?" Dell said as he dried his wet hair on his shirt.

"Mother's boyfriend, Karl, had one just like it back in Reading."

"That's where you're from?"

"Yup." She stirred the chili. "Dinner will be ready in two minutes."

"Why'd you leave?" He glanced at Willow to see if his question was too personal.

CHAPTER 7: WALKING WITH WILLOW – DAY ONE

Tara snuffled the pot and looked up at Willow as if to say, "Aren't I your best friend? Wanna share?"

Willow rubbed the dog's nose. "No, sweet girl."

"You needn't tell me anything if you don't want to," Dell said, as crickets chirped in the early evening.

Willow cleared her throat. She bit a fingernail and inhaled. "I kissed a girl." She eyed Dell warily.

Dell pressed a hand over his mouth and struggled not to laugh. "And?"

"My mother was drunk, as usual. Empty vodka bottles and beer cans were everywhere. She and Karl opened my bedroom door and saw us kiss. They went batshit." Willow swallowed hard and clasped her hands. "Mother screamed at the girl I kissed. Karl slapped me again and again, and he slammed my head into the wall." With her hands still clutched together, Willow cleared her throat and shook her head. "They shouted that I was a 'prevert.'"

"Pervert." Dell corrected her.

"Whatever." Willow wrinkled her forehead.

"Chili's ready," Dell said.

They ate the warm red mush with their only spoon, which they passed back and forth. Tara got kibble.

"Mother screamed that I was 'queer,' a 'slut.' Karl took his deer rifle out of his pickup and pointed it at me. He said I had ten minutes to get out of the house . . ." Willow pressed her hands to her face and sobbed, "or he'd shoot me."

Dell was stone quiet, his heart in his throat.

Willow's lips and chin quivered, her eyes full of fear. She pulled Tara close and held her tight. "I grabbed some clothes, stuffed them into my school pack, and ran out of the house. Mother shouted after me that she'd have me arrested."

Dell stood and hurled the empty food pouches and some scraps into the fireplace by the shelter and lit a match. "Karl and your mother should be the ones prosecuted—for child abuse, abandonment, assault and battery, and assault with a deadly weapon."

"But I kissed Laurie."

"There is nothing illegal or, as far as I'm concerned, immoral about a girl kissing a girl, a toad, or a pink flamingo."

Willow stared open-mouthed at Dell for several seconds. "How's that? You sure?"

Tara pushed up against her.

Dell tossed Tara a dog biscuit as the sun sank over the horizon. "I'm an attorney. I'm sure."

Willow gasped, looked at Dell with wide eyes, and confessed—"You know Gramps, I've also kissed *boys*."

"Hot damn!" He took her hand and held it between both of his. "If there's a God, and I hope there is, he or she loves you whether you kiss a girl or a boy."

Willow hugged. "Think so?"

"Absolutely."

Dell wrapped his arm around her shoulders and squeezed. With that, they entered the shelter. He hung their packs from the ceiling with a nylon cord to keep them away from the ever-present mice. Willow crawled onto the mat wearing Dell's sweater, covered herself with his wool shirt, and fell asleep.

Dell sat on the floor of the shelter and leaned against the back wall, legs tucked into his sleeping bag. Tara was curled up between him and Willow. *Why am I here with this young girl?* he wondered.

A piercing "*Kruck, Kruck*" sounded somewhere nearby, shattering the silence and startling him. *The one-eyed raven?* Dell realized he hadn't thought about the murderer all day, except when Bump showed up. A full moon lit the forest with a yellow glow. The moonlight cast shadows on everything but revealed nothing.

CHAPTER 8
AFFINITY

Dell and Willow woke as rays of light peeked over the horizon. Willow didn't protest the early hour, unlike his daughters when they were teenagers.

After getting dressed, Dell boiled water for instant coffee while Willow dished out their granola and fed Tara. As they prepared to hit the trail, Dell noticed one of Willow's shoulder straps had torn off from her pack and the other was frayed. He lashed her pack to his and jammed her small canteen into one of his pack's side pockets. The couple with the lab sleeping next to them in the shelter hadn't stirred.

Tara led them out on the trail under a clear sky, past poison ivy-covered stone ruins—remnants of old abandoned buildings, and onto a State Game Lands service road, what the A.T. guidebook described as a former railroad bed.

"You did great yesterday," Dell said. "Twenty-six miles, blisters and all."

"Bring it on Gramps." Willow pumped a fist in the air. Her sneakers were threadbare, and a tear in the left one exposed her toes. "You're hauling all the weight today," she said, "so I can fly."

Dell pointed his hiking stick up the trail. "Can you fly twenty-three miles?"

"Sure, it's cooler than yesterday. You've got the map. Where are we headed?"

"Hertlein Campsite." Dell traced his finger on the trail map. "It's near a stream."

"Sounds good, but won't we be hiking in the dark if it's that far?"

Dell shook his head. "Probably not, yesterday's hike was longer, but let's get a move-on."

Two hours and six miles later, they crossed the one-hundred-year-old iron truss Waterville Bridge that spanned the lushly wooded Swatara Creek. Within an hour, they'd ascended to the 1,500-foot-high ridge of Blue Mountain that they would follow for the rest of the day. The irregular rocky pathway meant their eyes had to be on their feet so they wouldn't trip. With trees and dense brush on both sides of the trail, a few vistas were obscured, but bypassing some viewpoints, along with Willow's exuberance and athleticism, enabled them to maintain a constant three-mile an hour pace.

* * *

Tara's growl brought them to a dead stop. The hair on her back rose as she anchored herself in front of Willow. Dell tensed. He shouted at Tara to "Stay!" Willow let out a shrill scream as a black bear a bit bigger than a large sheep dog emerged from a clump of scrawny pines and looked their way. *Omigod,* the bear seemed to say, *what was that hideous noise?* He scurried across their path a few yards in front of them and attempted to hide behind a birch tree. The bear's butt protruded from one side of the tree's trunk while its head peeked out at them from the other side.

"Wow, what a treat," Dell said, relieved that it wasn't a human threat.

"Treat. Are you crazy? He could eat us." Willow clutched Dell's arm.

Dell laughed and poked her ribs. "The bear might munch on you and eat our snack food, but he'd spit me out."

Willow was not amused. She clung to Dell until the frightened bear turned and hustled off into the underbrush.

Before long Tara spotted a rabbit, sprinted after it, and vanished behind a boulder. Dell and Willow continued on, confident Tara would soon catch up to them. Seconds later, they heard a sharp yowl and she exploded from the bushes with her tail between her legs, ears pinned back. She came up from behind and shot past them, leaping over rocks, eyes wide with a look that said—*Holy shit, what's happening?* Tara bolted down the trail and was soon out of sight.

"Damn!" Dell slapped a yellow jacket on his leg, and another stung his back. "Run Willow, fast! Follow Tara."

Sprinting alongside him, Willow shouted, "Why are we running?"

Before he could answer she shrieked, "Ouch!" A wasp had stung her arm.

They picked up their pace. After a quarter mile, they found Tara on the ground chewing one of her several stings.

"She must have stirred up a hornet's nest," Dell said, shaking his head.

He bent down to examine her. Except for a solitary wasp still clinging to Tara's ear, which Dell crushed between his thumb and forefinger, they'd outrun the wasps.

"What's next?" Dell asked.

Almost 11 a.m. and still making good time, they came to a narrow side trail that descended from the ridge through a tunnel of vines and brambles to the Blue Mountain spring, which bubbled out from under a quartzite boulder. They'd come more than thirteen miles. Dell and Willow stopped to relax, gobble gorp, and replenish their canteens. Five lean, well-tanned men who looked to be in their late twenties and had A.T. patches on their packs rushed in on the side trail, eager to refill their canteens.

"Hi. Where you from?" Dell asked the men. He turned to Willow and said, "These guys are serious hikers."

"Oakhurst, California. We're with the Sierra Club, speed-hiking the A.T. from the Susquehanna to Mt. Katahdin," said a blond bearded guy with a green bandanna and a 'Katahdin or Bust' T-shirt. "We've been following you for a while."

"Did the yellow jackets get you?" Dell asked.

"Yeah." He pointed to the tallest of the five men. "Gus got zapped."

When the men were ready to head out Dell asked them if the trailhead across the river from Duncannon was still closed.

"The cautionary sign is still there," said the one wearing the 'Katahdin or Bust' T-shirt, "but we ignored it." And Gus added, "Figured if the murderer was still on the trail he wouldn't mess with the five of us. But just in case . . ." Gus pulled a folded Buck knife from a nylon sheath on his belt and flicked open its five-inch blade. "I'll cut off his balls."

Dell glanced at Willow. She just shrugged.

"Where you headed today?" Dell asked.

Gus smiled, raised his hiking stick high in the air, and said, "Port Clinton, but it'll be well after dark."

"Wow. That's twenty-eight miles from here."

"Yup. We move. In fact, it's time to go," he said, waving his arm.

Dell heard the last man to leave comment to Willow, "Looks like you could use some new shoes." The guy glanced back at Dell with a cheeky grin.

His remark, and the look on his face, hit Dell hard. Dell's mind had wrestled with Willow's situation for the past two days, but he'd concluded early on, as he'd told Grace, that it would be an unconscionable betrayal to deliver her to CPS, assuming it was doable—which, given her fierce resistance, it probably was not. Even if feasible, her horrendous past experience with a public institution charged with child protection meant there was little reason to believe she would benefit.

Like his daughters Amanda and Joanna at her age, Willow was hardy, adaptable, and bright. And, like them, she took naturally to the A.T. Yes, the trail can be hazardous, not to mention the killer. But the A.T. was also a mentor; it nurtured, toughened, and could turn fellow hikers into comrades. Properly outfitted, Willow would acquire the survival skills of an experienced hiker. *If Patricia was here, she'd agree that it's best for Willow to grow on the trail, to find out who she is and who she wants to become.*

Although constantly aware of the legal risks of being alone with a runaway, Dell remained comfortable with the ethics of his decision not to turn her over to CPS. However, he resolved to again call Grace for moral reassurance. Willow was not being abducted or abused; she'd joined Dell of her own volition and against his initial advice. While she might someday benefit from therapy for the abuse she'd suffered, Willow seemed poised to grow into a mature and confident young woman.

Dell knew he'd grown attached to Willow. He was certain Patricia would never forgive him if he didn't look after her. Nor could he forgive himself.

CHAPTER 9
TRAIN

When Dell and Willow arrived back on the A.T. from the Blue Mountain spring they were soon immersed in wanton floral revelry, a magnificent display of mountain laurel, Pennsylvania's state flower. Both sides of the trail were adorned with seven-foot-high laurel bushes festooned with pink and white blossoms resembling miniature porcelain teacups.

"Wow!" said Willow, as she stuck sprigs of mountain laurel in her hair.

Dell smiled and said, "If we wake up before sunrise tomorrow, we could be in Port Clinton by early afternoon."

"Do we have to get up in the dark?"

"Only if you want a shower, a nice dinner, and your own room at the Port Clinton Hotel. And what about new sneakers?"

Willow leaped into the air. "Yes!" She wagged her finger at Dell and yelled, "You're kiddin', Gramps. Right?" Willow looked at her sneakers, toes sticking out of both.

"Manny Kopeki, the hotel manager, is a friend. We need a break, and you need good equipment and decent sneakers."

Willow stepped up her pace. She skipped and swung her arms in wide arks as she walked. "Come on Gramps. Let's go, let's go." To the tune of the 1930s-hit song, "We're in the Money," she belted out: "We're in a hotel! We're in a hotel! We've got just what it takes to move right along."

"How do you know that old song?" Dell asked.

Willow shook her head from side to side. "My ninth-grade math teacher always sang it."

By late afternoon, they arrived at the Hertlein Campsite, a level area just off the ridge where they found two unoccupied wooden tent platforms in a patch of young oak trees.

"Let *me* set up the tent," Willow said. "You go find the stream."

"Sure you can manage?"

She sighed and planted her hands on her hips. "Gramps, take the cooking pot and canteens and fill them up. Tara can stay with me."

"Yes, Ms. Willow."

Dell gave a military-style salute, grabbed the pot and canteens, and walked down a well-worn path that appeared to lead to the stream which, it turned out, was almost a tenth of a mile away. When he returned with water, Willow had pitched the tent, unrolled the sleeping bag, spread out the mat, and set up the stove on a picnic table beside two beef stroganoff pouches.

"Impressive," Dell said, "You'll rule the trail."

Willow tilted her head back and flashed a see-what-I-can-do grin.

After dinner and a walk with Tara down to the stream and back, they crawled into the tent at 8 p.m. even though it was still light. Tara stayed outside on the other tent platform.

"Good day," Willow said, pulling Dell's sweater on and stretching out on his mat.

"Good day," Dell agreed, sinking into his sleeping bag.

"Dell."

Uh, oh. She never calls me Dell.

"How'd you meet your wife?"

A breeze had come up, rustling the leaves. Dell flipped onto his back, took a deep breath, and his mind bounced back a quarter century to when he was a newly hired young assistant professor.

"I remember walking into a classroom to teach my very first course at the law school. Patricia Anne McKenna sat in the front row. One look, that's all it took."

"Oh," Willow said, "Patricia must have been hot."

Dell chuckled. "Beautiful. Mini skirt, blue eyes, long dark hair. A first-year law student. Patricia smiled at me."

"What'd you do?"

"My face flushed; my pulse raced. I clutched the lectern with both hands, trying desperately to steady myself. To this day, I don't know how I managed to finish the class." Dell took a deep breath.

"*Really?*" Willow rolled over on her side to face him. "What then?"

"Miss McKenna came to my office the next morning wearing what might politely be called a fetching pink blouse."

"Oh boy."

"Patricia looked me in the eye and flashed a mischievous grin. I stood when she entered, knocked over the trash can as she sat down, and stammered, 'It's Miss . . .'"

"McKenna," she said, giggling.

"I could barely talk because I was wondering how to ask her out without asking her out."

Suddenly, Tara barked and growled. They heard a thump as a snarling Tara leaped off her tent platform onto the ground.

"Omigod, what's that?" Willow said.

Dell peered out the front of the tent. Tara, hair raised, was circling a terrified raccoon who was standing up on his hind legs trying to face the dog.

"Whew! It's only a raccoon," Dell said before calling Tara. "Come! Tara, come!"

She retreated reluctantly, eyes on her quarry, until the coon turned and fled into the brush.

Dell slid back into his sleeping bag. Willow reclined on the mat and resumed asking questions. "Wait a minute. I don't understand. Either you ask Patricia out or you don't."

"Not that simple. Universities don't want their professors dating students."

"That's stupid. What happened next?"

"Patricia sat calmly. She clearly relished watching me squirm. I leaned so far back in my desk chair that it tipped and almost flipped over. I caught myself, then asked her what she thought about students and faculty who date one another?'"

Willow giggled. "Clever Gramps, clever."

"Patricia said, 'Sounds great to me.' Four weeks later we were engaged. Four months after that we were married at the Old South Mountain Inn near Boonsboro, Maryland, just a stone's throw from the A.T."

"Wow! Just one look at Patricia and you went bonkers?"

Dell cleared his throat and sang the last line of The Hollies

1960s classic hit song—"Just one look, that's all it took," stretched out in his sleeping bag, and said, "Goodnight, my dear."

Willow exhaled and whispered, "Night Gramps." She turned over and fell asleep.

* * *

At 4 a.m. Dell nudged Willow. "Be right back, nature calls." He grabbed his flashlight and went outside to pee.

Tara made it a twosome when she hopped off her tent platform and squatted next to him.

Willow and Dell dressed quickly and stuffed gorp into their mouths. While he made coffee and packed, she fed Tara.

"Hurry up, old man," she said.

Dell's headlamp lit the way. Light bounced off the ground, rocks, and fallen branches as the two of them walked shoulder-to-shoulder on an unusually wide trail until the sun came up. They sped along the same 1,500-foot elevation ridge they were on the day before and, despite a heavy mist, covered ten miles by the time they stopped for water at the Eagle's Nest Shelter, an unremarkable structure similar to many others along the trail.

They sat down on a bench by the shelter, stretched their legs in the warm sun, and Dell took off his pack. Tara's tail started to twitch. Out of nowhere, a young backpacker in red polyester shorts appeared. He walked right up to Tara, which was risky, especially for strange men. Tara remained calm. The hiker scratched her head.

"My German shepherd is back in Ohio," he said.

Dell nodded and swore that this square-jawed six-footer with eyes like trapdoors, dark and deep, could have modeled for Michelangelo's statue of David. The hiker removed his pack as he and Willow focused on one another. WHAM! The jolt raised hair on the back of Dell's neck and his paternal instincts kicked in. But Dell stood and extended his hand.

"Hey, David . . . sorry, I mean . . . I'm Gramps and this is . . ."

"Willow," she said. "My trail name's Fly Swatter." She stood up, wide-eyed.

The hiker's warm smile was reciprocated by Willow, much too eagerly, in Dell's opinion. Her cheeks flushed.

"Hi Fly Swatter, I'm Train. Theo Payne is my real name."

Their handshake lingered. Dell noticed. As Train chugalugged water from his canteen, he arched his back and licked his lips. Willow's eyes locked on him. Train stepped to within two feet of her and said, "Willow's such a pretty name."

Dell clenched his jaw. *What a creep.* He crossed his arms, moved closer to them, and glared at Train. He was primed to protect the underage Willow he'd taken under his wing.

Still flushed, Willow stroked her forearm, stood tall, and smiled. "Thank you. Theo's a nice name, too. Why did you pick Train as a trail name?"

"Because," Train said, sweeping his arm through the air, "I'm thundering down the tracks—clickety-clack, clickety-clack—all the way to Maine."

Dell rolled his eyes. *What a bullshit line.*

"Did Georgia to the Susquehanna River last year," Train said. "Now, it's the rest of the A.T., to the summit of Mt. Katahdin."

Uneasy about Willow being beguiled by this total stranger, Dell hoisted his pack and stepped toward her. "If we're going to make our destination by this afternoon, we'd better get going."

"Um . . . okay . . . um . . . I guess," she said, as her eyes flicked back and forth between Dell and Train.

"Don't you have a pack, Willow?" Train asked.

"Not anymore."

Train furrowed his brow and eyed Dell. "Not anymore?"

"Her pack disintegrated," Dell said. "It's lashed to mine."

"Disintegrated?" Train glanced at Dell again and scratched his chin. "I should be off."

Dell, Willow, and Train headed out together, following Tara. Despite the narrow trail, Willow and Train hiked, or tried to hike, shoulder-to-shoulder. Dell took up the rear. In trail talk, he was the sweep. Train and Willow chatted nonstop, laughing, and brushing against one another. They seemed to be a "natural item." *Suppose that's what Patricia and I were, but Willow's a minor—and this guy's swagger makes me uncomfortable.*

About an hour later, after everyone hopped from stone to stone across a small stream, Train announced: "Afraid this Train has to leave the station. The engineer wants to pull into the Eckville Shelter tonight."

Train and Willow gazed at each other for several seconds—too long, in Dell's mind. Willow glowed; Dell glowered.

"Maybe we'll see each other again," Train said to Willow.

She moved closer, tilted her head, and smiled. "Hope so. Be safe."

Train took off, not like a lumbering freight train, but more like a Harley-Davidson at full throttle. He was soon out of sight but not out of Willow's mind. Dell was certain. *Why did he take such an inordinate interest in a fifteen-year-old girl? Half the hikers killed on the A.T. in the past year were young women.* Dell bit his lower lip, then tightened his waist belt.

He and Willow walked for a while in silence until he asked, "Did you have a good chat?"

"Uh-huh. He's *really* nice."

"Remember what I said about strangers. There's a murderer at large. This guy can't be ruled out."

She shrugged her shoulders and mumbled, "Yeah."

"How old is he?"

"Twenty-three. Said he's a chemist. Played basketball in college. Some place called Kerniggy Molon."

"Ha! Carnegie Mellon, a fine university, if he's telling the truth." Dell looked at Willow. "Did you tell Train you were my granddaughter?"

She gave him a sly grin. "Maybe not."

CHAPTER 10
PORT CLINTON

A red-tailed hawk circled overhead as Dell and Willow stood on the bluff overlooking Port Clinton and the Schuylkill River. Dell thought he could make out the roof of the Port Clinton Hotel far below. Their late morning descent into the little town began with a knee-straining thousand-foot drop in elevation and, thirty minutes later, the trail led them almost up to the front of the hotel.

Three hikers stood outside chatting as Willow, Tara, and Dell walked into the old stone Port Clinton Hotel shortly after noon. The hotel, revered by hikers for the quality and, especially, quantity of its food, dated from the early 1800s when it was a stagecoach stop. Like The Doyle, although with fewer rooms, the Port Clinton had few fancy amenities, but it was warm and welcoming.

They walked to the reception desk where Manny Kopeki, the hotel's owner, stood. "Well, look what the cat dragged in," he said.

Dell laughed.

Manny took off his thick-lensed, badly smeared eyeglasses and rubbed them with a crinkled handkerchief that had never seen soap and water. "I know the dog," Manny said, "but who's the girl? Too young to be one of your daughters." Manny held his nose. "Whew. How long you two been on the trail?"

"Only three days." Dell tapped Willow on the shoulder. "This is a waif I found along the way. Her name is Willow."

"What's a waif?" Willow asked with a quizzical look.

"A forsaken or abandoned child." Dell grinned and elbowed her.

Willow hung her head and murmured, "Oh."

Oops, a sore spot. Dell gave her a shoulder hug.

Manny cleared his throat, motioned Dell to come closer, and whispered in his ear, "Should I call the police or child welfare?"

"That won't be necessary or helpful. I'm caring for her as long as she needs and wants my help. Charge her room and meals to me."

Manny rolled his eyes. With hands folded as if in prayer he leaned over the reception desk until his face was close to Dell's. "You're the only selfless lawyer I've ever known." Then he guffawed. "Selfless lawyer." Another belly laugh. "Do you know what's black and tan and looks good on a lawyer?"

"Yes. A Doberman," Dell said with a straight face.

Manny roared. "Correct!" He bowed and extended both arms toward Dell in mock supplication. "Behold, His Most Pious Eminence, Saint Dell the Good. He comes to save lost souls and needy hikers."

Dell made a sign of the cross and said, "What we'd like, Blessed Emmanuel, are two rooms, one for me and Tara, another for Willow."

Willow leaned forward, straining to hear the conversation.

Manny slapped his hand on the desk. "Um. . . . Good, 'cause I only got two rooms."

Tara was at Willow's feet, ears up, head tilted. "Can Tara stay in my room?" she asked.

"If it's okay with Manny."

"Sure honey," Manny said, "but the dog can't go in the restaurant."

Dell removed his pack and paid Manny, who handed him the room keys. He gave one to Willow.

"Manny," Dell said, "I've been wanting to speak with you about the matter that brought me back to the trail: the recent murders at the Clary Shelter. Do you have time?"

"And *that's* what I want to talk to you about," Manny replied. "Late this afternoon would be best."

Dell turned to Willow. "I'll be down in a minute, and we'll go get something to eat."

"Okay," she said. "I'll wash up down here in the restroom. Hot water, what a treat."

Dell brought his pack and Tara upstairs to his room. The instant he opened the door and saw the faded damask wallpaper with its a green floral pattern and inhaled the room's musky odor, he recalled the last time he and Patricia had stayed in this very room three years ago. They had splurged on New York strip steak and, after dinner, with full stomachs, tipsy from wine, chased one another up the stairs, into this room, and onto the bed. Today, Dell sat at the foot of the bed, felt the loss well up in his chest, and stared down at his hands.

When he returned downstairs, having left Tara in the room, he asked Manny how to get to Hamburg for some shopping. Manny leaned over the counter and looked down at the shredded remnants of Willow's sneakers.

"I'd say shopping is in order. Ruthie, our cleaning lady, will drive you. Ben's Taxi in Hamburg can give you a ride back."

Ruthie, a large quiet woman with a face as round and innocent as a cabbage, spoke little English. She dropped the two of them off in Hamburg, which calls itself "Hometown America." It was an attractive old town of four thousand with family-owned shops, flower boxes on balconies, and a German heritage dating to the eighteenth century. Dell gave Ruthie a few dollars for her time.

After finding some knockwurst and potato salad at a delicatessen, Dell and Willow walked along State Street to Kramer's Outfitters where he restocked their supply of trail food and snacks. Dell bought Willow a Gregory internal frame backpack, a down sleeping bag, and a pair of hiking sticks. He also got her three pairs of wool-blend socks, her own ground mat, a spoon and fork, Sierra cup, flashlight and headlamp with extra batteries, rain gear and hat, two one-liter canteens, and bug repellent. Her new clothes included a pink wool sweater, long and short hiking pants, two long-sleeved shirts, two T-shirts, and underwear, most of it polyester or nylon for fast drying.

They walked out of Kramer's with Willow wearing her new pack and Dell carrying bags full of clothing, food, and gear.

"When we reach the Delaware Water Gap, I'll get you a tent and hiking boots. That is, if you decide to continue north."

Willow's eyes went saucer-wide. "I don't deserve this."

"Well, you've sort of grown on me, Fly Swatter."

She teared up, covered her eyes, then gave him a hug. "Thank you, Gramps."

When they were about to enter Sassy Sasha's Shoes, Dell said, "The parable of the Good Samaritan has always been my favorite."

"Isn't that Bible stuff?"

"Yeah, Bible stuff. The Samaritan came to the assistance of a traveler simply because the person needed help."

When they entered the shoe store, Willow headed straight for the fashionable rainbow-colored sneakers with thin soles. Dell insisted on heavy fabric and thick soles. They compromised on gray sneakers with green stripes, heavy fabric, and thick soles.

Another half block down State Street brought them to Saperstein's Drugs, where Dell gave Willow cash to round out her supplies with a hairbrush and toiletries before they took Ben's Taxi back to the Port Clinton Hotel.

Late afternoon, when they walked into the lobby, Willow said, "I need a hot shower, NOW." She ran upstairs to her room wearing her new backpack and holding bags full of her acquisitions.

Manny sidled over to Dell holding a couple of bottles of Rolling Rock beer. "Got a minute, Dell?"

"Absolutely," Dell said.

The two of them sat in the hotel lobby on creaky, over-stuffed, heavily stained lounge chairs. The stains were so varied and intricate that the cigarette burns didn't detract from their striking resemblance to the abstract expressionist paintings of Jackson Pollock. Aromas of pot roast and onions wafted in from the kitchen.

"Ya know," Manny said, "Been thinking 'bout those murders." He bent forward and planted both elbows on his knees. "Day or two before they occurred I was standing outside shooting the breeze with some hikers when a Ford-150 pulled up. The driver ate lunch here. For some reason, he was awfully curious about the Pocahontas Campsite."

"Three miles north of here on the A.T.," Dell said.

"Right." Manny sat back, scratched his head, and swigged some Rolling Rock. "The campsite is 'bout the same distance from here that the Clary Shelter is from Duncannon. I recall one of the hikers telling the guy that it was popular and had a good spring."

Dell scooted his chair closer to Manny's. "What else?"

Manny chugged down the rest of his beer, burped, and said, "This fella was too heavy and out of shape to be much of a hiker. And get this, he wore friggin' L.L. Bean boots. Can you believe that?"

Dell jumped up, sloshing beer on the floor. "Great!"

Manny tilted his head to the side. "Great?"

CHAPTER 10: PORT CLINTON

Wiping up the spilled beer with a napkin, Dell asked, "Do you remember anything else about his appearance, behavior, color of the F-150, or whatever?"

"Not much. Short hair, I think. Truck was red; that I do recall. Oh, yeah, had a Maine license plate."

Both of Dell's arms shot into the air. "Holy cow! That jibes with what Jamie Doyle said. I could kiss you."

Manny grimaced. "Spare me, man."

A rush of adrenaline had Dell pacing the floor. "The authorities should know about this right away. I've got to call Harper's Ferry."

"Phone's in your room," Manny reminded him.

Dell patted Manny on the back. "We'll be down for dinner in a bit," he said, and dashed upstairs.

Dell knocked on Willow's door and heard a muffled, "Who is it?"

"Willow, it's Dell," he shouted. "I'll be on the phone a while."

"Take your time. I'm never getting out of this tub."

Dell entered his room, across the hall from hers, and called Brad Hornbeck's home phone. It rang and rang. Someone finally picked up but dropped it on the floor. Seconds later a female voice said, "Hornbecks' residence."

"Is that you Cherie?"

"Dell?"

He heard rustling, and a loud "Oh shit" in the background, followed by the thud of what sounded like bare feet hitting the floor.

"Yes. Hope I'm not interrupting something," he said.

"No, no. We were just . . ."

"Dell, Brad here. Cherie and I were handling some business at my place. What's up?"

"We got a break, one I never anticipated." Dell paced the floor and relayed his conversation with Manny.

"Fantastic. This gives us more to go on. I'll call the feds and state police right away."

"Good, but the cops haven't talked with Manny Kopeki. They *must* speak with him. He's the one who spoke to the guy. Willow and I will be out of here early tomorrow. Hope to reach the Delaware River in four days and be back in D.C. soon thereafter."

"Willow. Who's she?"

"A fifteen-year-old runaway. She's been with me and Tara the entire hike."

"You okay with that?"

"She needed help, and I'm helping."

Brad chortled. "Goddamn man, there you go again. You simply can't resist the unfortunate, distressed, wretched, or just plain screwed up. I still remember when you gave those shivering potheads in Tennessee your jacket and most of your food."

"Well, maybe I'm in the wrong profession. Talk to you later."

"Okay. I'll tell Scaperelli and the state police to talk with Kopeki."

Dell hung up the phone, showered, and changed clothes just as Willow rapped on his door.

"Wow!" Dell blurted out when he opened the door. "The drowned muskrat has transformed herself into a Fairy Queen."

She flashed a bemused smile and curtsied. Willow the winsome wonder sported her newly acquired wardrobe and sneakers. Her face glowed and her mostly dry hair curled over her shoulders and down her back.

Dell offered an arm, which she took. "May I have the honor of escorting milady to dinner?" She flashed a wide-eyed grin.

With Yuengling beer posters hanging from its off-white walls, the dining room was unpretentious. But even the most mundane item on the menu was the piece de resistance for Willow. For an appetizer, she settled on the fried shrimp. Dell had steamed clams. She hesitated before selecting a main course.

"Mother always talked about filet mignon. She said it was 'the best of the best.'" Willow glimpsed at Dell. "Guess that's why it's so expensive, huh?"

"Go for it."

She did, medium rare. Stuffed flounder with crabmeat was his choice. Willow ordered a Dr Pepper while Dell risked a glass of table wine labeled "Vinnie's Choice."

Willow asked about Dell's daughters and the university, and she wanted to hear more about Patricia. After a few minutes, she put her fork on her plate, looked across the table at Dell, and said, "You loved Patricia *so* much."

Dell nodded and took a sip of water.

"I loved my dad," Willow said, "but they wouldn't let me visit him in the hospital before he died. Were you with Patricia?"

Dell nodded again, looked down, and said, "Yes."

CHAPTER 10: PORT CLINTON

"What happened?"

He pushed against the back of his chair, bowed his head, and twisted the wedding ring that was still on his finger. Dell took a deep breath and looked at Willow.

"Patricia had been in a coma for three days at Georgetown University Hospital in Washington, D.C., when I mustered the courage to ask the cancer doctor, the oncologist, 'How long?' She said, 'I'm sorry, Dell. Not long.'"

Willow cupped her hand over her mouth. In a soft voice, she whispered, "Oh, God."

Still fingering his wedding ring, Dell continued. "When the doctor left me alone with Patricia, I held her hand. A peculiar silence flooded the room, then I heard a faint whistling. I *felt* it. My neck tingled, the hair on my arms rose, and the sweet scent of lilies-of-the-valley that Patricia so adored drifted through the room. Something otherworldly, spiritual even, touched me, tried to ease my suffering. Patricia's light went out forever that day. November 9, 1990, 5:47 a.m. So, too, did mine."

"That's so sad," Willow said, extending her hand across the table to Dell.

He reached over, touched her fingertips, and smiled.

Willow wrinkled her brow and tugged at a strand of hair. "You're an old guy, but life's not over." She picked up her fork and took a bite.

"What are you saying?"

"Well, you will marry again, won't you? You should."

Bizarre. Here's a runaway teenager from a dysfunctional family instructing a once happily married guy on how to live his life?

"Don't know yet," Dell said. "Patricia left my life, not my heart."

Willow's mouth was stuffed with mashed potatoes as she waggled her fork at him. She swallowed, took a gulp of Dr Pepper, and paused for several seconds before asking—"Don't you get lonely?"

"It's only been six months."

"Remember Bump?" said Willow. "We met him on our first day of hiking. Miserable and lonely. He was so heartbroken after his wife and kids left him."

"Okay, okay. Maybe you scored. Now it's my turn to pose questions."

"Sure." Willow went back to devouring her steak and potatoes. "I don't know your last name."

She shifted in her chair. "Monroe. Willow Monroe."

"What did you think of Train?" Dell asked.

She wiped her mouth with a napkin and flashed a Cheshire-cat grin. "Oh, he was . . . friendly, *real* friendly."

Dell raised an eyebrow but thought it best not to press the subject. "What will you do when we reach the Delaware Water Gap and I return to Washington?"

Willow put down her fork and took a deep breath. "I can't ever thank you enough. But I'm staying on the trail for as long as I can. After that, don't know." She sat up straight. "I understand now how you came to see the A.T. as family. Maybe it'll be mine as well."

"You'll have me, too." Dell smiled.

She nodded and returned his smile.

Dell spread both hands flat on the table and looked her in the eye. "You're a marvelous young woman, and a great hiker. Tough, too."

Willow grinned, then reached over and lightly touched Dell's hand. "Gramps, why don't you carry a gun. Wouldn't it be safer?"

He leaned back and thought a moment. "Well, I'm a lawyer, not a cop. Distance hikers on the A.T. don't carry guns because they don't want the extra weight; nor is gun-toting either necessary or compatible with the ethics of the trail. Patricia made me throw out my guns when we were married. Perhaps it's irrational, but I still honor her values. I can wield a mean hiking stick, and should I ever need a formidable weapon and early warning system, I have Tara."

The waitress came over and asked about dessert. Dell passed. Willow ordered something called "The Chocolate Bomb."

The thought of Willow hiking alone gave Dell chills. He knew that hikers, particularly distance hikers, look after one another. They form an informal protective community, one Willow could well link up with. But somewhere out there lurked a psychopathic murderer who got his kicks from killing and mutilating hikers, especially young female hikers.

With a tense gut, Dell rubbed his wrist and said, "I can't get the murderer out of my head."

CHAPTER 10: PORT CLINTON

Willow waved her a finger at him. "Don't you worry about me."

"I worry." Dell twisted his wedding ring yet again.

After dinner, they headed upstairs to their rooms. At the top of the stairs Willow turned to Dell and gave him a mile-wide smile. "Best dinner ever! Thanks, Gramps."

Dell winked. "Best dinner companion ever. See you in the morning."

Tara had been isolated in Dell's room for some time. So, before bringing her to Willow's room, Dell took her outside behind the hotel and fed her. The hotel's kitchen lights provided only faint illumination, but Dell made out a barely visible large bird perched in silence on a woodpile a dozen feet away from the back of the hotel. Light reflected off the blind eye of the raven.

When Dell got back to his room, he called Grace at her home in D.C. to talk about Willow. He was also anxious to connect with her. She had been on his mind for some time.

"Be careful," she cautioned, "Willow could be a loose cannon and get you into trouble." But in the very next sentence she said, "I miss you. That is, I miss our conversations. . . . Sorry, that was . . . awkward."

She misses me! Dell dropped down on the bed and flipped onto his back, phone in hand. He remembered what Willow had said at dinner about Bump and loneliness.

Closing his eyes, he said, "Grace."

"Yes."

"Ever have dinner at the Inn at Little Washington?"

"Never. A Michelin star place like that costs a month's salary."

"Maybe a week's."

Grace went quiet for several seconds. "Are you suggesting a . . ."

"Date. Yes." Dell crossed his legs.

"You're on, counselor."

After putting the phone down, Dell hurled his pillow across the room, sat up on the edge of the bed, and yelled, "Whoopee!" *Wow, Grace. 'You're on counselor.' Patricia's gone; time to join the living. Yes!*

CHAPTER 11
LOG MESSAGES

Old Glory snapped in the wind outside the Port Clinton Hotel on May 27th, Memorial Day, as Dell and Willow searched for a white A.T. blaze. Spotting one on a telephone poll, they adjusted their packs, tightened waist belts, and, with sun on their faces and Tara heeling next to Dell, followed the blazes onto and across a long-abandoned, iron railroad bridge that took them over the Schuylkill River.

They ascended a now familiar rocky trail onto Blue Mountain whose seemingly endless ridge slanted south from the Delaware Water Gap across much of eastern Pennsylvania. More than an hour later, they arrived at the Pocahontas Spring Campsite that Manny had mentioned. Only hard-packed dirt tenting spaces, no shelter. Dell poked around to see what he could find while Willow sat on a smooth granite stone, with Tara at her feet. Nothing unusual caught his eye other than some damp, partially disintegrated toilet paper with a residue of feces. *No A.T. distance hiker would ever be so inconsiderate.* Dell was confident the murderer was too smart to leave such obvious evidence. And since he knew the police would comb the area soon after contacting Manny, he and Willow returned to the A.T. and continued their northward trek.

By midmorning, they were immersed in a profusion of spring wildflowers. Most glorious were the tri-pedaled white and pink trillium that adorned patches of the forest floor. But less impressive flora caught Willow's eye. She picked up a large-leafed plant with a simple white blossom that grew in abundance twelve to eighteen inches off the ground.

"What's this?" she asked.

CHAPTER 11: LOG MESSAGES

"Mayapple," Dell said. "When my daughters were young, they called mayapple 'umbrella plants' and held them above their heads."

Willow raised the plant above her head.

"Oh, and they're very poisonous."

She flung the Mayapple into the bushes and pinched her lips shut.

"But only if you eat them."

By late morning, shortly after they'd begun walking on glassy, sharp-edged, black slag from long ago deserted pig iron works, they took a blue-blazed side trail to the Windsor Furnace Shelter for a water break. Dell thumbed through the shelter's dog-eared lined notebook, the kind that served as a log at many lean-tos along the A.T. Hikers often leave their trail names as well as messages. Dell read some of the messages out loud to Willow: "Jitterbug, meet me at Bake Oven Knob Shelter, Toad;" "Great burgers at the Port Clinton Hotel, Mooky;" "Miss you, Mom, Sheri-baby;" "RATTLESNAKES AHEAD!"

About half the entries had a date next to them. One message caught Dell's eye. It was undated but appeared among notes dated between May 7th and May 20th. Unlike other entries, which were scrawled with the stubby remnant of a pencil dangling from the log by a string, this one was written clearly in blue ink. The message read: "In the midst of life we are in death. Fr. Monson."

Strange. It's vaguely familiar, but I can't place it. Dell copied it down on a piece of notepaper for future reference and stuck it in his pack's side pocket. The content of the message was odd. So was the messenger, Father Monson. Like other long-distance A.T. hikers, Dell was well-aware that the tiny hamlet of Monson, Maine, was the jumping-off point for northbound backpackers heading into what hikers call the "Hundred Mile Wilderness," remote country running all the way from Monson to Mt. Katahdin. Dell also noted that the Pennsylvania trail map showed the Windsor Furnace Shelter to be disturbingly close to civilization. A nearby trail led a half mile downhill to a popular RV campsite located on a paved road. Anyone could easily walk up to the shelter and return to their vehicle in under an hour. *Was this shelter scouted out by the murderer?* It was much closer to a road than the murder site at the Clary Shelter. Dell knew the town of Monson well. *Was there a tie between Father Monson and the town? Was Father Monson a pseudonym? Why was his name and weird message in the logbook?*

Dell and Willow returned to the trail, and forty-five minutes later walked onto the massive rock outcropping at Pulpit Rock Overlook with sweeping views below of quilt-like patterns of farms stretched across the Lehigh Valley. A steep side trail from the overlook led up to the summit of 1,635-foot-high Pinnacle Rock. They drank from their canteens, and Dell told Willow how he, Patricia, and their daughters once shivered through a wet blustery night huddling under the Pinnacle's cave-like rock ledges.

They were about to leave Pulpit Rock when Tara tensed and her ears shot up.

"Sit. Stay," Dell said.

Two backpackers, a young couple in their twenties, hiked in from the south and walked up to them.

"I recognize you," Dell said.

"You do?" they replied in unison.

"Doyle Hotel, several days ago. Jamie Doyle and I were sitting at the bar when you two arrived. Actually, you first asked for a bed, then a room."

Dell winked at the young man who appeared to be in his mid-twenties. His short blond companion winced; then they both grinned. The young hiker scuffed his boot on the trail and said, "Well, yeah. We're newlyweds. Been on the trail every day for two weeks before stopping at Duncannon."

Dell chuckled. "Boy, can I relate. Two days after my late wife and I were married, we hiked a section of the A.T. The bugs, sweat, smell, and grime were hardly conducive to . . . uh . . . conjugal bliss."

Willow elbowed Dell. "What's that?"

The young woman glanced at Willow who, head cocked, was listening intently. She stepped over to Willow and whispered in her ear, though not too quietly, "Sex."

They both laughed.

Willow wagged her finger at Dell. "I know about that stuff. If you and grandma hadn't done it, I wouldn't be here."

Everyone smiled.

Leaning forward on his hiking stick, Dell said, "I'm Gramps. This is my granddaughter, Willow. Her trail name's Fly Swatter."

"I'm Skip," the young guy said, "Trail name's Skipper."
"And I'm Shirley. Trail name's First Mate."

First Mate Shirley said they'd gotten on the trail at Pen Mar, on the Pennsylvania-Maryland line. Skipper said they'd hoped it would be "a three-month honeymoon, hiking to Mt. Katahdin." He shook his head. "It's been tougher, much tougher, than we thought, but we're not giving up." Skipper looked at his wife. "Right, love?"

First Mate forced a pained smile, said nothing, and scratched a swollen mosquito bite on her neck.

Dell gave them a nod. "There's no better way to get to know one another, *really* know one another."

First Mate took Skipper's hand and looked up at him. "I guess, but R&R at The Doyle was critical that night, as were the clean sheets and shower."

Dell wished them good luck, and Skipper and First Mate went on ahead. He expected to see them again before he and Willow reached the Delaware River. Dell and Willow resumed their hike a few minutes later, maintaining a steady pace until they came to Hawk Mountain Road and nearby Eckville Shelter, where Train had said he'd spend the night. They'd covered fifteen miles since leaving Port Clinton. Concern about their time dissuaded Dell from detouring to the Hawk Mountain Sanctuary to show Willow the first reserve in the world for raptor conservation.

They did stop at the shelter, which differed from others on the A.T. It appeared to have once been a small barn. The shelter had a large front door, was painted white, and had wood platforms for sleeping bunkbed style.

Willow made a beeline for the shelter's log. With eyes glued to the notebook's entries, her finger traced the signatures and messages.

"Wow!" She shot a fist in the air. "Train said he would stay here, and he did."

Willow pogoed up and down on her toes.

"Train wrote that, get this, he 'L-O-V-E-D' meeting me. He 'VERY MUCH' wants to see me again." Willow wiggled her hips and danced around in a circle, hands held high.

Damnit, Dell thought. "Anything else?"

Willow grimaced. "Maybe"

"Let me see if Father Monson left a message," Dell said.

Willow shook her head and reluctantly surrendered the notebook.

Nothing from Father Monson, but Dell read aloud what else Train had written—"I'll be at the Bear Mountain Inn, near the Hudson River, for three or four days with my brother. He's driving up from New York City with his girlfriend. Hope you can make it. The Inn's phone number is: 914-786-2731."

Dell glanced at Willow. Her face reddened, but she jotted the number down on a blank page of the notebook and stuck it in her pocket.

When they left the Eckville Shelter to return to the A.T., Willow was so elated Dell feared she might float away. With wide eyes, she beamed at him, at Tara, at the trees, and at everything in sight. She bounced and skipped along as if in another world for the final eight miles to their tenting site. Willow remained in a haze until the next morning when rain and hunger brought her down to earth.

* * *

Sheets of rain fell on May 28th, so they called Tara into the tent and ate breakfast there. In Port Clinton, Dell had coached Willow on how and where to stash various items in her pack for maximum comfort and convenience. She now got to use her new rain gear and waterproof pack cover. Later in the day, after they'd arrived at their destination, Dell watched Willow wring out her wet wool socks the way he'd shown her and stuff them into the bottom of her sleeping bag so they'd emerge drier and warmer the next morning.

Dell and Willow hiked eighteen miles along another of Blue Mountain's long ridges, leaning headfirst into fierce wind gusts that knocked them backward and sideways as the rain beat down in horizontal torrents. They slipped and fell on slick, moss-covered rocks, sometimes pitching forward and tumbling into the mud. Thinking it was some kind of game, Tara would run over, wag her tail, and lick their faces.

Wiping his muddy hands on his pants, Dell's mind floated off to Patricia. *Wasn't it Dante who said the greatest pain is to remember happy times when you're in misery?* Dell gave Willow a hand as she stepped over a dead tree that had fallen across the trail.

CHAPTER 11: LOG MESSAGES

After crossing four dirt roads and PA Route 309 and walking a thousand feet above the muffled roar of eighteen wheelers passing through the Pennsylvania Turnpike's Lehigh Valley Tunnel, they arrived at the run-down George Outerbridge Shelter. The shelter was empty. Like the Windsor Furnace Shelter, this one was only a half mile from a highway. The ground was littered with broken glass, cigarette butts, discarded condoms, and crushed beer cans—the very antithesis of wilderness. Easily accessible to anyone, it invited the kind of visitors who could be hostile to hikers.

Standing in the rain surveying the scene, Dell hesitated. He looked at his watch, scratched the stubble on his chin, and said, "Well, Fly Swatter, it's pretty sketchy. What do you think?"

Willow said, "I think I'm tired and wet."

The rain hadn't let up. It was 5 p.m. and much too far to the next shelter. And despite a leaky roof, mouse droppings on the floor, the smell of urine, and spent shotgun shells on the picnic table, they would be out of the rain.

Dell shrugged and sighed, "Okay."

They threw their wet packs on the warped floor and watched as Tara pounced high in the air and skidded along the loose floorboards to the shelter's far interior corner, her jaws snapping. She flipped a dark object over her back in their direction. It plopped at Dell's feet. Dell and Willow looked down to see a gray mouse, or what was left of it, bloody entrails splattered across the floor.

"Oh, gross," cried Willow.

Dell picked the mouse up by its still twitching tail and flung it outside.

"Good girl," Dell said to Tara, petting her head.

She flashed her German shepherd smile. A few minutes later she whacked another mouse, then another.

Stepping over one of Tara's victims to get to the shelter's log, Willow said, "Maybe Train left another message." She scanned the log, her shoulders drooped. "Train wasn't here."

Then she waved Dell over and said, "Look at this."

An undated blue ink entry by Father Monson read: "Man that is born of a woman hath but a short time to live, and is full of misery."

"I know that!" Dell said. "It's from the *Book of Common Prayer*. It's depressing but was read at my grandfather's funeral service.

That's why I remember it. Bet that's also where Father Monson's log entry at the Windsor Furnace Shelter came from."

"What does it mean?" Willow asked, taking off her raincoat.

"I could hazard a theological meaning, likely from the Old Testament, but why it's up here in an A.T. log only a few days hiking from the Clary Shelter is unsettling."

Willow squinched her face up and clutched Tara's neck. "I'm scared."

"Yeah, me too," Dell said, "but we need to eat."

They ate dinner and tucked into their sleeping bags, but slept uneasily that night. When Tara wasn't dispatching field mice, she snuggled up against Willow who draped an arm over her damp canine companion.

Dell fell into a nightmare. He was with Tara. They were searching for Patricia who would sometimes morph into Willow. In the dream, he waded through a muddy marsh, then hiked in a trackless spruce forest where Train (of all people) had told him to look. Two-foot-long rats swarmed Tara. She snapped the necks of several, but their sheer numbers overwhelmed her. The rats ripped off her ears and tail and gnawed her legs and hind quarters to the bone. Then they surrounded Dell, Tara's blood dripping from their faces. A sulfurous smell filled the air. A shadowy figure of a man appeared in front of Dell with a long black knife in his hand.

Kruck, kruck. Dell bolted awake, breathing heavily and sweating. In the early morning light, a raven alighted on the picnic table outside the shelter. The bird flew off with a dead mouse in its beak.

CHAPTER 12

SNAKES

The rain had cleared by morning as Dell and Willow started the twenty-one-mile hike that would take them over the Lehigh River, up to the open ridge of Blue Mountain, and along a somewhat level A.T. scattered with scrawny twisted oak and birch trees, to the Leroy Smith Shelter. Seeing bags under Dell's eyes Willow said, "You look tired. You okay?"

"Didn't sleep too well," he replied.

Not long after reaching the mountain's ridge, composed mostly of granulated schist and crystalline quartzite, Willow stooped down to pick up an odd-looking black stick laying across the path. She screamed when it moved. A four-foot-long rat snake with shiny black scales and white chin was sunning itself in the middle of the trail.

"Eek! I hate snakes," Willow screeched. She jumped back, shook her hands frantically, and tried to hide behind Dell.

"But why?" Dell asked, as he stepped to within three feet of the snake.

"What . . . what's good about them?" she shrieked. "They bite, they're slimy, and they freak me out."

A prominent bulge in the snake's midsection indicated it had devoured some hapless critter not too long ago. Tara sniffed its tail and walked away. Dell leaned over and gently lifted the blacksnake off the ground with open hands so as not to apply pressure to its body.

Willow screamed again—"Don't! It'll bite. Don't!" She cringed and grabbed onto Tara, who seemed confused by the ruckus.

The snake flicked its tongue, exuded a musky odor, and wrapped itself around Dell's arm. "Willow, snakes have gotten a bum rap ever since Adam and Eve. This is the same kind of snake I had as a pet when I was a boy. Come over here. If you handle blacksnakes with kindness they won't harm you."

"Yuck. No way!" She wrapped her arms around her chest.

"Tara wasn't afraid of him. I thought you were curious and adventurous. Tell you what—if it bites you, I'll bite the snake." Dell flashed a wide grin, exposing his front teeth.

Willow pursed her lips, wrinkled her nose. "Don't bite it." She inched closer, stretched out her hand, and touched the snake that engirdled Dell's arm with her fingertip. "So smooth."

Dell returned the snake to the ground, where it slithered off his arm and went straight for the nearest tree. They watched as the blacksnake wound its way up a gnarled oak and draped itself over a branch a few feet above their heads.

Hours later, as the sun began to sink in the western sky, Dell and Willow eyed a hawk soaring in wide circles high above them.

"Probably a red tail," Dell said.

The hawk's wings were spread wide and raised at the tips to catch air currents as it drifted overhead. It seemed to follow them as they hiked along. Twenty minutes of soundless elegance—until an ominous buzz, like an angry hornet in a jar, raised the hair on the back of Dell's neck.

Ears up, Tara had stopped ten feet from a rattlesnake coiled on a flat rock by the side of the trail. She didn't sniff this one. Instead, she barked a high-pitched warning as the fur on her back rose.

Willow clutched Dell's arm. "What's *that* snake?"

"Eastern timber rattlesnake. Give it a wide berth. Leave them alone, and they'll leave you alone." Dell looked Willow in the eye. "Look at that snake very closely. I want you to remember its diamond-shaped head and dull brown and yellow markings. Not as aggressive as its western cousins, but one of North America's most venomous snakes."

Willow's eyes glommed onto the rattler. "I'm more scared of snakes than some crazy dude killing people on the trail."

She didn't ease her grip on Dell's arm until they'd stepped off the trail with Tara and skirted around the snake. Once past the snake Dell then stopped, put an arm around Willow's shoulders, and looked her in the eye. "Listen. Rattlesnakes bite people only when threatened. Snakes are important creatures in the natural

CHAPTER 12: SNAKES

world. The murderer, who is still at large, kills for the *joy* of killing. He murders and mutilates young women just like you. *Never forget that.*"

Willow looked down, red-faced. She mumbled, "Sorry. I won't forget."

A few miles later they arrived at the small, six-person Leroy Smith Shelter and its usually reliable spring. Without any prompting from Dell, Willow got down on her hands and knees in the dirt and peered under the shelter. "No snakes," she announced. "No murderer either."

Dell remained on alert. They dropped their packs and hiking sticks on the floor of the shelter, ate dinner, fed Tara, cleaned up, and tucked themselves into their sleeping bags before nightfall.

"Something new happens every day," Willow said, as she snuggled down in her new bag.

"Indeed," Dell said. "On the A.T. you might be anxious, thirsty, in pain, or sometimes lonely, but you're rarely bored." With that, he rolled over and dozed off.

They'd been asleep for a couple of hours when Tara's muffled growls woke Dell. He sat up in the dark and heard twigs snap and the rustle of heavy footsteps crunching high brush somewhere toward the back of the shelter. Through a crack in the rear wall, he saw two lights bobbing toward them, but the lights soon disappeared from sight. *Good God! Why aren't they on the side trail to the shelter? No one would walk right through the brambles and trees, especially at night.* Dell picked up his flashlight, always ready by his sleeping bag, and clicked it on. Tara's low growls grew into loud snarls. She pinned her ears back and bared her teeth. Dell jumped out of his sleeping bag with his trousers on, stood, and seized his only weapon—the hiking stick. He shook Willow.

"What's wrong?" she asked.

"Shhhh! Someone's coming. It's strange, I don't like it. They're off the trail and crashing through the woods. Quick, get dressed. Grab your hiking stick and be ready to run."

Trembling, Willow pulled her pants and sneakers on muttering, "Oh no. Oh no." She stood up in the shelter, breathing rapidly, poised to flee. A boot scuffed the dirt nearby. Still inside the shelter, Dell raised his hiking stick in the air. "Tara . . .," he said. She growled and crouched low, muscles tensed.

"Sorry to bother you at this hour," said a woman who came up from behind the shelter and whose appearance Dell couldn't quite make out. "Is your dog friendly?"

Dell exhaled, tossed his hiking stick to the floor, and held Tara by the collar. "Well, she is now. She likes women, but not strange men. I thought you were the friggin' murderer."

From somewhere behind the woman, Dell heard a man's voice, probably the woman's husband or boyfriend, say, "Not too reassuring about the dog, but we're so bushed I'll take my chances."

Willow was shaking, almost in tears.

"We're so sorry," the woman said, looking at Willow. "Didn't mean the frighten you." She tossed her pack into the shelter. "Somehow, we strayed off the side trail and ended up plowing through the woods."

The couple turned in almost immediately, without eating dinner or washing up.

Dell wrapped his arms around Willow. "It'll be okay, honey." He had Tara lie down between the two of them. But a quiet calm was not restored. Neither of them slept well, and Tara's anxious grumbles continued throughout the night.

CHAPTER 13
DUST-UP

Pale orange rays from the early morning sun were creeping into the shelter when Willow woke.

Grunting, scratching, and gnawing sounds came from behind the lean-to. She leaped out of her sleeping bag and dressed quickly. Tara tilted her head and uttered a muffled growl. Dell and the couple who had arrived in the night were asleep.

Willow shook Dell awake. She whispered, "Someone's scratching at the back of the shelter. I'm scared."

Dell rubbed his eyes and yawned. He rolled out of his bag, pulled on his trousers, and told Tara to, "Sit. Stay." Careful not to disturb the sleeping couple, he whispered, "Think I know what's making that sound. Take Tara's collar. Hold it tight. I don't want her involved."

Willow held the collar, Dell grabbed his hiking stick. "I may need this."

He slipped his boots on, hopped to the ground, and tip-toed to the back of the shelter. There, chewing on a corner of the lean-to and making a noise strikingly similar to a cooing baby, was a porcupine, a twenty-pounder about the size of a Welsh corgi. Its black, white-tipped quills rose when Dell approached, and a quill-studded tail swished a warning. Dell poked the rodent with his hiking stick. "Get lost, prickle pig." Surprised, it screeched and backed away from where it had been gnawing on the shelter's pine boards. The porcupine grunted, chattered its teeth, and wobbled off into the woods. Dell returned to the shelter.

"What was it?" Willow asked, still holding Tara by the collar.

"Porcupine. They love salt. Some guy probably peed on the back of the shelter."

Gripping Tara's collar tighter, Willow gasped, "Porcupines shoot their quills at people."

"No, that's a myth. Leave them alone, and you'll be fine."

They stepped to the picnic table in front of the shelter, gazed out at the farms and fields below, and ate breakfast. They then fed Tara, packed, and were ready to go when a curly-haired man stuck his head out of his sleeping bag and they heard him say, "Do you know how porcupines make love?"

"Yes, dear," said a woman's voice, "very carefully."

Dell and Willow chuckled and waved to the couple as they headed back onto the trail.

With a smile and quick wink, a self-confident Willow asked, "Where to today, Gramps?"

"Not too far: fourteen miles to the Kirkridge Shelter. Afraid we'll have lots of company. The shelter is on federal land in the very popular Delaware Water Gap area, and it's close to a major highway that runs through Fox Gap."

Two hours of easy rock hopping brought them to a sweeping vista at Lookout Rock, where they took a short break. It was a favorite destination for day hikers, most of whom hiked up from the nearby town of Wind Gap on PA Route 33. Several people sat or stood on the shelf of fractured rock that jutted out over a cliff. Some were photographing one another, others gazed out at the distant, cloud-shrouded Pocono Mountains to the north and Aquashicola Creek meandering through the valley below.

Shortly after leaving Lookout Rock, Dell and Willow encountered a young man of maybe nineteen or twenty walking uphill toward them. His lip was swollen, and an ugly purple bruise marred one side of his face. He had no pack, no hiking stick, and he stared down at the ground to avoid looking them in the eye. He shoved his hands deep into the pockets of torn trousers that appeared to be bloodstained. He did manage a barely audible, "Hi."

Tara sniffed him cautiously and flicked her tail.

"My gosh," said Willow, instinctively reaching out her hand, almost touching him. "You okay? Did you fall? I'm Fly Swatter, what's your trail name?"

"Don't have one. Real name's Sam Welch."

"Dell Peterson, Appalachian Trail Conference. How can we help?" *Poor guy. Looks like he could break down and cry at any moment.*

"Don't know. Yesterday, two men beat me pretty bad near Fox Gap. And . . ." Sam rolled up a pants leg, exposing red, puffy puncture wounds on his calf. "I was mauled."

Willow winced. "Ouch."

"Dog bites?" Dell asked, as he moved in closer to take a look.

"Uh-huh." Sam touched his swollen leg.

Tara trotted over to him. Sam cringed and stepped back.

"Don't worry, she likes you," Dell assured him as Tara sat down next to Sam.

Sam stroked Tara's head and said, "Their dog, a nasty pit bull, had just killed a wild turkey. I saw it happen. As I walked by, I said, 'Wildlife are protected here.' That was my mistake. They laughed, punched me in the face, knocked me to the ground. That's when their dog attacked. They stole my brand-new Kelty backpack with everything in it."

Willow clenched her fists and shouted, "That's shitty!"

Dell raised an eyebrow and gave Willow a stern look.

"Sorry," she said. "I mean, how awful."

"Look Sam," Dell said, "let's walk down to Wind Gap where you probably were a little while ago. We're headed that way anyway. I will call the state police."

Sam shrugged. "Yeah. Guess that's a good idea even though I'm going back home to Vermont. My parents are driving down from Burlington. They'll meet me at the Meadows Motel in Wind Gap where I stayed last night. I walked up here today for something to do before they arrive."

"Fine," Dell said. "We'll call the cops from the motel. Need anything? Water? Snickers?" Dell pulled a small bottle of iodine from his pack. Here's something for that leg, but you'll probably need an antibiotic."

After Sam took a candy bar and applied iodine to his wounds, they slow-walked the short distance downhill on the rutted, well-traveled trail to PA Route 33 where the motel manager let Dell use his phone to call the Bethlehem Barracks of the state police. Dell identified himself and explained why he'd called.

"We might be able to get someone to the motel later this afternoon Mr. Peterson," said the woman who answered the phone.

"Madam, Sgt. Clayton Ward in Harrisburg asked me to call him anytime if I needed assistance. I can give you his number."

"Oh. I apologize, sir. Everyone knows Clay. Someone will be at the Meadows Motel in a few minutes."

A state police car pulled up to the motel ten minutes later. Out stepped a towering officer with sharply creased black trousers and a tailored gray shirt with black epaulets. Willow held Tara on a leash while Sam and Dell briefed Officer Sean Driscoll.

Driscoll listened intently, asked several questions, grimaced, shook his head, and said, "This isn't the first incident at Fox Gap or, for that matter, at the nearby Kirkridge Shelter. We'll contact the National Park Service because both the shelter and Fox Gap—where the Appalachian Trail goes across Route 191—are in the National Recreation Area." Driscoll assured them he'd poke around in the Fox Gap area later that afternoon.

Sam, Willow, and Dell thanked Officer Driscoll, who returned to his squad car and drove away.

Dell put his hand on Sam's shoulder and said, "Things will work out. Don't let this color your opinion of the A.T. Most of the trail is magnificent, and safe."

"You've been a great help. Thank you," Sam said with a gentle smile.

Tara nuzzled against his uninjured leg and Willow said, "You'll be okay."

Dell and Willow lifted their packs and, with Tara on a leash, walked the short distance from the motel along Route 33 to where the A.T. crossed the road.

"Wouldn't be surprised to see Sean Driscoll again this afternoon," Dell said.

"Could the murderers have been the ones who hurt Sam?" Willow asked.

Dell shook his head. "Unlikely. Probably just thugs who saw an easy mark. The murderer or murderers would not have let him walk out alive. Also, the killer has always struck at night and, at least so far, he has only attacked couples. And there's no evidence the murderer has had a dog with him. Overall, the killer of A.T. hikers seems to be far more sophisticated than the creeps Sam ran into."

"Whew! That's a relief," Willow said, stepping up her pace.

"But," Dell said, "it's not impossible, and you're asking the right question. It pays to be vigilant."

CHAPTER 13: DUST-UP

A gradual ascent out of Wind Gap brought them to the ridge of what was now called Kittatinny Mountain. They hiked north along the stony but level trail for nine miles until, by midafternoon, they arrived at the paved road passing through Fox Gap. Dodging speeding cars, they crossed to the other side of PA Route 191 where a white blaze marked the trailhead. A blue Chevy van without hubcaps was parked by the roadside. The ground was littered with broken glass and stained with what looked and smelled like motor oil. The Kirkridge Shelter was less than a half mile away.

Recalling Officer Driscoll's remarks, Dell said, "The shelter's closeness to the highway invites the kind of trouble Sam encountered. Even the Clary Shelter murder site was at least three miles from the nearest highway."

Willow wrinkled her brow.

Within minutes after entering a sparsely wooded area, they smelled, then saw, the mangled headless carcass of a wild turkey by the side of the trail. Black feathers tipped with bronze and white were strewn about on the trail and forest floor. Tara set off a cloud of flies when she nosed the partially dismembered, fetid remains. Right away, Dell knew Tara had detected something more than a decaying turkey—another dog. With a low growl, she tensed, ears back, hair raised. Another ten minutes of easy hiking in the direction of the Kirkbridge Shelter brought them within earshot of loud music.

"We're not staying there," Dell said.

Willow lifted her stick in the air. "Good call."

The brown-stained boards at the rear of the shelter soon came into sight. So, too, did a pig-eyed, muscular pit bull with only one ear. The dog snarled, then bounded toward them, rushing straight for Tara.

"Oh, no!" Willow screamed.

"Willow, hold your pack up in front of you with both hands," Dell shouted.

He threw his backpack to the ground and gripped his hiking stick with two hands, like a baseball bat, ready to whack the beast. Tara crouched on the ground in front of Dell and Willow, prepared to pounce. She waited until the onrushing cur was almost on her before leaping out of the dog's path. The dog skidded past her, frantically digging its claws into the thick leaf litter trying to regain traction. Before the beast could turn to resume the attack, Tara lunged, slamming all of her eighty pounds into the snarling brute. Tara clamped her jaws onto the scruff of her assailant's neck, twisted sharply, and flipped him over on his back. In an instant, she had the dog's throat in a mortal vice-grip as she whipped her head fiercely from side to side. The dog whimpered, peed on himself, foamed at the mouth, and went limp.

"Tara, enough!" Dell shouted. "Come!"

Caught up in the thrill of the kill, she ignored his command. Dell seized her collar with both hands and yanked. Never taking her eyes off the enemy, Tara stood up and straddled the fallen dog. The defeated aggressor laid on his side, twitching, panting, and exhaling a bloody froth.

Dell was only a few feet from the dogs while Willow stood at a distance, trembling. Hearing the commotion, two potbellied middle-aged men, one bald and wearing a gray sweatshirt, the other with straggly dark hair and a yellow Don't-Tread-on-Me T-shirt, duck-walked toward them as fast as their swaying paunches would allow.

"Hey, you shithead!" one man shouted, "Control your fuckin' dog." A younger, heavyset woman wearing blue jeans and holding a can of beer watched as she leaned against the outside rear wall of the shelter.

Gray sweatshirt was the first to arrive. He kicked at Tara, but she hopped out of the way. Eyes bulging and exuding a putrid odor not unlike the turkey's, but with a little beer and urine mixed in, he turned on Dell.

"Your goddamn dog should be shot!" he snarled as he threw a punch.

Dell stepped back and the blow just grazed his shoulder. When the assailant raised his fist to try again, Dell swung his hiking stick, striking the bridge of the guy's nose with a sharp crack. He crumpled to the ground on one knee, face and sweatshirt splattered with blood.

Willow shouted, "Watch out, Gramps! Here comes the other one."

A few yards away, an even more obese guy, the one with disheveled hair and T-shirt, toddled toward Dell clutching a knife with a curved six-inch blade. Tara barked a sharp warning and positioned herself in front of Dell, poised to spring at the attacker.

CHAPTER 13: DUST-UP

"Back off! Drop the knife." Officer Driscoll had his pistol drawn, as did the National Park Service ranger who was with him.

The woman tossed her beer can aside and raced toward the two men screaming, "Nick, don't do it!"

He threw his knife to the ground. Both men were handcuffed and read their Miranda rights by the ranger, who introduced himself as Jerry Kulikowski.

Driscoll chuckled as he picked up the knife and said, "Well, how about that. I know these Russo brothers—recidivists and bail jumpers."

He and Kulikowski looked inside the shelter. So, too, did Dell and Willow. Along with blankets, bags of junk food, a cooler of beer, and a still blaring radio playing Garth Brooks, "Friends in Low Places," was a new, green Kelty backpack—no doubt, Sam Welch's.

"I'll see that Mr. Welch knows we have this," said Driscoll.

Willow walked over to the officers, her hands pressed together as in prayer. "Omigod. Thank you, thank you."

"Indeed," Dell added. "Things would have gotten much worse if you hadn't shown up. We're grateful."

"Well," said Ranger Kulikowski, "you and your dog did pretty damn well." He pointed at Tara, who was licking her paw. "No way I'd ever cross that dog."

The two officers prepared to leave with the handcuffed Russos, the woman, their limping dog, and Sam's backpack. Sean Driscoll looked at Dell and tipped his hat.

"Clay Ward told my captain good things about you, Mr. Peterson. We owe *you* a debt of gratitude—not only for helping us get the Russos, but for assisting us with those Appalachian Trail murders outside of Duncannon."

Dell told Driscoll about the odd log messages they'd found from Father Monson, he stressed that they should be checked out, and asked, "Anything new about the murderer?"

"Don't know," Driscoll said. "I'm not on that case. But no suspect has been apprehended."

While Dell was talking with the officers, Willow thumbed through the shelter's log and found Train's signature, but no message. She and Dell shook hands with Driscoll and Kulikowski. Then the officers and Russos walked down the trail and out of sight.

Dell turned to Willow. "This place is unsafe. Much too close to the highway. I know a spot that's not far away." He pulled out his trail map and pointed a finger to Nelson's Overlook. "That's where we're going."

"Good. Let's get away from here. This place gives me the shivers."

Dell took her hand. "You're safe with me and Tara, honey."

She gave Dell a hug.

Before moving on, Dell looked back at the Kirkridge Shelter and noticed something yellow underneath the lean-to. He knelt down, flopped onto his chest, and extracted a slender, dirt-streaked book with his hiking stick. The water-damaged hardcover book was entitled, *Wilderness Survival Strategies and Techniques*. Its warped inside cover had a faded blue stamp:

Miller Library

Colby College

Waterville, Maine

Dell crammed the book into his pack, and they walked north down the trail.

CHAPTER 14
HOLY SPIRIT MOMENTS

Kirkland Shelter was just a half mile from Nelson's Overlook. At 1,534 feet in elevation, the rocky ledge offered an unobstructed view to the south of the small towns of Bangor and Roseto with their several churches, to the southeast of the winding Delaware River, and, directly below them, the Minsi Lake–Bear Swamp County Park. After the violent confrontation at the shelter, which further sharpened Dell's constant concern about the murderer, he and Willow pitched their tent a hundred yards away from the overlook and A.T., down a faint deer path Dell knew about on the western side of the ridge where they were well-hidden behind a dense tangle of blackberry bushes, laurel, and pine.

They finished their freeze-dried mush of a dinner labeled "Chicken Surprise" as the sun melted into splotches of peach and purple and smudged the western sky like a Rothko painting hung above the distant hills. As darkness descended, they heard the whispering of black-shadowed pines and the solitary *kruck* of a raven hidden somewhere in the trees.

Although Dell knew how Willow would answer, he asked, "Are you still determined to continue north by yourself when we reach the river tomorrow?"

She glanced down. "Uh-huh."

Dell brushed Willow's hand and looked at her. "I told you early on I'd be getting off at the Delaware. That's much more than the ATC asked of me, but I don't regret it for a minute." He rubbed his forehead. "When we get to the Kittatinny Visitor Center on the New Jersey side of the river, I'll give you my contact information. Promise you'll call whenever you're near a phone to let me know you are okay and, especially, if you need something."

Willow let out a huge breath. She pressed his hand and said with a radiant smile, "Promise."

"Good, that's what I wanted to hear. Grab your headlamp; the overlook should be magnificent tonight."

Tara's nose, more surely than any headlamp, led them out of the thick brambles and onto the overlook. They sat on a massive rock shelf on this cloudless night, staring at the heavens and the scarcely visible outlines of farms and fields below.

Dell's head filled with an ancient hymn he'd sung as a child, some forty years ago. He was a lousy singer, but out came "Now sunset comes, but light shines forth, the lamps are lit to pierce the night. Praise Father, Son, and Holy Spirit: God who dwells in the eternal light."

And light there was on this warm evening in late May. Fireflies, spots of yellow and green luminescence, flitted about. Stars sprinkled the half-moon sky, and far below in the distance scattered lights winked at them from towns and farmhouses.

The redolent smells of spring wafted up from Minsi Lake and Bear Swamp with the earthy scents of a verdant marsh, resiny odors of poplar buds, the wind-pollinated fragrance of willow catkins, and the sensual aroma of jasmine. Waves of sound rippled up from the black swamp below in an undulating din. Spring peepers were in full and frantic song. That evening on Nelson's Overlook cast a spell, a peculiar mystique that would never be forgotten.

They lingered at the overlook for an hour. A pensive Willow sighed and half closed her eyes. Tara's muzzle rested on her lap. Willow stroked the head of her forever-friend.

"Gramps?"

"Yes?"

"When we first started hiking together you said you hoped there was a God."

"Can't recall, but it is something I could've said."

"Why do you hope there's a God?"

Uh oh. Better not flub this one. Silence.

"Well?" Willow asked.

"Our lives are our bodies, of course, but something more. Think about it. You know this."

Willow pulled her knees against her chest and held them tight. "I do?"

"Holy Spirit moments is a phrase I sometimes use."

"What's that mean?"

"Christians—I'm a Christian but not a very good one—believe that something called the Holy Spirit, kind of like the breath of God, is inseparable from God himself and Jesus; that God expresses His or Her presence and power to people through the Holy Spirit. When such expressions occur, we have Holy Spirit moments." Dell patted Tara and scuffed his boots on the rock ledge.

Willow sighed and stared at the stars. "Like what moments?"

"Like Tara's love for you; like the sound of those marsh peepers; the smells of springtime; the delicate beauty of mountain laurel blossoms; and the twinkling stars you're gazing at that tell us, even after death, there is no perpetual darkness."

"Life's wonders?"

"Yes. Like when I first saw Patricia and . . ." Dell's voice broke, and a solitary tear rolled down his cheek. "And when I first met you."

He reached over and held Willow's hand. She gripped it and leaned her head on his shoulder.

"Like Patricia, you brought me joy and light. For this, and for our Appalachian Trail, I'm forever grateful."

"For Tara, too!" said Willow.

Dell chuckled and patted Tara's head again. "Yes. For Tara, too."

"And," said Willow, "that's why you want to catch the murderer. He threatens what you love."

"Well put."

Dell stood and stretched his arms over his head. "Well, my dear, tomorrow will be a short hike, but a big day."

Willow got up. They turned on headlamps and followed Tara along the overgrown deer path through clinging vines and dark shadows to their campsite.

Before entering the tent on this starlit night, Willow asked, "What day is it?"

"Thursday, May 30th."

"Thought it was close. Tomorrow's my birthday."

Dell wrapped his arm around her shoulders and squeezed. "Happy birthday, sweet little sixteen."

CHAPTER 15
PARTING

Still in Pennsylvania, Dell and Willow approached Lunch Rocks, a stony outcropping with a view to the north into New Jersey. It was the morning of Friday, May 31st, Willow's birthday and their last day together on the A.T.

Shoulder-high azaleas with voluptuous pink and white blooms lined the trail, perfuming the air with nutmeg-like fragrances. A summery weekend had started. A slight breeze rustled the leaves on this bright day, and they had already encountered people flocking to the trail.

"Reminds me of Times Square on New Year's Eve," Dell said to Willow.

Two stone-faced women in matching uniforms, gray skirts and tops, sat on a granite slab in the scant shade provided by a scrub oak. When the women saw Dell and Willow, they looked away. Some of their charges, girls not much younger than Willow dressed in blue and white parochial school uniforms, shaded their eyes from the sun's glare and waved at Willow as they scrambled over the rocks. Other girls munched snacks and chattered to each other like a flock of chirping sparrows.

Willow stared at them without saying anything.

"What are you thinking?" Dell asked.

She adjusted her backpack and thought a moment before speaking. "Someday I'll go back to school, but I'm not like them. I'm not a schoolgirl anymore."

"No, you're not."

Over the next four miles on the way to Mt. Minsi, where they would begin a long, winding descent to the Delaware River, they met many people—earnest sixty-something bird watchers with

CHAPTER 15: PARTING

binoculars, other school groups, couples holding hands, picnickers out for the day, and a troop of Boy Scouts hurling sticks and acorns at one another. None of these people were long-distance hikers, but Dell and Willow heard the scout master shout out in their direction, "Keep on truckin'!

At 1,461 feet in elevation, Mt. Minsi commanded the Pennsylvania side of the Delaware Water Gap. Across the river on the New Jersey side loomed the equally imposing Mt. Tammany, with its wavy, diagonal strata and sheer cliffs plunging down toward the Delaware. Dell and Willow took a brief water break on Mt. Minsi before beginning their last descent on the A.T. together. The spring green river snaked through the gap between the mountains with water so clear that boulders on the riverbed far below were as visible as the kayakers riding the currents. Despite the distraction of an unbroken stream of tourists over the first mile of their downward climb, the beauty of the river combined with tall arches of white blossomed rhododendron had Willow exclaiming, "Wow! Wow!"

Trees and brush obstructed the view of the Pocono Plateau to the northwest, but Dell remarked to Willow that the plateau's remnant glacial wetlands had one of the most reproductive populations of black bears in the country.

"We're *not* going there!" Willow said.

"No, sadly."

She elbowed Dell in the ribs.

When they arrived at Lookout Rock, a stone ledge the size of a basketball court overhanging the river which flowed five hundred feet below, they sat down and reclined against their packs.

"Another half hour," Dell said, waving his hand, "and we'll be at the river."

Willow was quiet. Dell slid over and put his hand on her shoulder. She drew up her knees, bent forward, and laid her head on folded arms. Tara snuggled up beside her.

"Are you reconsidering?" Dell nudged his shoulder against hers.

"No. I've decided. I'll keep hiking north by myself."

"Well, . . . okay. Soon we will come to the village of Delaware Water Gap, then walk across a bridge to the visitor center. But first there's a stop at an ice cream shop and a visit to the Pack & Paddle."

"Yum." Willow sat upright. "What's the Pack & Paddle?"

"That's where the birthday girl will be provisioned for her breakneck trek north to meet up with Train."

Willow's eyes widened. She gave Dell a playful swat with her hiking stick. "He's too old," she quipped with a sheepish smile.

Dell grinned.

A boisterous group of middle school hellions invaded the ledge, laughing and squirting one another with water pistols.

"Time to leave," Willow said.

She and Dell stood, hoisted their packs, cinched waist belts, tightened shoulder straps, and resumed their descent to the village and Delaware River, with Tara in her customary lead.

When the first building came into sight Willow, who was walking ahead of Dell, stopped and turned. Her eyes were red.

"Gramps, I hate, really hate to leave you. I don't want to lose you." She wiped tears from her face.

Dell pointed his hiking stick to a nearby bench where they sat down. He took both her hands in his.

"Willow, you're in my heart. You will *never* lose me." Dell's eyes glistened with tears.

"Are you sure?" She frowned and squished her eyes together as tears streaked her face.

"I'm sure."

How to put this? Dell released her hands, stretched his back, and looked up through the branches of the tall sycamore they were sitting under. Its leafy fingers fluttered far above, sending down flickers of sunlight.

"Love comes in many strange and surprising forms. So, I love blacksnakes, black bears, and even black ravens. I love the A.T. and this sycamore tree. I love my daughters, and I'll always love Patricia. And I've grown very attached to you, an emotional attachment. For this, I'm thankful. Life is a mystery we do not and cannot comprehend. In the end, the Beatles were correct—love is all we need."

"Um, yeah." Willow tilted her head. "Emotional attachment, I get that Gramps. Me, too." Tara looked up at Willow and thumped her tail on the hard ground. Willow petted Tara's head. "And, I love you, Tara."

* * *

CHAPTER 15: PARTING

Long-distance hikers fantasize about two things—ice cream and a hot shower.

"Order something that'll hold you until dinnertime," Dell said.

"Anything?"

"Yup, anything."

Willow went for the Moo Cow Creamery's seven-scoop Chief Tammany—three pistachios and four mint chocolate chips, topped with whipped cream and drenched in hot fudge sauce. Dell ordered a three-scoop banana split. She wolfed hers down before he'd finished.

Two doors down at the Pack & Paddle they met the store's owner, Lisa Purcell, a short, wiry, high-octane woman with a perpetual smile, someone who never seemed to age and who was known to everyone as Auntie Lisa. She remembered everyone who'd ever stepped into her store, including their dogs. Like Jamie Doyle and two or three other longtime proprietors along the A.T., Auntie Lisa was a legend. She gave interest-free "loans" to penniless hikers so they could replace torn up boots. Borrowers usually repaid her, although she conceded it sometimes took them three or four years.

Lisa was with a customer when they walked in, but she looked up and shouted, "Howdy Dell! Heard you were headed this way. Be with you shortly. Tara's welcome."

"Take your time. We've got some looking and buying to do."

"Now, that's what I like to hear."

They soon scooped up most of the smaller items Willow would need, including: the A.T. trail guide for New York and New Jersey, a hiker's micro-filter for when water quality was questionable—as it was most of the time—a lightweight stove and fuel canister, and a packet of waterproof matches. "Invaluable," Dell said, holding the matches up for Willow to see.

He also picked out a small aluminum pot, a Swiss Army knife, and a five-ounce emergency blanket. "Just in case," Dell said.

A wide-eyed Willow hummed, bounced on her toes, and pirouetted from aisle to aisle as they moved around the store.

"I'll repay you, someday."

"No way. It's your birthday, remember," he said with a cheeky grin.

She smiled and twirled, Tara at her heels.

In the food aisle, Dell said, "I'll give you what's left in my pack, and you pick out freeze-dried dinners, mac and cheese, and snacks for an additional two weeks."

"Will I need that much?"

"No, but it's good to have extra food. You're strong enough to handle the extra weight. This'll cover you for the 115 miles from here to Bear Mountain Inn. You can buy more at the Inn or in Connecticut."

"Gramps, you know I have no money." Willow's voice trailed off and she stared at the floor. Tara pressed against her.

Dell nudged her. "Don't worry, it's covered."

She gave him a quick hug just as Lisa approached.

"So, Dell, who's your friend? Too young to be one of your daughters."

Dell nodded toward Willow, who then looked Lisa in the eye and said, "My name's Willow Monroe."

"Uh . . . Lisa," Dell said, "Willow ran into a bit of difficulty on the trail. When I return to D.C. this afternoon, she'll continue north on the A.T. She needs a few things, including boots and a tent."

"A *few* things! I'll say." Lisa tilted her head and pursed her lips. "With this killer on the loose, I've seen exactly zero women, let alone young girls, hiking by themselves on the A.T. Stepping closer to Willow, Lisa whispered softly, "What kind of difficulty, honey? Auntie Lisa's here to help."

"No difficulty! I'm just fine now," Willow blurted out, crossing her arms. Tara, who was at Willow's side, tensed.

"Forgive me, dear. I apologize." Lisa took Dell's arm and looked at Willow. "The patron saint of good fortune, whoever that might be, sure connected you with the right guy."

Even with the poles, stakes, and fly, the tent weighed only a little over four pounds, and

Willow loved her new Merrell hiking boots.

"They'll be needed in New Hampshire's White Mountains and Maine's Mahoosucs, Bigelows, and Chairbacks," Dell said. "That is, if you get that far. Your sneakers can be relegated to camp shoes."

"I *will* make it." Willow gave him a thumb's up.

When Dell handed Lisa his credit card she grinned. "Why don't you come in more often, Dell?"

CHAPTER 15: PARTING

He smiled. "Who told you I was coming north on the trail?"

"Several people. I think the first was some FBI guy with a crew cut who was asking questions about those murders outside of Duncannon. Claimed he knew you."

"Yeah. Scaperelli is a hard charger."

"Two or three days ago a nice young couple who were hiking north came in to replenish their food supply. Said their trail names were Skipper and . . ."

Willow cut in—"First Mate. We met them after we left Port Clinton."

Lisa took a deep breath, glanced at Willow, and continued to tell Dell, "Brad Hornbeck called. No urgency. Wanted you to call when you get back to Washington."

"Uh-huh." Dell signed the credit slip.

"And there was one other: that cute ranger across the river at the visitor center—Jerry Kulikowski. He's taken a liking to the girl who sometimes works with me."

"Oh?" said Dell. "Nice guy. Came to our assistance at the Kirkridge Shelter."

"Jerry came in yesterday afternoon. Said, 'That Peterson with the ATC is a pretty tough cookie.'"

Dell stepped away from the counter. "Don't know about that, but thanks for the information."

Once outside, Willow rearranged her pack to accommodate the new acquisitions. Dell estimated her pack's weight to be about thirty-four pounds—a shade too heavy but she seemed unfazed.

A brief stroll took them onto a crumbling concrete sidewalk affixed to a four-lane toll bridge over the fast-flowing Delaware River and, shortly thereafter, to the Kittatinny Visitor Center. It was now 1:30. A sign by the visitor center pointed toward the A.T. trailhead and indicated four miles to Sunfish Pond. Dell waved his stick toward the trailhead.

"Remember, *always* be suspicious of strangers, especially older men," he said.

"Uh-huh. Older men. Like you," Willow said smiling.

Dell wrinkled his brow.

"I'll be careful. Promise."

"This is it," he said, as they removed their packs. "There's a good spring a mile past Sunfish Pond. It's also a safe tenting site."

Willow was on her knees hugging Tara, who wiggled and swished her tail. "Good," she mumbled.

When Willow stood, she was crying. So was Dell.

He tore a page from his Pennsylvania trail guide and wrote down his name and phone number, along with Grace Lombardi's number. He handed it to Willow, who stuck it in her pocket.

"Remember, call me collect when you need something. Money, anything. If you can't reach me, try Grace. She's a good friend."

Dell removed his wallet from his pack, extracted $230, all he had except for one twenty-dollar bill, and handed the cash to Willow.

She shook her head and said, "No."

He inserted the cash into one of his small plastic bags and stuffed it into the top pocket of her pack. They hugged for a long time before she hoisted her pack. Dell couldn't help but fear for her safety, but he somehow knew he'd see Willow again, if only because in some unfathomable way the heart often knows what the mind does not.

They parted in the shadow of an ancient, gnarled white oak whose trunk was at least four-feet-wide. Willow started walking north on the A.T. toward Sunfish Pond as a raven strutted across the path in front of her. Tara whined and strained at the leash to join her and continued to whine long after Willow had vanished around a bend. Less than two weeks before, Dell had met her as he and Tara bounded around a curve in the trail. This time, he watched as she disappeared around a curve in the trail.

CHAPTER 16
LEV KOMAROFF

Dell tied Tara's leash to a black metal hitching post, left his pack with her, and walked up the steps of the Kittatinny Visitor Center, a simple, brown-stained wood structure of an architectural type so common to national parks that it must be mandated by the National Park Service. He entered the building and signed the guestbook—Dell Peterson, ATC. He looked around and saw Jerry Kulikowski standing a few yards away. Jerry was in his late twenties with an athletic build and wavy dark hair that covered his ears and curled down his neck. His appearance was probably as close to a "hippie look" as his park service superiors would tolerate. He waved and sauntered over. Grinning, Jerry shook Dell's hand with both of his.

"Good to see you under less threatening circumstances than we had the other day at the Kirkridge Shelter. Those Russo brothers won't be getting bail again any time soon," he said. Jerry tipped back his straw Smokey-the-Bear hat. "What can I do for you?"

"Glad to see you, too, Jerry. My car is parked in Duncannon. I need to get back there today. Do you have the names of Trail Angels or anyone else who'd like to make a few bucks by driving me there?"

"Hmm." Kulikowski wrinkled his brow and rubbed his neck. "It'll be tough finding drivers on such short notice, especially as it's a more than two-hour drive, one way. But I'll make some calls."

"Mention I have a dog, but I'll pay for gas. Oh, and Jerry, can I thumb through the signatures in your guest book?"

"Sure, help yourself."

Dell flipped the guest book's pages back to May 1st and ran his finger down the long list of entries, leafing through, page by page until—Bingo! May 12th.

"He who will overcome you is working in silence. Fr. Monson."

Dell took a deep breath. *Unlike Monson's other entries, this one sure isn't from the Book of Common Prayer.* He tightened his hand into a fist, then relaxed it and jotted the sentence down on a piece of paper and slipped it into his pocket.

When Kulikowski returned from calling prospective drivers, Dell asked him about this entry.

"Afraid we don't pay much attention to what visitors write unless they criticize us."

We're primarily interested in the number of signatures, so we can show headquarters how popular we are and keep our budget from getting cut." Jerry shook his head. "Called all four Trail Angels on my list. None were available for this afternoon." He sighed and swallowed hard. "Despite real misgivings, I phoned a guy who is not a Trail Angel. Name's Lev Komaroff. He's a bit of an iconoclast. Unsociable, is the best I can say about him. I've tapped him only twice before, when hikers were desperate for a driver. Got negative feedback both times. Komaroff said he'd do it for $80, plus gas. Up to you."

"Like what kind of negative feedback?" Dell grimaced.

"Unfriendly, uncommunicative, borderline hostile. One hiker said, 'Slugs have more personality than Lev.' A woman hiker said, "Creep! Glad my boyfriend was with me.'"

Dell shrugged and glanced at his watch. Almost 2:30. "What the hell. Fine. Tell him I accept his offer and that I'll need to stop at a bank in Stroudsburg."

"Will do. I suspect he could use the money. Komaroff's cabin is near a pass that cuts through Kittatinny Mountain where it crosses the A.T. It won't take him long to get here."

Dell thanked Jerry, walked outside, untied Tara from the hitching post, and waited.

Twenty minutes later, a mud-splattered, red Ford-150 pickup truck with a loud muffler pulled in front of the visitor's center. A man with a military-style buzz cut wearing an army green T-shirt and bib overalls stepped out. He was a little shorter than Dell, maybe five foot ten, but heavier and with what looked like size fifteen boots. Dell guessed his age to be about fifty.

"Peterson?" the man asked.

Dell waved. "Lev Komaroff, I presume. I'm going to The Doyle Hotel in Duncannon."

CHAPTER 16: LEV KOMAROFF

Komaroff said nothing, gave a perfunctory nod, and did not offer to shake hands. Tara was still, eyes fixed on Komaroff.

"Dog goes in back," he said, pointing at Tara. "On the truck bed."

"Can't she sit on the floor at my feet? It's unsafe back there, and probably illegal."

"No."

Son of a bitch. Dell threw his pack in the back of the truck and called Tara. "Come!" She whined, hesitated, then leaped onto the truck bed and laid down. Dell hopped into the front seat. "To the bank."

They stopped a few minutes later at the Keystone Bank on Stroudsburg's Main Street. Dell withdrew $150 from the ATM and gave Lev thirty dollars to fill up an almost empty tank at the gas station across the street. Within half an hour, they were heading southwest on a highway that would take them to within a few miles of Duncannon.

"Live in the area long, Lev?" Dell asked.

Dell noticed a jagged scar under Lev's right ear. It ran down his neck to his jaw, and along the jawline to his chin.

"Yup."

"Must like it."

Lev shrugged.

"Army vet?"

Lev grunted. He neither confirmed nor denied military service.

"Travel much?"

"Only New England." *Aha, an opening.*

"Where in New England?"

"Places."

This guy is no conversationalist. At *least he doesn't have a Maine license plate or wear L.L. Bean boots.*

Komaroff seemed intent on maintaining a steady sixty-mile-per hour speed; no more, no less. He didn't ask Dell any questions and made no unsolicited comments. Every so often Dell peered through the truck's cracked rear window at Tara. She was hunkered down, flush against the cab, ears pinned back, fur ruffled with wind. Fortunately, it wasn't raining. They drove for almost an hour in silence before Dell hazarded another question.

"Any relatives in the area, Lev?"

"No."

Noticing a magazine on the seat next to Komaroff, Dell asked, "Read much?"

Komaroff flipped it over, revealing a naked young woman on the cover of *Hustler*.

"For the quality of the writing?"

"Yeah."

"What do you do for entertainment?"

"Not much, except hunting. Most people irritate me, especially women."

"What?" Dell flinched. "Women?"

"Yeah, women."

Glad Willow's nowhere near this sleazeball.

"What about dogs?"

"*Especially*, dogs. Shoot 'em."

Dell clenched his jaw and asked no more questions.

Komaroff exited I-81 and drove up the west side of the Susquehanna to Duncannon. He knew exactly where on Market Street the Doyle Hotel was located but, without explanation, he parked more than a block away. Tara jumped from the truck onto the sidewalk. Dell lifted his pack out of the truck bed and handed Komaroff four Andrew Jacksons for the drive. Lev took the money without saying a word, stuffed it in his shirt pocket, and drove away.

It was going on 6 p.m., and Dell had to be on the road to Washington. He put Tara and the pack in his Jeep and walked into the hotel to thank Jamie Doyle for letting him park by the hotel. Jamie stood behind the bar in a red plaid shirt.

"How are you doing my lad?"

"Afraid I'm in a hurry. Have a long drive to D.C. in front of me. Wanted to thank you for looking after my Jeep."

"No problem." Jamie held both his palms up high. "Wait here!" He disappeared into the kitchen, reappearing a few minutes later with two huge corned beef sandwiches on rye. "One for you, one for my dog."

Dell gave Jamie a bear hug.

As Jamie hugged back, he said, "God bless you, my boy."

Dell dropped a twenty by the cash register and before walking out the door asked Jamie, "Ever heard of a Lev Komaroff?"

CHAPTER 16: LEV KOMAROFF

"Can't say that I have."

* * *

Dell pulled into his driveway in northwest Washington at 9 p.m., lifted his pack off the back seat, let Tara out of the Jeep, and shouldered open the front door of a musty smelling house. Tara wagged her tail and raced from room to room, sniffing, until she plopped down beside Dell with a happy look that said, *Everything's in order.*

The phone had fifty-three voice mail messages, but Dell only listened to four: three from Grace, all of them from the day before wondering if he'd returned, and one from Brad. Both wanted him to call. Grace had been on his mind since well before Port Clinton, but it was late and he was bone-tired. *Tomorrow.*

Dell went into the dining room and ran his fingers along the edge of the small cedar box holding Patricia's cremains. "Love you, babe. You would've adored Willow. She grew into a strong, self-confident young woman on the trail. Hurts that she's gone. Hurts that you're gone." He rubbed his eyes, walked into the bathroom, and brushed his teeth before entering the bedroom where Tara was curled on the floor at the foot of the bed.

"Quite a day, girl," he said, falling into bed. "Quite a trip."

CHAPTER 17
GRACE

Tara poked her cold nose into Dell's neck around 7 a.m. This, and dog breath, roused him. *Where am I? Tent? Willow!* Dell shot up in bed. *God, hope she's safe.*

After a shower, scrambled eggs and coffee, and a walk with Tara to the corner market, he returned to the house, proceeded to his office, and pushed open the door. Except for the stale smell of a closed-up room and a solitary spider dangling undisturbed in a corner, nothing had changed during his absence. He opened an office window while standing on the frayed red and blue Sarouk rug his late father brought back from Iran in the 1950s. Tara loved that rug; she'd munched on it as a puppy. Bookshelves lined the cedar-paneled walls, crammed to the ceiling with dust-covered legal briefs and mostly unread law review journals. On his desk was a coffee-stained Baltimore Orioles mug and extra copies of Patricia's death certificate he hadn't yet consigned to the file cabinet.

Family photos hung on the wall by Dell's desk, none more cherished than one of him and Patricia kissing as they draped themselves around the weathered wooden sign at the summit of Mt. Katahdin. Not a cloud in the sky. Carved into the sign were the words:

KATAHDIN
Northern terminus of the
APPALACHIAN TRAIL

Dell sat down at the desk, picked up the phone, and called Brad. "Hi, old man. Got in last night."

"How did it go? Been a week since I've heard from you," Brad said.

"Not bad. The cops may want another meeting."

CHAPTER 17: GRACE

"Oh? What'd you find?"

"Lisa Purcell at the Pack & Paddle said the FBI had spoken with her, but did anyone speak with Manny Kopecki at the Port Clinton Hotel?"

"Don't know," Brad said. "Probably. I told Tony Scaperelli and Sgt. Ward you thought Manny should be contacted. The authorities, FBI especially, don't always keep me in the loop."

Dell leaned back in his desk chair. "You know Monson, Maine, right?"

"You bet. I've been there."

Dell sat up. "Well, in mid-May some weirdo calling himself Father Monson signed the logs of at least two shelters and the guest book at the Kittatinny Visitor Center and left disturbing messages about death."

"What! No hiker would do that."

"Right. That's not all. Another wacko drove me from the visitor center back to my Jeep in Duncannon. The police must interview Lev Komaroff. Among other things, he lives in the woods near the A.T. and told me he hates women. A ranger at the visitor center, Jerry Kulikowski, knows how to get in touch with him."

"Think Komaroff could be Father Monson?"

"He wasn't anywhere near as articulate as Father Monson appeared to be, but I don't know."

"Okay. I'll pass it on."

"Well, guess that's about it." Dell closed his eyes and kneaded his forehead. "Oh, yes. One more thing. I found a water-damaged book under the Kirkbridge Shelter titled, *Wilderness Survival and Techniques*. It had a library stamp from Colby College in Maine. Might be insignificant, but it's something else to check out. Tell Scaperelli. The FBI needs to see it."

"This is helpful, but pretty circumstantial. Look, it's Saturday. I'll call the authorities Monday morning and fill them in on everything. By the way, whatever happened to that runaway you took under your wing?"

"Willow's still on the trail, headed north to New York. She's amazing—resilient, determined, and a fast learner."

"That's good to hear. You keep in touch."

After hanging up, Dell went through the rest of his voice mail messages, including two from his daughters. *I'll call them later.* He started to dial Grace's number but put the phone back down. The photo of him and Patricia on Katahdin again caught his eye. Dell's watch read 9 a.m. He stood, paced across the office floor, bit his lower lip, and sat down on top of his desk. *I'd rather wrestle a bear than ask a woman for a date.* This simple act had always unnerved him, but especially now. It had been twenty-five years since he'd dated. *Maybe Grace will think it's too awkward to go out with the husband of her best friend less than a year after Patricia's death.* Rapping his knuckles on the desk, he took a deep breath. *But she did accept a dinner date when I called her from Port Clinton.*

With sweaty palms, Dell tried to call Grace once again. But he misdialed her number. *Calm down Peterson.* On his third attempt, the phone rang and rang until he heard a recording—"I'm unavailable right now. Please leave a message."

"Uh, hi Grace. Dell. The rolling stone has returned. Tara and I were kind of hoping you might like to go for lunch and a walk on this beautiful . . ."

"Dell! I'd just gone out the door when the phone rang. Almost missed you." Grace sounded out of breath.

"Well, I was sort of wondering if . . ."

"I'd love to."

Dell hopped off the desk, his back on the photo of him and Patricia, and exhaled. "What about Shepherdstown?"

"Never been there."

"Oldest town in West Virginia, about an hour and a half away. On the Potomac. Great restaurants. After lunch, we could walk on the C&O Canal. It's just across the river, on the Maryland side."

"Sounds great. I was about to go for a walk of my own, but this is much more interesting. My sneakers are on. I'm ready."

"Tara and I will be there in twenty minutes."

Grace lived less than a mile away, near Dell's church, St. Columba's Episcopal. Wearing a T-shirt and shorts, he grabbed a daypack and threw in a canteen, hat, windbreaker, and some dog biscuits and jumped into the Jeep with Tara. Two blocks down Windom to Wisconsin Avenue, north through Tenley Circle, and a quick left on Albemarle brought him to 43rd Street NW, where he pulled into the driveway of an imposing, turn of the century, brick and stucco, Tudor style house. He walked up the boxwood-lined brick path and remembered how much he'd admired the house's triangular gables and its striking resemblance to an English country manor. Grace's ex-husband had been chief lobbyist for the pharmaceutical industry. Their divorce settlement awarded the house to her. Before Dell reached the front step, she came out the door, daypack in hand, wearing a light cotton blouse and shorts. Grace was a devoted hiker who, Dell suspected, saw hiking as one way to maintain her shapely legs that even Radio City Rockettes would envy. They pecked one another on the cheek.

At thirty-eight, Grace was as stunning as when she was younger and one of Dell's best law students. Her jet-black hair was longer then but it still swept down below her shoulders. She was five foot nine with olive skin and an aquiline nose. But Grace's pale green eyes were her most striking feature. Dell knew they could twinkle to signal, "Let's play!" or, as he had witnessed more than once in a courtroom, flash a cutting, "Don't bullshit me!" to an opposing attorney or evasive witness.

Patricia often said, "Grace and I are like sisters." Patricia and Dell had both liked Grace immensely. Indeed, if he hadn't been so hopelessly in love with his beautiful wife, well, who knows. After Grace divorced, she often joined Patricia and Dell on weekend hikes with Tara, usually in the Shenandoah National Park. So, Tara greeted Grace like the old friend she was by spinning around in circles and swishing her tail.

On the drive to Shepherdstown, Grace asked, "Heard from your daughters?"

"Only got in last night."

She tapped his arm with her fingertip and winked. "You called me."

Dell looked over and was greeted with a mischievous grin. His face felt hot; he knew it was probably red. "They left voicemail messages," he said. "I'll call them soon."

Grace touched his shoulder. "What happened to Willow?"

Dell glanced at her. "We parted ways at the Delaware River. She's headed north to New York to meet up with a young guy who calls himself Train, a hiker we met on the trail."

"Are you concerned?"

"I grew really fond of Willow, and maybe a little too protective. But, yes, I can't help but worry." Dell tightened his grip on the steering wheel. "I'm not that concerned about Train, although his all-too-obvious attraction to Willow bugged me and triggered my paternal instincts. But it's more the unknowns, especially the whereabouts of the killer, that unnerves me."

"I'd worry, too," Grace said. "Children in these situations, especially if they're let down by Child Protective Services, don't have a safe home to go to."

Dell raised his hand. "She's a survivor—physically strong, sensitive but tough-minded, fiercely independent, and reflective."

Grace pushed her feet against the floorboard, stretched her tanned legs, and said, "Me, too."

Dell chuckled. "Yes. Maybe that's why . . ."

"We get along so well?"

Without taking his eyes off the road, Dell extended his right hand to Grace. She held his hand between both of hers.

"Does Willow have decent equipment, like a tent, sleeping bag, boots, etc.?" Grace asked.

"The best money can buy, and a little money as well."

Grace reached over and again touched Dell's shoulder. "Why am I not surprised?"

Two miles from Shepherdstown on Route 34 they passed through the small Maryland village of Sharpsburg. With a population of about eight hundred, it looked like many other rural American towns—a few shops, a couple of restaurants, and a gas station—except for all the granite and marble monuments and American flags.

Grace stared out the window. "Something important happened here."

"Battle of Antietam, 1862. Bloodiest single day of the Civil War." Dell pointed down a narrow road on their right. "Lee's advance was halted over there. Ten months later he tried again, at Gettysburg. Antietam puts on quite a show every Fourth of July. We could go next month."

He looked at her. She grinned and said, "You're on, professor."

Crossing over the Potomac on the James Rumsey Bridge, they entered Shepherdstown, a village of two thousand and home to Shepherd College, founded in the 1870s. Much of the town revolved around German Street, lined with brick row houses, shops, and cafés. They drove down the street and parked in front of the Yellow Brick Bank restaurant, situated in an old brick bank build-

CHAPTER 17: GRACE

ing. Dell rolled the car's windows down for Tara, and they walked inside. A young woman seated them by the window in a semi-circular, white-walled room with a cast iron chandelier. A middle-aged waiter came over with menus.

"Haven't seen you for a while, sir."

Dell nodded.

"You know this place?" Grace asked.

"One of Patricia's favorites. Thought her dear friend might like it."

"She was such a joyful person. I do miss her. That you'd bring me here. . . . Well . . ." With soft eyes, Grace smiled and reached across the table and patted his hand.

So much touching. Good sign. "Speaking of fine dining," Dell said, "we have dinner reservations at the Inn at Little Washington for June 22nd. I called the Inn from Port Clinton, but I can always change the date."

"No way!" Grace cried out so loudly that everyone in the room turned to look, and the waiter started to walk toward their table. "But what can I wear?"

"You'd look marvelous in anything," he said. "Let's order lunch."

Grace ordered the trout, Dell had scallops, and they shared a bottle of chardonnay. They chattered away with the ease and frankness of friends whose lives had been entwined for years. Even the silences were comfortable. Her green eyes lit up and, maybe it was Grace's Italian heritage, but her arms and hands gestured freely as she spoke. Again and again her fingers touched his.

After lunch, they drove back over the bridge to the Maryland side of the river where they parked and walked west with Tara along the towpath of the C&O Canal. Dell had walked and biked all 185 miles of the canal that ran from Washington, D.C. to Cumberland, Maryland, many times with Patricia.

The hard-packed, twelve-foot-wide, clay and gravel towpath follows the Potomac. Many people were out strolling along the grassy bank of the wide, slow-flowing river. Others were fishing, picnicking, or throwing Frisbees for their dogs on this sunny day. Canoeists floated downstream, kayakers raced one another, and bicyclists shouted "on your left" as they zipped past.

Dell confided to Grace about what he'd found on the A.T. relating to the murders, and he spoke of Willow and their experiences together. He did not mention the violent encounter with the Russos at the Kirkridge Shelter.

Four miles of easy walking brought them to the mouth of a man-made cave cut into a limestone bluff. Dell explained how some women and children took refuge in the cave during the Battle of Antietam.

"Let's explore it," Grace said.

"Not much to see. Goes in only about ninety feet. Pretty dark and spidery." Dell pointed to empty beer cans on the ground. "Think local teenagers party here."

"Oh, come on."

Grace grabbed his hand and pulled him into the musty smelling cave. Tara trotted after them, sniffing the ground. Without flashlights, they had to feel their way in the dark along cold, damp walls.

"Told you. Nothing here," Dell said, when they reached the back wall of the cave.

"Except me," Grace said.

She wrapped her arms around his waist and pulled him close. They kissed, and kissed again, as her hands slipped under his T-shirt and up his back. *Yikes! Green light.* Dell loosened her blouse and let his fingers do the talking. From the small of her back, up the spine, to where he met the enemy, formidable hooks securing her bra. She pressed hard against him as they continued to embrace, triggering an embarrassing and all-too-obvious stirring in his shorts. *Much more of this, and I'm in launch mode.* Her hands moved to his chest and descended. He finally managed to unclasp the bra and had just begun to caress her with his fingertips when they heard voices.

"Think anyone's in there?"

"Don't know. Can't see too well. Thought I heard something."

Tara growled. They froze, dressed quickly, and, red-faced, waved sheepishly to the family standing at the mouth of the cave. They hurried out. A woman who looked to be the wife shaded her eyes and laughed. Grace and Dell walked back to the Jeep with Tara, giggling like teenagers and holding hands. They continued talking, not about what had just happened, but about her work, the kids inner tubing on the Potomac, Willow, and especially the A.T. murders.

CHAPTER 17: GRACE

Dell mentioned the messages left in the logs of some shelters by "Fr. Monson."

Grace said, "They could hold important clues to the murderer's identity. He seems intelligent and well-read."

He squeezed her hand. "Maybe you should be on this case."

She kissed his cheek. "With you? That'd be fun."

After stopping for dinner at the Taste of Saigon in Rockville, Maryland, they returned to her place at about 8 p.m.

"Come in?" she asked, as he pulled the Jeep into her driveway.

"Love to, but I need to feed Tara and unload my backpack from the Pennsylvania trip. Maybe even call my daughters. What about coming to church with me at St. Columba's tomorrow morning?"

"Sure."

Dell walked Grace to the front door. "We can meet at the church a little before eleven."

They kissed with an intensity that promised more.

CHAPTER 18
MOVING ON

After dropping Grace off at her place, Dell returned to his house just before dark. He fed Tara, walked into his office, and lifted the Mt. Katahdin photo with Patricia from the wall and kissed it. *God knows, I love you. Please forgive me.* He carried the photo into his bedroom, wrapped it in the blue dress shirt Patricia had given him for his birthday, and placed it in a dresser drawer.

Returning to the office, Dell sat down at his desk and deleted all his voice mails, except for a few from colleagues, and those from his daughters—both of whom wondered where he was. Dell first dialed Amanda in Boston because, unlike Joanna, she had always liked Grace. She was putting his grandson to bed and only had time to say, "Glad you are home safe, dad. Anything new?"

"Went for a walk today with Grace Lombardi."

"Wow! That's *great!* Did you have a good time?"

"Yeah. We talked and talked and walked and walked."

"I think Grace is your cup of tea. She's a wonderful person. Love you dad but can't talk now. Call me again soon."

As Dell dialed Joanna, who lived in nearby Alexandria, Virginia, he noticed Tara slip furtively into the office to curl up in the only uncluttered corner.

"Dad," Joanna said, "I phoned the ATC in Harper's Ferry this morning. A woman named Cherie told me you'd gotten back last night. I called the house three times today. Where were you?"

This could be delicate. Dell leaned back in his desk chair.

"Tara and I were walking on the C&O Canal near Shepherdstown."

"Nice area. Mom loved it. If you'd called, I would've gone with you."

CHAPTER 18: MOVING ON

"Remember Grace Lombardi?"

"Uh-huh. Good friend of Mom's. She and her husband came over for dinner a couple of times when we were younger. One of your former students, right?"

"Yes, years ago. Grace was with us on our walk today."

"Oh. Oh!" Joanna gave out a long breathy sigh. "Thought she was married?"

"Divorced."

"Well, was it a . . . date?"

"Just a walk." Dell scratched the back of his neck. "Don't know much about dating anymore."

Joanna paused for several seconds until she said, "Well, I'm relieved you are back home dad. Keep me posted about . . . uh . . . developments with Grace."

"Of course!" No way, he thought to himself. By now, whatever doubt or guilt Dell might have felt about dating Grace had melted away. He was eager to see her again.

* * *

The tower bell at the nineteenth century St. Columba's church was calling parishioners to worship on that first Sunday of June. Dell hurried up the gray fieldstone steps to where Grace stood—rather, stood out—in a lavender A-line dress, sprinkled with white apple blossoms. She smiled and hooked her arm in his. They entered together and found a pew near the back of the church. The processional had just begun—Beethoven's glorious "Ode to Joy." She held his hand and a joy of a more temporal sort washed over him.

The rector looked in their direction from the pulpit as he concluded his sermon with, "God's love can appear any time, in any place, and at any stage of life."

Grace pressed Dell's hand. The organist struck the first notes of "The Old Rugged Cross," the closing hymn, and one not often heard in Episcopal churches, although it was sung frequently in the Methodist church when Dell was a child. His mother loved it. He thought of her, and his eyes welled up as he sang the refrain from memory:

> So I'll cherish the cross, the old rugged cross,
> Till my trophies at last I lay down;
> I will cling to the old rugged cross,
> And exchange it some day for a crown.

Grace noticed his reaction and put an arm around him. After the service, most congregants left through the main entrance, but Dell saw the associate pastor, Rev. Joe Wingate, standing by a side portal. Although not long out of seminary, Joe had presided at Patricia's memorial service, and he'd been a comfort to Dell in the painful months following her death.

Gesturing toward where Joe stood, Dell said to Grace, "Could you wait just a minute? I need to have a word with the pastor."

"Afraid I've got to run. I'm late for a Sunday meeting downtown with two of my associates. We have to be in court first thing tomorrow morning."

He took her hand. "It was good of you to come. What about a hike next weekend in the Shenandoah?"

"It's a deal." She pecked his cheek and dashed out the door.

Rev. Wingate was six-foot-four and, if not for his vestments, could've been mistaken for a linebacker on the Chicago Bears. With wavy blond hair that covered his ears, Dell knew his mother would have labeled him a "hippie priest."

Rev. Wingate put his hand on Dell's shoulder. "Haven't seen you for a while, Dell."

"Been in the woods, Joe. Literally." Dell clasped his hands behind his back. "Patricia's cremains have been on my dining room table since last fall." Dell felt a heaviness in his chest. He fought back tears and stammered, "It's time."

Joe nodded.

"Some months ago, I acquired a space for her in the columbarium. Could we . . ."

"Lay her to rest?" Joe said.

Dell bowed his head. "Yes."

"Of course." Joe touched Dell's arm. "When would you like to do that?"

"This week, if possible."

"Would Wednesday work? 10 a.m.?"

Dell looked up. "Yes, that's good. Thanks, Joe. I'll be there." Dell smiled. "With Patricia."

Joe winked.

* * *

Interment of cremains is usually a family affair. Dell knew Amanda would not make the trip down from Boston because she'd often told him she wouldn't attend when that time came. "No one was dearer to me than Mom," she'd said. "Her memorial service was very painful. I can't take another reminder that she's gone forever."

Joanna was close by in northern Virginia. He hoped she might accompany him to St. Columba's on Wednesday. Dell phoned her from his office.

"No, that's okay. Amanda and I said our goodbyes." Dell heard Joanna's breathing deepen as she asked, "How much of this has to do with Grace Lombardi?"

"Mom wanted her ashes at St. Columba's and there's space for her now."

"Mom has only been gone six months . . . I gotta go. Bye, dad." Joanna hung up.

Dell caught his breath. He bent forward, elbows on his desk, and cradled his head in his hands.

* * *

A little before ten o'clock on Wednesday, Dell drove to the church alone. He met Rev. Wingate in his office and surrendered the cedar box with its precious contents. Before the two of them went outside to the columbarium, and while they were standing, Joe took Dell's hand, bowed his head, and offered a prayer.

"Lord, take me where you want me, let me meet who you want me to meet, and keep me out of your way."

They both grinned.

Like the church itself, the adjoining outdoor columbarium was constructed of gray fieldstone. It was encircled by pink azaleas and white blossomed dogwood trees. Dell could hear children's voices from a distant playground. *Patricia would like that.*

The priest leaned over and lowered the box of Patricia's ashes into the hollow of a fieldstone receptacle affixed atop a stone base. He covered the open space with a fitted bronze plaque engraved with Patricia Peterson, and the dates of her birth and death. Tears ran down Dell's face as Joe read from the *Book of Common Prayer*—"Give rest, O Christ, to thy servant Patricia with thy saints, where sorrow and pain are no more..., but life everlasting."

Dell tripped over the steps leading out of the columbarium but regained his balance. *Where did I park the Jeep?* Joe walked him to the street, where together they located his car. Dabbing his face with a handkerchief, Dell thanked him. "This got to me."

"Listen, Dell," Joe said. "Drive *very* carefully."

Before Dell got in the Jeep, Joe rested a hand on his shoulder and said, "Father of mercies and giver of comfort, deal graciously, we pray, with he who mourns; that, casting all his care on you, Dell may know the consolation of your love."

Dell drove home in a daze, Patricia on his mind. *What would she think of me and Grace? Why is Joanna so upset?* When he pulled into the driveway, Dell hung his head and sat for a few minutes before heading inside. As he opened the door, he heard the phone ring. He ran into his office to pick up.

"Peterson. Scaperelli. I'm calling from FBI headquarters downtown. Hornbeck called me Monday. Have a minute?"

"Yes. What's up?" Dell sat down at his desk.

"You found some kind of book. We'd like to see it."

"Of course. I haven't gone through it but, like some other things, it points to Maine."

"I can have someone pick it up in a half hour."

"I'm on Windom Place, off . . ." Dell stood up.

"I know where you live."

Of course, he'd know.

"Did the Bureau interview Manny Kopeki in Port Clinton?" Dell asked.

"Yes. Our Harrisburg and Allentown offices scoured the whole area between Duncannon and the Delaware River, and we checked out every damn shelter. Well, Peterson, that's about all I need from you."

"Did you find the trail log entries by someone calling himself Father Monson?"

"We interviewed Jerry Kulikowski on Monday afternoon. He showed our agent the entry written in his guest book on May 12th. Wait, did you say entries, plural?"

"Father Monson left log messages at two shelters, both of which are within a half mile of a highway: Windsor Furnace and George Outerbridge." Dell let out a loud breath.

"Holy Mother of God!" Scaperelli jumped up from his desk.

CHAPTER 18: MOVING ON

"Our guys will be back at those shelters tomorrow. We've contacted some people in Maine, including in the town of Monson."

"What about Komaroff?"

"Who?"

Dell shook his head. "Lev Komaroff. He should be thoroughly vetted."

"Kulikowski or Hornbeck might have mentioned his name, sounds familiar. If so, we didn't follow up."

Dell slammed his fist on the desk so hard that an empty coffee cup bounced onto the floor. "Tony, the FBI is supposed to be a professional outfit."

"Watch it Peterson! Cut the bullshit, or I'll kick your ass off this investigation."

"Listen Tony," Dell said, "This character lives in the forest near the A.T.; he admitted to me that he doesn't like women; Komaroff goes nowhere *except* New England; and when he drove me back to Duncannon, he knew exactly where The Doyle Hotel was located, yet refused to park in front of it."

"Damn!"

Dell heard what sounded like a wastepaper basket being kicked across a room.

"Good tip, Peterson. We'll be on Komaroff immediately."

Fifteen minutes after they ended their call, the doorbell rang. A young man in a dark suit and narrow tie flashed his badge.

"Sir, Mr. Scaperelli sent me."

He left with the wilderness survival book Dell had found under the Kirkbridge Shelter.

* * *

Dell and Grace had lunch downtown and they talked several times on the phone during the week. When the phone rang, he thought it was Grace calling again. He sat at his desk and picked up the phone.

"I have a collect call from a Miss Willow Monroe. Will you accept it?"

"Yes."

"Gramps?"

Dell closed his eyes. "I am so relieved to hear your voice. Are you at the Bear Mountain Inn?"

"Yup. Got in today. Despite the mosquitos, ticks, another bear, and some rain, I moved right along. Met lots of other hikers; most were really friendly."

"Most?"

"Everyone was friendly, except for one scary and weird guy early this morning."

Dell sat up. "What happened?"

"Right after I'd walked over the New York State Thruway, a man came out of nowhere, blocked my path."

"What the . . ." Dell shot up from his chair and paced around the room.

"He said he wouldn't budge unless I told him my name, where I was headed, and where I would spend the night."

"What did he look like?"

"Maybe about your age," Willow said, "but overweight, short hair. Definitely not a backpacker. I was scared but told him nothing."

Dell looked up at the ceiling. "Then what?" Dell sat back down in his desk chair and started taking notes on a yellow legal pad. "How tall was he?" Dell asked.

"Tall, but shorter than you. He seemed educated, spoke well. I was lucky because three hikers heading north, college guys who shared a shelter with me last night, came up the trail."

"Oh, Willow. Thank God."

"They circled the weirdo and told him to 'push off.' Like me, they were headed for the Bear Mountain Inn, so we all walked together. As the creep was leaving, he pointed a finger at me and said something unnerving I won't forget."

"What was that?" Dell asked, pressing the phone closer to his ear.

Willow took a deep breath. "He said, 'Our days on the earth are as a shadow, and without hope.'"

Stunned, Dell rubbed his forehead. *Fuckin' Father Monson! Sounds biblical, maybe Chronicles.*

"Gramps, you okay?"

He leaned back in his chair, pulse racing. "Thank goodness, you're safe." Tara sat down beside him and looked up. Dell scratched her head. "You made great time. Is Train still at the Inn?"

"Yes, but he's returning to the trail tomorrow morning. That is, we are returning to the trail."

Dell looked down at his hands for a moment and said nothing.

"Gramps?"

"Um . . . I'm here."

"Don't worry. He's really nice, and I have my own room."

"Good." *I will worry, but she'll be safer with Train.*

They talked for another fifteen minutes until Willow said, "The restaurant is paging us for dinner. I miss you, Gramps, and love you. I'll stay in touch."

"Miss you, too, honey. I love you. Call again, often. Bye."

When they got off the phone, Dell called the Bear Mountain Inn and spoke with the manager. Dell gave him his credit card information and said, "Put all of Ms. Monroe's expenses—lodging, food, hiking supplies, and a hundred dollars in cash—on my card."

"Yes, sir."

Dell put his arm around Tara. "Thank God she's no longer hiking alone." He then called Scaperelli and related everything Willow had told him.

CHAPTER 19

LOVE AGAIN

Dell and Grace had both done the Cedar Run–White Oak Canyon circuit hike in the Shenandoah National Park, but never together. Dell was fortunate to find a space for his Jeep when they arrived midmorning at the crowded Hawksbill Gap parking area because this was also the trailhead for the popular hike up Hawksbill Mountain, the park's highest peak. The plastic thermometer on Dell's waist pack registered ninety degrees on this early June day. No wind, clear blue sky. Tara spun around, eager to go, as Grace tightened the shoulder straps on her daypack. Dell, Grace, and Tara walked across the Skyline Drive into a patch of oak and ash and onto a rutted horse trail which they followed past the Cedar Run trailhead for a half mile to the start of the White Oak Canyon Trail.

The circuit hike was less than ten miles long, yet it traversed two of the deepest and steepest ravines in the park, with an elevation change of 3,200 feet. The Potomac Appalachian Trail Club's trail guide rated the hike "strenuous."

Leaning on their hiking sticks, they descended the steep, boulder-strewn White Oak Trail, by far the most frequented section of the circuit because of its six rushing waterfalls. One waterfall that was neither as sheer nor as impressive as the others was popular with hikers because the stream slowed as it washed over a twenty-foot-wide, water-smoothed granite incline coated with slick moss. Dell slid down that very slope with Patricia into the clear pool below on one of their first dates. He could still hear her scream as she hit icy water, and even recalled the resinous scent of pine and hemlock in the air that day. Her water-drenched hair framed a beaming face and the bluest of blue eyes. When he kissed her, she

CHAPTER 19: LOVE AGAIN

tasted like the Reese's peanut butter chocolate she'd eaten minutes earlier. The memory was as fixed in his mind as when he first held their new-born daughters, when he and Patricia scaled the summit of Mt. Katahdin, and as fresh as the precise minute Patricia took her last breath. Dell gazed at the pool with a far-off look.

A bemused Grace glanced at Dell, tilted her head to one side, and said, "Grace to Dell, Grace to Dell. Come in. Can you hear me?"

Only when the mists lifted did he realize he'd been holding his breath. As Dell exhaled, his eyes focused on the strikingly beautiful woman standing next to him—his present and, he hoped, future love.

"Sorry. Day dreaming."

Grace took his hand and squeezed.

About fifty feet from where they stood a group of young men and women slid down the slippery incline into the pool and cavorted in the cold water at the foot of the waterfall. The men were bare-chested and some of the women sported wet, blue and orange, University of Virginia T-shirts. One topless woman rode on her boyfriend's shoulders as he waded up to his chest in the water.

"Party's on, pretty crowded," Dell said. *Young people just like them are being murdered on the A.T.*

"You're right, it is crowded," Grace agreed. "They look like undergrads." She touched his arm. "Oh, to be twenty again."

Dell gazed at the frolickers. "Life's not over."

She took his hand. "No, indeed."

This spot reminds me too much of Patricia. Dell wrapped an arm around Grace's waist, drew her close, and kissed her. A guy in denim cutoffs who was poised to slide down the waterfall looked up, saw them, and waved. He shouted what sounded like, "Wahoo wah!" and pumped his fist in the air.

Dell and Grace continued to hike downhill until they arrived at the base of the White Oak Trail, where they hopped over lichen-covered stones along a winding side trail that soon connected them to the Cedar Run Trail. No hikers were in sight as Dell and Grace started to walk up this partially overgrown path, a steep, four-mile ascent that would eventually take them back to the trailhead and his Jeep. The trail snaked through a narrow ravine along Cedar Run which cascaded over and rippled around school bus-sized boulders. They came to a pool about thirty feet long and a dozen feet wide, shaded by hemlocks, where the otherwise rollicking stream was momentarily serene. Dell's thermometer read ninety-two degrees as he peeled off his sweat-soaked T-shirt and stuck it in his pack. Grace's face was flushed and wet with perspiration. They looked at one another. Grace smiled, said "Yes," then reached for Dell's hand.

Holding hands, and using their hiking sticks for added support, they hopped from rock to rock down an embankment to the pool. Tara zipped past them, belly flopped into the water and dog paddled around the pool's perimeter, sending Jesus Christ bugs skittering across the surface.

They removed their boots, sat on a flat rock, and dangled their bare feet in the frigid mountain stream while they munched on ham and cheese sandwiches Grace had prepared. Tara made gurgling noises when she dipped her snout into the water as she swam. She plunged her whole head deep into the pool and climbed out with something wriggling in her mouth.

"Drop it!" Dell shouted.

A greenish black, three-inch-long crayfish with pincers at the ready fell from her maw.

"Wow!" Grace said. "How'd she do that?"

"Don't know, but she has an incredible sense of smell and . . ."

Tara shook hard, and shook again, soaking them.

"That does it!" Grace lifted her sweaty T-shirt up and over her head. Then off came her bra. "Have been wanting to do that." She slung the shirt and bra into a sunny spot on a nearby log. "Twenty-year-olds can't have all the fun."

Dell's heart pounded and blood rushed to his extremities. All his extremities. Wearing only hiking shorts, they held hands and waded waist-high into the pool with their bare feet stepping on smooth, slippery, river rocks. They turned to face one another. Dell rested both his hands on Grace's hips and pulled her close.

"No," he whispered in her ear, "college students can't have all the fun."

The only sound was the swirl and babble of Cedar Run as they embraced. When they waded out of the water, Grace stuffed her damp bra and T-shirt into her pack, and they put their boots on.

Back on the trail, they hiked uphill for about a half hour until they heard male voices descending toward them. With no time to dress, Grace hid her bare chest against Dell's back and giggled.

CHAPTER 19: LOVE AGAIN

Two young guys grinned as they passed. One of them sang out "Oh Happy Day!"—the opening words of a popular gospel song. Grace hurried to dress as soon as the hikers were out of sight.

When they got back to the Jeep Dell and Grace changed into dry clothes and comfortable shoes and drove four miles down the road to Skyland Lodge. Dell had eaten there many times with Patricia and his daughters and loved its familiar casualness. The wide-open, pine-paneled dining room probably sat two hundred, prices were reasonable, and the menu never changed. The basic family dining menu always included fried chicken, Virginia country ham, catfish, and corn bread. Dinner lasted for a couple of hours, although neither Dell nor Grace were too certain about its duration because they downed a bottle of merlot and almost another full bottle of cabernet franc. They finally staggered up from the table, leaned on one another for support, and wound their way out of the dining room into the lobby, where Grace hiccuped and poked a finger into Dell's chest.

"No DUI," she slurred.

"No, no," he agreed, wagging a finger back at her. "We sh-shtay here."

The lodge had only one vacancy, a cabin. After letting Tara out of the Jeep, Dell and Grace set out to find it in the dark. The wine didn't help their search, as they laughed and bumped into one another. Dogs were prohibited at Skyland, but Tara was a skilled infiltrator. She hugged the ground as they hunted for the cabin and followed close on Dell's heels to avoid being seen. She slinked into nearby bushes when other guests approached and, when the cabin was finally located, Tara popped inside the instant Dell opened the door.

Tipsy and dead tired, they took turns taking off one another's T-shirts and hiking shorts. Grace unclasped her bra, flung it on a chair, and grinned.

"Ladies first."

She peeled off her panties, then stared at Dell's boxer shorts and chuckled.

"Well, that hoss wants out of the barn."

Dell threw the barn on the floor and freed the hoss.

Their first time was electric, if tentative and a bit awkward. What he remembered most clearly was Grace pleading, "not yet, not yet."

Next morning, he awoke with Grace's hand on his thigh, Tara's muzzle in his face, and a throbbing headache.

"Good morning, Mr. Quick Draw," Grace said.

Tara was telling him something else—*Gotta pee real bad.*

Dell kissed Grace on the cheek and said, "Tara first."

He rolled off the bed and located his boxer shorts on the floor. It was 6 a.m. when he eased the cabin door open a crack and peeked out. *No one.* "Tara. Come. Make it fast girl."

She trotted ten feet away onto a patch of dandelions, squatted, and ran back inside flashing her German shepherd happy face. When Dell shut the door and turned around Grace was sitting naked at the foot of the bed.

"You may approach the bench, counselor," she said with a mischievous smile.

Dell stepped toward her.

"Closer, Mr. Quick Draw," she demanded.

"May it please the court." Dell removed his boxer shorts and edged closer.

"You must assure me," Grace said, pointing to the offender, "that the hoss won't be so quick out of the gate."

"Yes, your honor."

She held his hips with both hands and pulled him close. Grace's ministrations proved beyond a reasonable doubt that her judgeship was one of considerable discernment and unparalleled professionalism. No hesitancy or awkwardness.

Before the point of no return, Dell pulled back so they could *both* tango. Their dance was sensuous and unhurried. As they kissed, she shuddered. Afterward, now headache free, they reclined on their backs, heads on pillows.

"Wow!" she said, resting her head on his chest. "No more Mr. Quick Draw."

Dell rolled her over and nuzzled her neck as his index finger traveled down between her breasts.

"Your honor," he said, "if you weren't so damn beautiful, I would have been slower last night."

Grace snatched Dell's meandering finger and put it to her lips. "So naughty." Poking his chest, she said, "Shower together?"

While showering, Dell determined that Grace required a thorough above-the-waist lathering and washing, and she found that

CHAPTER 19: LOVE AGAIN

his lower reaches demanded special attention. After the shower, Dell dressed, snuck Tara through the woods back to the Jeep, and returned to the cabin. Squeaky clean and (for the moment) lust-free, they had omelets and waffles at the lodge. They were back in D.C. by noon.

Over the following two weeks, Dell and Grace saw each other almost daily, attending musical and theatrical performances at the Kennedy Center and Folger Theater. Dinner conversations and pillow talk sometimes hinted at, but always skirted around, the matter of formalizing the relationship. But Dell did tell Grace more than once how "very special" she was.

* * *

On June 22nd, they drove to the Inn at Little Washington, located in the town of Washington, Virginia, once surveyed by George Washington. The tiny village is about an hour and a half south of Washington, D.C. Dell parked his beat-up Jeep next to a silver Bentley with an ostentatious VA-MD license plate.

With a slight bow and a "your honor," Dell opened the Jeep's passenger door for Grace. She stepped out, elegant in a fitted black dress and pearl necklace. Arm-in-arm, they walked into the blue and white Main Inn. The red, white, and blue flags of France and the United States fluttered from a second-story porch. Dell patted his back pocket to assure himself that his wallet was still there because the Inn's Michelin star rating insured that his wallet would be lighter when they left.

The *maître d'*, perfectly attired in a white tuxedo with black tie, white-gloves, and highly polished black leather shoes, greeted them. He whispered in Dell's ear, "Your request for dessert has been taken care of, sir." He led Grace and Dell to their table, where waiters (plural) were so attentive they almost spoon-fed them. After the salad and appetizer, Grace ordered the Inn's popular "Carpaccio of Herb-Crusted Elysian Fields Baby Lamb Loin with Caesar Salad Ice Cream," while Dell settled for a simple "Chartreuse of Maine Lobster and Savoy Cabbage with White Wine Butter Sauce." Of course, all courses were paired with French wines selected by the sommelier, starting with a 1985 Bordeaux, Château Montrose, Saint-Estephe.

Dell laughed and said, "This sure beats mushy freeze-dried trail food with canteen water."

"With cuisine this exquisite," Grace said, fluttering her eyelashes and flashing her green eyes, "why bother with sex?" She winked and added, "Well, maybe for dessert."

Dell glanced at a hovering waiter and gave him a slight nod. "Yes, sir," the waiter replied.

He disappeared but soon returned with a "Chocolate-Hazelnut Mousse Napoleon" for two. He then placed a small crystal dish next to Grace.

"*Voila!*" he said.

On it, was a sizable square of white chocolate with "Grace—I love you—Dell" written in script with dark chocolate. Grace gasped, gave Dell an incredulous stare, and cried out.

"Omigod!"

She rocketed out of her chair, upsetting a water glass, drenching the linen tablecloth. Grace rushed around to his side of the table and kissed him in full view of everyone. "And I love *you*," she said loudly.

Waiters whisked away the wet tablecloth and replaced it with another. Guests smiled and clapped.

The following weeks were the happiest of times. On weekends, they often hiked in the Virginia and West Virginia mountains. On the Fourth of July, they watched fireworks at the Antietam Battlefield, and later spent a week at Ocracoke Island on North Carolina's Outer Banks.

* * *

Willow called twice more while Dell was in Washington—once in July, from just across the Vermont line in Hanover, New Hampshire, and again in early August from Rangeley, Maine.

"We're doing great, Gramps."

"We?" Dell asked, knowing the answer.

"Train and I are making good time and meeting wonderful people."

"Do you need anything?"

"No, not really."

So, Dell arranged for them to spend a night at the boutique Hanover Inn on the Dartmouth College campus, and he picked up the cost for both of them to stay at the Appalachian Mountain Club hut system in the White Mountain's Presidential Range, through which the A.T. runs.

CHAPTER 19: LOVE AGAIN

When Willow called from Rangeley, Dell said, "Be sure to phone me when you get to Monson. That's another hundred miles north. I'm concerned. The murderer is still at large. He could well be in Maine. And don't forget about that weirdo, Father Monson."

"I won't. Promise I'll call. Love you, Gramps."

"Love you, too, honey. Be careful."

Dell never stopped worrying about Willow, but he and Grace were so enwrapped in and enraptured by each other that his mind sometimes floated away from the fiercely self-assured young woman he'd watched come into her own.

His daughter Amanda was delighted that he and Grace were together. "I know Mom would approve," she told Dell.

But Joanna remained skeptical. "Dad, are you sure about this?"

"Yes, absolutely," he assured her.

By mid-August, the humid dog days of a Washington summer enveloped the city. Life slowed. Dell closed all the windows in his house, turned on the air conditioner, and walked into the kitchen to make a tuna sandwich for lunch. Tara stared up at him hoping some would drop to the floor. The phone rang.

"Dell, Brad. There's been another murder. This one is painful, horrible."

Oh, God, don't let it be Willow! Dell gasped, dropped the phone on the kitchen floor, and slumped onto a chair.

"Dell? You still there?" Brad asked again in a louder voice, "Dell?"

Hand trembling, Dell reached for the phone, brought it to his ear.

"Yeah, I'm here."

"A couple. They were stabbed to death . . ."

CHAPTER 20
THE CALLS

"Listen," Brad said. "It happened last night. They were in a tent by the trail."

A high-pitched buzzing in Dell's ears made it hard to concentrate. "Where?"

"Maine."

"What! What?" Dell pressed the receiver hard to his ear.

"Not far from the Pierce Pond Lean-to, close to the Kennebec River."

Dell felt faint, nauseated, short of breath. He rested his elbows on the kitchen table, chin on his chest as he struggled to speak. He let out a sigh and asked, "Victims' names?"

"Don't know. Maine state police and FBI were on the scene early this morning. Scaperelli wants you up here in Harper's Ferry at one o'clock tomorrow. Can you make it?"

"Um, um, I mean, of course."

"Scaperelli said he and someone named Barbara Hopper will fill us in."

"Uh, okay. I'll see you, uh, tomorrow at one."

"You okay, old buddy?" Brad asked.

"Yeah, yeah. I'm . . . okay."

Dell hung up, walked into his office, and sat with both palms flat on the desk trying to steady himself. *God, please not Willow.* He picked up his office phone and dialed Grace.

With as calm a voice as he could muster Dell said, "Hi love, something has come up. Afraid I'll have to leave town for a while."

"What came up?" Her voice was a bit curt.

"Oh, just some business . . ." he paused ". . . relating to the A.T. I should be back in a week or so."

CHAPTER 20: THE CALLS

"A week! You sound a little too nonchalant, and more than a little evasive. What the hell is going on?"

Dell bit the inside of his cheek. "Well, it's another couple. Murdered. I'm leaving for Maine tomorrow, right after a meeting with the FBI and Brad at Harper's Ferry."

"Listen, sweetcakes. You are *NOT* going anywhere without me."

"Now, Grace . . ."

"Don't 'now Grace' me! I'll be at your place in a couple of hours, after getting my boots and hiking gear at the house. We'll use your tent. Love you."

"Wait! There's no way . . ."

She hung up.

"Damn!"

Dell slammed his fist on the desk and stood up. Grace had told him weeks ago she could take a month's vacation any time, but this would be no vacation. The danger was real. Dell knew Brad wouldn't welcome her involvement, and Scaperelli would be pissed and probably order her to butt out.

True, Grace was no neophyte in criminal matters or the out-of-doors. She was an assistant district attorney early in her career, and he knew that she was an outstanding hiker and backpacker, someone who had done the Maine A.T. south of the Kennebec River to the New Hampshire line when she was an undergraduate at Bates College in Lewiston, Maine. But her principal attribute, the only conceivable reason to bring her along, was her intellect. She was a gifted problem-solver who could recall, organize, and adeptly apply complex facts and suppositions to evolving situations. Few attorneys were better.

Through his own inquiries and efforts Dell had learned that the FBI failed to follow up on Lev Komaroff until he prompted Scaperelli to do so; the Bureau interviewed Manny Kopecki in Port Clinton only after he'd told Brad they should do so; and FBI agents had initially located just one of Fr. Monson's several messages, not to mention the Miller Library book that Dell, not the Bureau, found under the Kirkridge Shelter. Such sloppiness would never have happened with someone like Grace running the investigation. But Dell did not want Grace anywhere near what could only be a hazardous search in the Maine woods. He'd told her in strict confidence everything he knew about the murders, the possible murderer, and Willow, but Grace was not fully immersed in the case and her presence could invite tension in what would probably be an all-male law enforcement team. More importantly, she had no familiarity with the vast wilderness north of Monson or any relationship with Brad, Scaperelli, or the legendary person Dell called next.

Everyone knew him as "Old Man Shaw" but, to Dell, he was just his good friend Keith. No one was more closely identified with the Maine A.T. If anyone had information about Willow, it would be Keith Shaw, owner of Shaw's Boarding Home in Monson, Maine. With hound-dog-droopy eyes, bandy legs, and bottle shoulders, he stood barely five feet tall. He resembled a grizzled elf who just woke up from a deep sleep. But Keith had his finger on the pulse of the trail because Shaw's was a hikers' social and communications hub. For long-distance hikers, like Willow and Train, eighty percent of whom were northbound, Shaw's was the last taste of civilization before they plunged into the Hundred Mile Wilderness.

Dell sat at his office desk and phoned Keith.

Keith answered with, "How 'bout that. You won't believe this, but this morning I promised a young lady I'd call you today. Hadn't gotten around to it yet. She and her boyfriend headed north into the wilderness around seven o'clock, right after breakfast."

"Was her name Willow?"

"Willow?"

"Trail name's Fly Swatter."

"Ayuh! That's her. Fly Swatter and Train. "Good kids, nice couple."

"Yes!" Dell shouted, exhaling deeply. *She's alive. Thank God.*

"Oh. Sounds like that's a good thing. How do you know her?"

"Hiked the Pennsylvania A.T. with her in May. I'm relieved to hear Willow and Train are forty miles north of Pierce Pond. But the murderer is still at large. The bastard could be anywhere."

Tara came into Dell's office and sat down next to him on the Persian rug. He leaned over in his chair to pat her head and, with his face turned away from the phone, whispered to Tara, "Willow's in trouble, babe." At the mention of Willow's name, Tara's ears shot up and she let out a whine.

CHAPTER 20: THE CALLS

"State troopers left my place an hour ago," Keith said. "They're closing seventy miles of the A.T. from Monson south to ME Route 27. Told me they might also close the entire trail north of Monson—all the way to Katahdin, another 115 miles. If they do that, I may go broke."

"Don't worry. Most thru-hikers will ignore the closure. Tell you what, I'll give you some business on Friday if you hold a room for me and a friend."

"You've got it. See you then."

Willow and Train had entered the most remote section of the entire A.T. Dell was certain the murderer was in there somewhere. He closed his eyes, then got up from the desk and hurried to haul his boots, tent, sleeping bag, and other hiking gear up from the basement. He spread each item out on the living room floor, threw clothes into a separate pile, and scrutinized his checklist. There was plenty of trail food and bagged kibble for Tara.

Dell packed, returned to his office, and called the Miller Library at Colby College. The inside cover of the book he'd found under the Kirkridge Shelter and given to the FBI had the library's name. After introducing himself, Dell told librarian Diane Holden he was "assisting" the police in a murder case and needed information about a book checked out of the library that was never returned.

"Wilderness Survival Strategies?" she asked.

Dell leaned forward in his desk chair. "How did you know?"

"An FBI agent interviewed me and the provost back in June about Professor Henry Dubois, the person who last checked it out."

"Who is Professor Dubois?"

"Look, I'm very busy Mr. Peterson. Why don't you speak to Professor Katherine Ingham, chair of the English department?" Ms. Holden took a deep breath and added, with an edge in her voice, "Dubois was denied tenure last spring; he is no longer with the college. Good riddance, I say."

"Good riddance?" Dell said, jotting notes down on a pad of paper.

"I probably shouldn't say this, but everyone at the college knows Dubois despises women." Before hanging up, Ms. Holden said, "Professor Ingham's extension is 3117. She'll confirm that."

Tara's muzzle was on Dell's lap. Time to feed her. He walked into the kitchen, filled her bowl, returned to the office, and called Professor Ingham. She was leaving for the day but agreed to see him in her office in a couple of days to discuss her former colleague.

Not long after getting off the phone with Professor Ingham, Dell heard Grace's car pull into the driveway. She had a key to the house, but he and Tara went outside to greet her with a hug. Tara circled them both, wagging her tail. Dell hauled Grace's backpack and boots into the house and placed them by his gear in the living room. She opened a hot container of kung pao chicken she'd picked up for dinner, brought a couple of plates and forks to the sofa, and they sat to eat.

"Glad you agreed I could come along," she said with a wink.

"Only because I love you," Dell said. *And because you'd never accept 'no' for an answer.*

"That's *why* I'm coming. Because I love you." She took a bite of food and smiled.

They kissed, and Dell told her what Keith Shaw had said about Willow and Train.

"Wonderful! But they're still vulnerable," she said.

"Very much so. Those two can easily hike twenty miles a day, which means they were only two hiking days north of Pierce Pond Lean-to when the murderer struck. I suspect, and we should assume, the killer is very familiar with northern Maine, every friggin' deer path and gutted out logging road. The threat to Willow and Train and every other hiker, whether north or south of the Kennebec, is immediate."

Dell raised an eyebrow. "The FBI guy in charge of the investigation, Tony Scaperelli, is a hard ass who only barely tolerates me. He'll blow his top when I walk into ATC headquarters tomorrow with a drop-dead gorgeous, green-eyed bombshell."

Grace's eyes narrowed. "Oh yeah, we'll see about that. I'm a Lombardi. He's a Scaperelli. I can keep any *paison* in check."

"Yes, we'll see about that soon enough."

When Grace got off the sofa to take the plates into the kitchen, Dell called Brad at home to tell him about Willow.

"I'm bringing someone with me to the meeting tomorrow."

"Oh?" Brad said.

"Her name's Grace Lombardi. An attorney and a top-notch hiker who has done portions of the Maine A.T., and . . ."

"You're dating her."

"Well . . ." Dell hesitated for a moment. "Yeah. Look, she'll be an asset."

"Good thing we've known each other forever." Brad paused. "However, I'm warning you: Scaperelli will likely go into orbit."

CHAPTER 21
THE MEETING

Dell's mind was fixated on Willow as he, Grace, and Tara drove from Washington to the meeting at Harpers Ferry. It had been three months since his last visit to the town. A shiver shot up his spine. *Damn. She's in real trouble. I feel it.*

"You're worried about Willow," Grace said. "I can tell."

"Yes."

She slid across the Jeep's bench seat and patted his knee. "We'll find her."

Nodding, he stared straight ahead as Tara whined in the back seat.

After an hour and a half drive, Dell parked across the street from ATC headquarters. He and Grace walked over to the building where some hikers sat on an outside bench chatting and licking ice cream cones. Dell opened the front door and almost collided with Cherie Nardone.

"You're early Dell," she said, "but everyone's here."

Cherie gave him a lavender-scented peck on the cheek, then turned to Grace.

"You must be Grace Lombardi. Glad to meet you."

As Cherie led them toward the same room where the last meeting had been held she said, "Brad and I were worried about you Dell. Pennsylvania state police told us you, Tara, and some young girl tussled with pretty rough characters at the Kirkridge Shelter. Thank goodness you're still in one piece."

Grace clutched his arm. "What's this about? What happened?"

"Nothing much." Dell looked away.

When they entered the cedar-paneled room, Cherie excused herself. Brad was standing with his back to them at the far end of the oval oak table speaking with Scaperelli, who wore the same ill-fitting blue suit. Next to Tony stood a woman wearing a tailored gray suit and white blouse who looked to be in her mid fifties, a brunette with a shag haircut and tortoiseshell eyeglasses. A topographical map of the Maine A.T. hung on the wall by the door. On the wall to the far left was a framed black and white photograph of a craggy-faced man with a prominent chin and no-nonsense look. Conservationist Benton MacKaye was the first person to articulate the idea of a continuous trail along the crest of the Appalachians from Georgia to Maine. On the same wall, next to MacKaye, hung a smaller photograph of another A.T. legend. Pointing to this photo, Grace asked, "Who's that?"

"Grandma Gatewood," Dell said. "She was the image of an archetypal grandmother, a Norman Rockwell-type granny with white hair and a kindly smile. Except this grandma became the first woman to hike the entire A.T. solo in one season. She did it wearing Keds, with an army blanket, raincoat, and plastic shower curtain stuffed into a denim bag slung over her shoulder."

Brad walked over, patted Dell on the shoulder, and said, "You know Tony, of course."

"Good to see you," Scaperelli said, as the two men shook hands.

No bone-crushing handshake this time, Dell thought. He replied with a circumspect, "Good to see you," and glanced at the woman standing next to Scaperelli.

Tony introduced her as "Dr. Barbara Hopper."

"Barbara Hopper, behavioral analyst," she said. "The popular media call us profilers." She smiled warmly at Grace, who was standing at Dell's side.

Touching Grace's elbow, Dell said, "Let me introduce my friend Grace Lombardi, a senior attorney at Cloverdale, Thayer & Weiss. She's an experienced backpacker and former assistant DA who has offered her assistance, pro bono."

Brad said, "Welcome."

Tony frowned, but Barbara walked over to Grace with a wide smile and said, "My son, William Hopper, is with Cloverdale, Thayer. Do you know him?"

Grace lit up. "Why yes, William has a sharp mind and promising future with the firm."

Barbara beamed, but the furrows in Tony's brow deepened and he shot a reproachful look at his colleague.

Brad sat down at one end of the large table. "Now that we've been introduced, let's get started." Dell and Grace sat across from the two FBI officers.

"Tony," Brad said with an uneasy glance in his direction, "Could you brief us on events in Maine?"

Scaparelli squinted at Grace and snapped, "I'm unclear about exactly what Ms. Lombardi brings to the investigation." Without waiting for or, apparently, expecting a response, he extracted a sheet of paper from his briefcase. "If, and *only* if, I conclude Ms. Lombardi adds something of value to our investigation, and I don't know what that might be, this nondisclosure agreement must be signed." A brusque swipe of his hand sent the form sliding across the table.

Grace pressed her lips together and fixed a cold don't-mess-with-me stare on Tony before she scanned the familiar form and signed it with a curt, "Of course, Mr. Scaperelli." She pushed the signed form back to him.

Barbara adjusted her glasses so they rested on the tip of her nose. Brad and Dell glanced at one another. Tony stood and stepped over to the Maine A.T. map. He put his finger under a small blue dot, Pierce Pond, located about three miles west of the Kennebec River.

"The FBI's Bangor office received a call early yesterday from the Maine state police," he said. "Terrified hikers had called the police from the nearby town of Caratunk after they'd come upon two mutilated bodies splayed out directly on the trail between Pierce Pond Lean-to and the Kennebec River. We sent a response team immediately." Tony pointed to Bangor. "They arrived at the scene in three hours. The state police asked us to take the lead because of our prior involvement in the Pennsylvania and Virginia cases but assured us of their active support."

"It was a couple tenting?" Brad asked.

Tony looked at Brad. "Yes. The shelter was filled to over-capacity that night, at least a dozen people. The couple camped about a mile from the lean-to. They were isolated and vulnerable."

"Pierce Pond Lean-to is always full this time of year," Brad said. "We expect about two hundred northbound thru-hikers to be in Maine over the next month, plus many day and section hikers. Hardly surprising the couple decided to pitch a tent on down the trail away from the shelter."

CHAPTER 21: THE MEETING

Dell gave Brad a knowing look and added, "This also got them closer to the Kennebec River for an early morning crossing." Dell explained that the seventy-yard-wide Kennebec, with powerful currents and changing depths, presented the most formidable unbridged river crossing on the entire A.T. Hikers had drowned, which is why many try to reach the west side of the river early so they can be among the first ferried across by a small boat from the town of Caratunk.

"Good point," Tony said, rubbing his chin. "In fact, the hazardous river crossing reinforces our belief that the murderer drove in on the open logging road that crosses the A.T. a mile southwest of the shelter. That's how our agents got in."

Tony then described a tent slashed repeatedly with a sharp knife. As in Pennsylvania and Virginia, the couple was mutilated in a shocking manner, especially the woman. "Both of them were stabbed multiple times, and their eyes were gouged out. The killer sliced off one of the female victim's breasts and," staring directly at Grace, Tony said, "only the female victim was decapitated."

Grace didn't flinch. Speaking in an even voice, she said, "Those poor hikers who came across the bodies yesterday morning. How fast a pleasant walk in the woods can turn into a horror scene."

Barbara glanced over her eyeglasses at Grace and nodded.

Tony shifted his weight and continued. "We found another oddball message in the Pierce Pond Lean-to's log from the so-called Fr. Monson, apparently written a day or two before the murders." He removed a crinkled piece of notepaper that an agent had torn from the lean-to's log and read, "'If no one else, the dying must notice how unreal, how full of pretense, is all that we accomplish here, where nothing is allowed to be itself.'"

"Wow!" Brad said, leaning forward. "This guy's a nut case, but an articulate one."

"Yes," Dell agreed, looking at the message and jotting it down. "And the blue ink handwriting matches that of the other messages."

"Would you read that again Mr. Scaperelli?" Grace asked.

Scaperelli scowled, shook his head, and read it once again.

"I know who Fr. Monson is quoting," Grace said.

They all turned toward her.

"German literature was one of my college majors." She flipped a strand of hair from her face. "It's Rilke, Rainer Maria Rilke, one of the two greatest German-language lyric poets. He was deeply religious and unafraid to stare death in the eye."

Tony stepped toward Grace. Dell had anticipated that Scaperelli would look for a reason, any reason, to confront her, just as he'd confronted him at their first meeting. Scaperelli crossed his arms, smiled disparagingly, and said, "Oh, really? A friggin' poet?"

Dell was about to jump down Tony's throat when Grace stiffened, pushed her chair away from the table, and shot back, "Well, who do *you* think is being quoted?"

"I have no idea. And it probably doesn't make a damn bit of difference who it is."

A sly smile crept across Grace's face. "I wrote my honors thesis on Rilke. The quotation is from his *Duino Elegies*, number four."

She poked Dell under the table. With wide eyes, Grace delivered a coup de grace. "The poem ends with: 'The minds of murderers are easily comprehended. But to contain death so gently within oneself is indescribable.'" She drummed her fingers on the table. "And," she said with only a hint of sarcasm, "identifying the source of the quotation will likely prove significant."

A hush fell over the room as they glanced at one another.

Everyone but Tony uttered a collective, "Wow!"

Dell wanted to hug Grace but settled for a whispered, "Brilliant."

Thrown off balance, Tony stammered, "It's, it's. . . ." He pounded his fist on the table and shouted, "Damn! Let's get back on track."

Relishing the moment and grinning broadly, Grace said, "*Du heulst im Sturm.*"

Tony growled, "What the hell does that mean?"

"More Rilke," Grace replied. "Translates as, 'You howl in the storm.'"

Dell murmured to Brad, "In the wrestling world, we call that a takedown."

Barbara Hopper interceded, probably hoping to end the dialectic escalation. She folded her hands and turned toward Grace.

"Your observation about Rilke is very insightful. I'm curious, what else did you study in college?"

CHAPTER 21: THE MEETING

"Logic," Grace said, with a twinkle in her eye.

Brad leaned close to Dell, "Wow, where'd you find her? Another takedown."

Cherie opened the door and entered with coffee and soft drinks. Tension in the room eased as everyone took a break.

A red-faced Tony sidled up to Grace, who was standing sipping her coffee. "*Mi scusi*, Ms. Lombardi. I'm a cop, not a scholar. But maybe I will consider your poet."

Waving an arm above her head and smiling, Grace said, *Va bene Tony, noi italiani emozionati.* (That's okay, Tony. We Italians are emotional).

He sighed, "So I've heard."

Tugging at his shirt collar and loosening his tie, Tony regained composure. As the others sat down, he returned to the map and again pointed to Pierce Pond.

"Assuming the murderer came in on the logging road, he might have hung out in his vehicle or around the lean-to for one or two days. The couple's tent was only a short walk away."

"Do we know the victims' names?" Brad asked.

"Yes," Tony answered. "Their drivers' licenses identify them as Shirley and Skip Moore. They were . . ."

". . . In their early to mid twenties," Dell said. "Shirley was short and blonde. Her trail name was First Mate. Skip's was Skipper. . . . Excuse me." Dell pushed himself up from the table, hurried from the room, and quick-stepped from the building. He let Tara out of the Jeep to pee as a tear meandered down his face. His skin crawled as he thought of the sweet couple, the blood, and the cold steel blade piercing their bodies over and over. A hand touched his. Grace kissed him on the cheek.

"It's too damn personal," Dell said. "Willow and I spoke with First Mate and Skipper on the trail. That's exactly what awaits Willow and Train."

"We won't let that happen." Grace held Dell's hand tight and guided him back to the meeting.

"Sorry," Dell said, sitting down. "It won't happen again. Met those two on the Pennsylvania A.T. three months ago. Nice people. Newlyweds." He took a deep breath and asked, "What else do we know?"

Tony pointed to Barbara and sat down.

"We think we have a good fix on the killer's appearance," Barbara said.

She passed out copies of an upper body photograph of a man, along with a full-body FBI sketch of the suspect. The two items bore a resemblance to one another. The rendition by the Bureau's artist was based on descriptions of the suspect by two hotel proprietors, Manny Kopecki and Jamie Doyle. The drawing portrayed an overweight, jowly, middle-age man of somewhere between forty-five and fifty with short-cropped brown hair. Barbara put his height at about five foot ten.

Dell eyed the sketch for several seconds. "It matches Willow's description of the man who straddled the trail and blocked her path the day she called me from New York. Several young guys she knew came along and told the bastard to move on. I told you about this, Tony."

"Yes, you did, but remind me again who Willow is."

"She's a young runaway Dell took under his wing on the Pennsylvania trail," said Brad.

Leaning across the table toward Dell, Barbara asked, "Do you know where she is today?"

"On the A.T. with her boyfriend, Train, somewhere north of Monson."

The two FBI officers looked at each other, then at Dell. Tony asked, "Do you have a close attachment to this girl?"

Grace nudged Dell's foot under the table.

He got the message. "Not particularly."

"Good," Tony said. "Emotional attachments cloud judgment."

Grace tensed as she zeroed in on Scaperelli. "We wouldn't want to be *emotional*. No emotions, no humanity. No reality either. An emotional engagement can solidify commitment and intensify motivation to, for instance, solve a crime."

Tony didn't take the bait this time. Instead, he asked Barbara to comment on the photo. Barbara explained that the book Dell had found under the Kirkridge Shelter had, unsurprisingly, led them to Colby College, where an FBI agent interviewed librarian Diane Holden. Because of what he learned from Ms. Holden, the agent decided to speak with the college's provost, Ruth Silverman.

"She was the one," Barbara said, "who gave us this photo of

Henry Dubois, a former professor at Colby and the person who last checked out the book."

"I spoke with Ms. Holden yesterday on the phone," Dell said. "She told me Dubois was denied tenure. Even more interesting, she said, and I quote, 'everyone at the college knows Dubois despises women.' I would've called Tony about this but I knew we'd be meeting today."

Barbara's eyes widened. She peered at Dell over the rims of her glasses and said, "I'm impressed Dell."

Dell gave her a thumbs-up.

Barbara continued. "Because of the killer's singularly malicious butchering of his female victims, and what both the librarian and provost told our agent about his attitude toward women, we can assume he's a vicious misogynist." She paused and held up the photo of Professor Dubois as well as the artist's sketch of the suspect. "And I'm sure you've noticed similarities between the two."

Everyone in the room nodded.

"Moreover," Grace said, as if summarizing the prosecution's case to a jury, "it had to be Dubois who left the library book at the Kirkridge Shelter and," pointing to his photo, "he was likely in Duncannon, Port Clinton, and probably several other places along the Pennsylvania A.T."

"What about Lev Komaroff?" Tony asked. "Thanks again Dell for reminding me to follow up on him."

Tony explained that the FBI had obtained a warrant to search Komaroff's cottage. He'd disappeared, but agents found an old address book. Crossed out in black ink, was Henry Dubois's former address in Waterville, Maine, when he'd taught at Colby. "So, the two knew one another, although there's nothing so far that points to Komaroff as the murderer," Tony said.

"But it's conceivable, maybe likely," Dell commented, tilting his head to the side, "that Dubois stayed with Komaroff for a period of time before those murders at the Clary Shelter near Duncannon. He may not be the murderer, but he sure could be an accomplice. At the very least, he probably knows something."

"Yes, I agree," Tony said.

Absent another credible suspect, the cascade of evidence and conjecture pointed to Dubois as the probable murderer.

"But what was his motivation?" Brad asked. "I've known

some misogynists, and they weren't killers—just pains in the butt."

Barbara nodded in agreement.

"And where is Dubois today?" Brad wondered aloud.

Dell remarked that he and Grace would be meeting tomorrow morning with the chair of Colby's English department. "She might shed some light on motivation and Dubois's whereabouts."

Barbara took off her glasses and turned to Scaperelli with a caustic, "Why didn't *we* interview the English department's faculty?"

Tony's ears reddened.

With a glance at Grace, Dell thought, *Tony just lost his standing to challenge the value of Grace's involvement in the case.*

Dell leaned back in his chair and, hoping not to come off as a 'gotcha' smart-ass, said, "Grace and I will let *Brad* know what we find out."

Tony scowled at Brad, "Remember, Peterson is *not* law enforcement. Get back to me immediately on this."

"Of course," Brad replied.

Shifting the focus away from her chagrined colleague, Barbara said, "I haven't written *the* book on psychopaths, but I have written *a* book on the subject. Dubois could well be a psychopath, and that's what our profile of the murderer suggests." Barbara pulled a folder and some handwritten notes from her leather attaché case. With her elbows on the table, she said, "Based on everything we've learned from the Virginia, Pennsylvania, and Maine cases, it's clear the killer fits all of the many indicators of a psychopathic personality." Pointing her finger at Dell and then Grace, she said, "I'm only mentioning a few of these indicators, but you two might keep them in mind when you talk with people at Colby. Wish I could go with you, but I'm scheduled to brief senior officials on another matter tomorrow."

Grace nodded, and Dell removed a small notebook from his pocket and started taking notes.

Barbara put her glasses on and began. "First, the murderer is self-obsessed. His vanity leads him to believe he can avoid apprehension."

"Overconfidence is a weakness," Grace said. "It works in our favor."

"Absolutely," Barbara agreed. "Thinking he won't be caught will strengthen his desire to kill. And he's likely to make a mistake.

CHAPTER 21: THE MEETING

Next, our misogynistic murderer has accumulated real or supposed injustices committed against him, especially by women."

Dell sat upright in his chair. "Like being denied tenure by female colleagues."

"Good example," Barbara said. "A third element is that he dehumanizes others and blames them for his failures."

Tony leaned back, hands behind his head, "Yeah. Like young military recruits are taught to dehumanize the enemy. Makes it much easier to kill."

Barbara gave a crisp nod.

"A fourth consideration. While this guy is bright, calculating, and plans his crimes meticulously, he probably has poor anger-management skills in social and professional situations," said Barbara.

"We could confirm this tomorrow when we meet with his former colleagues at Colby," Dell said.

"Finally, and most obviously, the murderer may hold grudges against other classes of people besides women, like hikers or police. If so, women hikers would be extreme provocations."

"Oh! One more thing," Barbara said, gathering her notes. "Like misogynists, most psychopaths are not violent, but they can be and ours is. Indeed, most cold-blooded killers tend to be psychopaths. They have no conscience and live on the edge."

It was 3 p.m. when Brad asked whether there were any other questions or observations. Hearing none, he stood and thanked everyone for their contributions. They all walked out into the lobby.

With a half smile and hands jammed into his pants pockets, Tony said to Grace, "Welcome to the team."

He revealed that some FBI agents were already on the trail between the Kennebec and Monson; that he would arrive in Monson in "a couple of days;" and that a federal response team from Boston would soon begin moving south along the trail out of Baxter State Park where Mt. Katahdin anchors the northern terminus of the A.T. Tony said agents would be equipped with the newest Motorola mobile phones, although connectivity was notoriously poor in mountainous wilderness areas. He mentioned that the state police would provide a floatplane or helicopter if needed.

Dell and Grace walked out to the Jeep where Tara greeted them with yips and wags. Their five-hundred-mile drive to the Blue Mermaid Motel off I-95 in Portsmouth, New Hampshire, was grueling. They stopped once for refueling and a fast-food dinner and pulled into the motel after midnight, well-positioned for the next morning's drive to Waterville, Maine, and Colby.

CHAPTER 22
HENRY DUBOIS

Colby College sits atop a hill overlooking the small city of Waterville and the Kennebec River Valley, ninety miles south of the town of Monson and the A.T. Dell and Grace arrived at the college shortly before 10 a.m. and parked on a nearby tree-lined street. They rolled the windows down for Tara, walked onto campus, and asked a young woman in shorts and a blue and white "Colby Mules" T-shirt for directions to the English Department. She smiled and pointed to a multi-storied brick structure with a soaring white spire in the center of a grassy quadrangle lined with several smaller brick buildings. "It's in the Miller Library."

Dell and Grace walked to the library, which they later learned had been the tallest building in Maine when it was built in 1939 and took the steps. Probably because they looked so out of place, a man in a pink polo shirt with rimless glasses and a well-trimmed beard approached them and asked, "Can I help you find something?"

"Thanks," Dell said. "We're looking for Professor Katherine Ingham's office."

He introduced himself as Professor Randall Galloway—"You must be from the Appalachian Trail Conference. I'm headed to the same meeting."

Grace and Dell nodded and smiled.

"Our meeting is in seminar room 119," Galloway said. "I'll take you there and tell Katherine you've arrived."

On their way to the seminar room Dell said, "I recall a law school friend who was a Colby alum saying that the college had quite a history."

"Indeed. We were founded in 1813," Professor Galloway said. "One of the oldest liberal arts colleges in the country."

"Impressive," said Grace. "Would you know when women were first admitted?"

Galloway grinned. "1871. We were the first previously all-male New England college to admit women."

"Go Colby!" Grace said, raising both arms above her head.

Galloway led them through the library's spacious reference room, which seemed largely devoid of students in the summer, to a door that opened into a seminar room with casement windows looking out on the quad. A photograph of Major General Joshua Chamberlain, hero of the Battle of Gettysburg and former Governor of Maine, hung from a wall. Two large tables with folding chairs had been pushed together in the center of the room. A woman of about forty-five in blue jeans sat at one of the tables jotting something on a pad of lined yellow paper. She looked up when they entered. Gunmetal gray hair with streaks of ivory framed her face, partly obscuring her eyes. She bore a striking resemblance to an English sheepdog.

Randall Galloway introduced Dell and Grace to Professor Sylvia Alvarez who nodded, looked at them with a blank expression, and went back to whatever she was writing. Galloway then left the room but soon returned with the English Department's chair, Katherine Ingham, who had a welcoming, easy-going manner—"Just call me Katherine." She was maybe sixty, with a pageboy haircut.

Dell smiled and said, "I'd like to introduce my friend and fellow attorney, Grace Lombardi."

"Wow!" Katherine said, chuckling, "Hope you two don't charge by the hour."

Everyone laughed.

Katherine took an immediate liking to Grace and the two women greeted one another warmly.

"I didn't realize there'd be two of you," she said, "but I'm delighted to have a female attorney with us today." They sat down around the consolidated tables and Dell thanked the three faculty members for agreeing to meet with them.

"I asked Sylvia and Randall to join us," Katherine said. "Sylvia chairs the English department's Rank and Tenure Committee." Katherine turned toward Randall and winked. "Randall represents a distinguished minority of our department's faculty—men." Adopting a more earnest demeanor, she lifted her chin and looked Dell and

CHAPTER 22: HENRY DUBOIS

Grace in the eye. "Before we start, I'd like to clarify something. It's my understanding you two are representing the Appalachian Trail Conference in a criminal matter that may involve Henry Dubois."

"Yes," they replied in unison.

"And you're with law enforcement?"

"Yes," Grace said, nudging Dell's foot under the table. The word "with" was conveniently ambiguous. "The ATC has been working with the FBI for months concerning murders on the Appalachian Trail." Grace glanced at Dell. "That relationship is ongoing. Dell and I conferred yesterday with FBI agents at ATC headquarters in Harper's Ferry."

Katherine leaned back in her chair. "Fine. How can we help you?"

"Perhaps you can tell us about Henry Dubois," Dell said. "Librarian Diane Holden told me he was denied tenure, and, in her words, 'Dubois despises women.'"

Katherine gestured toward Sylvia who shifted anxiously in her chair as if preparing for battle. She took a deep breath, her face taut—"My committee voted unanimously to deny Dubois tenure," she said. "Katherine concurred with our decision, as did the college's interdepartmental committee, which I also chair, and, finally, Provost Ruth Silverman signed off on the matter."

"When I'm not hiking," Dell said, scratching his head, "I'm a professor of law with some experience in tenure decisions. Were Henry Dubois's scholarship and teaching really that bad?"

Sylvia clenched her jaw. "In the classroom," she said, talking through her teeth, "his command of substance was adequate. But misogyny permeated everything he said and did." Red splotches broke out on her face. "Our students, most of whom are women, complained bitterly about this to other faculty and in their written evaluations of Dubois's courses."

"Could you give us an example?" Grace asked.

"Examples are legion," said Katherine, who grimaced and folded her arms. "Dubois targeted women students, not men, for humiliation in class. His verbal assaults wouldn't stop until he'd reduced his victim—and victim is the proper word—to tears. Dubois showed no sensitivity, no remorse."

Katherine related one particularly egregious instance that was confirmed to her personally by several of Dubois's students, both women and men. A woman student whom he'd asked to read a poem in front of the class broke down in tears. She apologized, and explained that her mother had died a week earlier. Dubois was livid. He walked up to her, his face inches from hers, and shouted, "Don't be weak, woman! Death is part of life. No sympathy for you." She ran from the classroom in tears, dropped the course, and withdrew from Colby.

Sylvia and Randall Galloway nodded in agreement. Speechless, Grace covered her mouth with her hand.

Katherine stared at the ceiling for a moment to gather her thoughts. "Dubois was self-centered, a narcissist even. He was obsessively competitive with women, not so much with men. He'd explode in anger if a bright, confident female student challenged him in class." She flipped an opal pendant between her fingers and added, "Several of us witnessed his heated outbursts when our colleagues had their poems or short stories accepted for publication in *The New Yorker* after his multiple submissions were rejected."

Sylvia's eyes flitted from person to person and her hand trembled as she jammed something into her purse. "And," Sylvia said, with a reddening face, "Dubois would steal the ideas of his female colleagues, never his male colleagues. My committee substantiated two instances of his outright plagiarism of their work. Not only unethical, but dumb."

Dell kneaded his forehead and remarked, "Sounds like Dubois should've been fired long ago."

"Probably so," Katherine said, "but the plagiarism wasn't fully uncovered until late in his tenure review process. By that time, it was clear he would no longer be on our faculty."

Randall removed his glasses, wiped them with a white handkerchief, and spoke for the first time. "I probably knew Henry better than anyone at the college. Sometimes we'd go into town for a beer. He was always cordial toward me, and as far as I know, with most other men." Randall paused to slip his glasses back on. "But Katherine and Sylvia are correct. He harbored grudges, bitter grudges, against women. After his manuscript on Rilke's poetry was rejected by several academic publishers he blamed the rejections on, and I quote, 'the goddamn bitches who control the whole publishing business.'"

"Rilke!" Grace said. "Was Dubois a Rilke scholar?"

CHAPTER 22: HENRY DUBOIS

"He taught a course on Rilke and Goethe," Randall said, resting his chin in both hands and pausing for a few seconds. "Rilke, of course, was deeply religious. Henry was not. I think Henry was drawn to the darkness of so much of Rilke's work and the poet's emphasis on the impermanency of life. Henry was obsessed with the subject of death."

Grace's eyebrows shot up and she looked at Dell.

Sylvia noticed and said, "A misogynist fixated on death. Did that ring a bell with you two?"

"It did," Dell said, pushing his chair back and looking at his watch. "You've all been very helpful. Is there anything else we should know?"

"Yes," said Randall. "Dubois was convinced the tenure process at Colby was so female-dominated that it was stacked against him. Shortly before he left Waterville for good, and I remember this clearly, I heard him issue a direct threat." Randall lowered his voice and looked Dell in the eye. "Dubois said, 'There *will* be retribution.' He was deadly serious."

"Frightening," said Grace.

As they filed out of the seminar room Dell asked whether anyone knew where Dubois might be.

"I'd heard something about the little town of Monson," Katherine said.

Randall shook his head. "He once had some kind of tie to Monson, but he doesn't live there. Henry would occasionally mention a remote cabin on or near timber company land." Randall stroked his beard. "He knows the backwoods of Maine well but, except for hinting that the cabin was somewhere south of Baxter State Park, he was always vague about its exact location."

With that, Dell and Grace returned to the Jeep and Tara. They had a quick lunch in Waterville, where Dell called Brad to brief him on their meeting.

He ended the call with, "It's got to be Henry Dubois. Barbara Hopper was right. Dubois is a vindictive misogynist and almost certainly also a psychopath. After being denied tenure he vowed unspecified 'retribution,' conceivably against women simply because they are women."

"I'll call Scaperelli," Brad said, "but Tony will be in Monson in a day or two."

"Good. We might miss him, though. Tomorrow morning, we hope to be on the A.T. heading north toward Katahdin in hot pursuit of Willow."

"Be careful, buddy."

CHAPTER 23

MONSON

Drivers heading north to Moosehead Lake on Route 15 might not notice Monson with a population of 666 unless they slowed down, way down. But the town plays a disproportionate role in the lore and culture of the Appalachian Trail because it is the gateway to the A.T.'s most isolated and inaccessible section—The Hundred Mile Wilderness.

Dell did slow down. He drove twenty miles-per-hour as they approached the Monson post office, then hooked a left off Route 15 by the general store onto Pleasant Street. About two hundred feet down the street on the right was the renowned Shaw's Boarding Home, a plain white, boxy, two-story frame building.

The legendary Keith Shaw had welcomed and provisioned hundreds of long-distance hikers for fourteen years at his hikers' hostel. Dell spotted him. Even at a distance, Keith's squat, milk-bottle profile was unmistakable as well as his stained white T-shirt stretched over an ample belly. His baggy pants would've fallen to his ankles if not for the suspenders. He was standing out front, not far from several parked cars, chatting with someone.

"That's Keith," Dell said. "He's a teddy bear. Prepare to be hugged. He *loves* women."

"Oh great," Grace said, rolling her eyes.

Dell pulled the Jeep next to other cars parked by the hostel, one of which was encircled with yellow tape. Keith was talking to a thick-necked, muscular man with a buzz cut whose army green flannel shirt and heavy black nylon trousers looked like some sort of field uniform.

"Oh, oh. Something is up," Dell said. "That guy's no A.T. thru-hiker. He means business."

Keith's back was to Dell and Grace, and he was waggling his head like an old dog bothered by a horsefly. He hadn't heard Dell's Jeep, probably because he hated wearing his hearing aids. When Dell let Tara out of the car, she squatted in the grass, then paused for several seconds to sample the air until her nose detected Keith. She rushed straight to him, bumping into his backside.

"Whoa!" he shouted, spinning around. "Well, if it isn't my sweet Tara girl." He wrapped his arms around her as Tara stood on her hind legs with both front paws pressed against Keith's chest. She licked his face. "Only Willow and Jamie Doyle love Tara like that," Dell said to Grace.

As Grace and Dell approached, they saw Keith shake his head from side to side, this time as if grieving or in disbelief. Keith dabbed his eyes with a frayed yellow bandanna but forced a grin when he saw them. The other man dipped his head and peered over his sunglasses in their direction. He eyed them with an apprehensive half smile. When they got closer, Dell saw the holstered Glock pistol strapped to his side.

"So great to see you, Dell," Keith said, "especially at a time like this."

Unable to reach Dell's shoulders for a bear hug, he hooked an arm around Dell's waist and squeezed.

"What happened?" Dell asked.

Keith wiped his face with the bandanna, tried to speak, but could only say, "Terrible, so terrible."

"Stan Schneider, FBI," said the man with the Glock who'd heard Dell's name mentioned. Tony Scaperelli said you'd be here. Glad to meet you." Turning to Grace, he said, "You must be Grace Lombardi. Tony said—and these are his words—'She's one smart cookie.'"

Grace gave Schneider an incredulous stare before grabbing Dell's arm and saying, "Well, it isn't every day a girl receives a compliment—albeit second hand—from a wholly unanticipated source."

"Did Tony score big time?" Dell asked Grace.

She winked.

A red-eyed Keith shuffled over to Grace, looked down, touched her hand with one finger, and said in a hushed voice, "Any friend of Dell's is a friend of mine."

CHAPTER 23: MONSON

Sensing Keith's need for emotional support, Grace patted him on the shoulder. "Thank you. You're very kind."

Dell looked at Schneider. "Well?"

Schneider grimaced, glanced at Grace, then looked back at Dell. "It's pretty horrific."

"It's okay. She can take it."

Schneider nodded. "State police and one of our guys hauled her body out two hours ago. Appalling mutilation. She was disemboweled. Ravens were feeding on her entrails."

"Good God," Grace said, clenching her jaw.

"She was backpacking at night by headlamp. Not smart with a killer on the loose. Happened on the A.T. near a marshy place called Mud Pond, about five miles east of Route 15."

"Was she alone?" Dell asked.

"Apparently. Her driver's license indicated she was from Worcester, Massachusetts. Twenty-six years old. Her car is parked over there." Schneider pointed to the taped-off, dust-covered blue Toyota Corolla with Massachusetts plates. "State police have closed off the wilderness to hikers. Everything from Monson to Baxter State Park."

Keith blew his nose into the bandanna and shoved it into his pocket. "I've got a full house for tonight," he said. "This could put me out of business. Hikers are ninety percent of my lodgers."

Dell rested his hand on Keith's shoulder. "Think you'll survive. You know nothing deters hell-bent distance hikers, certainly not a putative closure of the trail."

As in Pennsylvania three months earlier, Dell knew most long-distance hikers would find any one of multiple ways around the yellow warning tape at the trailhead. Thru-hikers don't struggle for 2,200 miles in the heat and cold—through lightning strikes and driving rain; swarms of blackflies and mosquitos; rashes, bites, blisters and sprains, with one or more body parts usually hurting—to turn back when they can almost smell Katahdin's fresh breezes.

Dell grabbed their suitcases from the Jeep, and they followed Keith to an outside door with a red-lettered sign: TAKE OFF BOOTS. NO DOGS ALLOWED. Keith turned a well-worn brass doorknob and called out to Tara, "Come, babe."

Tara trotted inside at Keith's heels, followed by Grace, Schneider, and Dell—after they'd removed their boots.

To the right as they entered was a spacious kitchen with a ceiling fan the size of a Harley-Davidson. As always, the kitchen smelled of bacon grease. Years of oily buildup had left a brown film on what had once been blue and white wallpaper behind the eight-burner propane gas stove that Keith called "the Battleship Missouri." Keith, Tara, Grace, Schneider, and Dell walked past the kitchen and a hikers' fridge and entered the first and largest of three common rooms. Several hikers were whooping and hollering at one of two long, polished plywood dining room tables. They were caught up in a spirited game of hearts, and barely noticed the new arrivals.

Skirting the card players, they entered a smaller room with a noticeably warped pine-planked floor. A couple was pulling wet clothes from the washer and stuffing them into a dryer. Another hiker, barefooted and wearing only boxer shorts, folded clothes on a corner table. Tara led the way, prancing through spaces she knew well. She led them to a back room lined with bookshelves crammed with dog-eared paperbacks. In the corner was a cooler always filled with Budweiser beer and Molson ale. Grace claimed one of the two comfy armchairs and Schneider and Dell sat down on an unoccupied lumpy sofa.

Keith said all the boarders had been informed of the recent murder. He seemed surprised that none gave any sign of rushing to leave the hostel. To the contrary, Dell suspected most, if not all, would make every effort to sneak back onto the A.T.

Keith went to the kitchen to get coffee for everyone and a hot dog for Tara, who trotted behind him.

"Scaperelli will be in Monson tomorrow by midmorning," Stan said, pushing back in the sofa. "Tony will have another agent with him. The two of them hope be on the trail heading north shortly after noon. Don't know yet whether he'll want me to join them or stay here."

"Grace and I will enter the wilderness right after the 6 a.m. breakfast," Dell said.

Schneider scratched his head. "If it was my call, I'd stop you. Much too dangerous. But . . ." He tilted his head and sighed. "Tony made it clear that you two are free to go wherever you want. Fortunately, he'll probably catch up with you on the trail by nightfall."

Grace said, "We have Tara, and we'll be cautious."

Schneider put his feet up on a nicked, boot-scuffed coffee table. "Tim O'Connor, our guy who helped the state police carry out the woman's body, is back at Mud Pond, one of the many Mud Ponds in Maine. He'll still be there tomorrow gathering evidence."

"Sounds like there'll be plenty of firepower on the trail," Dell said. "Did Tony say anything about the baseball cap I found near the Clary Shelter in Pennsylvania?"

Schneider dropped his feet to the floor, bent forward, and said, "Damn! Almost forgot. Tony wanted me to tell you that our forensic people are convinced the cap would've lost whatever scent it might have had back in May. So, we didn't bring it."

"Probably right," Dell said, rubbing his neck. He smiled, then explained how Tara was both a trailing and an air-scenting search-and-rescue dog. She could track a person after smelling a personal item of theirs, often clothing, or, if an event was fairly recent, she could follow someone by the scent that individual gave off in the air."

"Impressive," Schneider said. "Not many dogs have both sets of skills." Schneider's eyes went wide as he scooched to the edge of the sofa. "However, the cap *was* important. We found a Pennsylvania phone number written under an inside flap. We only recently discovered it but, get this, it turned out to be Lev Komaroff's."

"Wow!" Dell and Grace said in unison.

Keith returned from the kitchen with a happy-faced Tara and four cups of coffee on a tray, which he handed out before sinking into the one remaining empty chair.

It was 4 p.m. Grace stood up. "Whew!" She shoved her heavy chair across the linoleum floor next to Keith's and sat down. With her forehead creased, she asked him, "Do the names Henry Dubois or Lev Komaroff ring a bell?"

Keith bent toward Grace, dribbling some of his coffee on the floor. "Didn't ever know Henry or Lev, but years ago when it was still operating, the Dubois family here in town owned the largest slate quarry in Piscataquis County. Several Komaroffs worked in the quarry and lived around here. The Komaroff and Dubois families were all somehow interrelated."

"Do any of them still live in the area?" Grace asked.

"Ayuh, but only Elise Dubois." Keith said Elise was an elderly widow who lived alone on Water Street, about a mile away. "It's on the left, can't miss it. Gray barn-like house with red trim. Heard her son, Henry—never met him—teaches at some fancy-pantsy college."

Grace hopped up from her chair and announced, "I'm paying a visit to Elise right now, alone. Think she will feel more comfortable around another woman." Staring at Dell, Grace said, "Give me the keys to the Jeep." She paused, then grinned. "Please, sweetheart."

"Uh. Yes, ma'am." Dell handed them to her.

"Be back by six for dinner." She flipped her hair back and headed out the door.

Dell chatted with Stan Schneider and Keith. He found out Stan had been an Army Ranger after graduating from Notre Dame and before attending law school at Boston College. He was a family man with two kids who joined the Bureau five years ago after passing the bar exam. A straight shooter. Dell liked him.

Keith excused himself to go help his wife Patsy in the kitchen. The two of them needed time to prepare chicken dinners for a full house of ravenous hikers.

Dell was very concerned about Willow, so before Keith left the room he asked, "Any southbound hikers staying with you tonight?"

"Ayuh. Two I know of: Clay and Clarence. They're out back tossing horseshoes." Keith disappeared around a corner.

Dell excused himself, and after a brief chat with some hikers in the laundry room, he walked outside to the horseshoe pit where he saw something that, in the year 1991, was rarer than a three-dollar bill—a Black long-distance hiker. The hiker had just thrown a ringer. *He's good,* Dell thought, before introducing himself. Turned out Clarence Young was a Gulf War veteran discharged from the Army in June. "Started going south on the A.T. from Katahdin more than a week ago," Clarence said, as he celebrated the ringer by pumping his fist in the air. He paused and said, "Will keep going, maybe with this honky." He grinned and pointed to the lanky white guy he was competing against, who wore a dull green USMC T-shirt and camouflage pants. "That is, until the snow stops us. Saw stuff in Iraq I have to get out of my head."

The "honky" was Clay Johnston, a scar-faced Marine Corps

veteran from South Carolina who drawled, "Listen up Peterson. I stumbled across this wimpy city boy on Rainbow Ledges. He was in a *real* bad way. Being a Southern gentleman and a caring Christian, I offered to help him out."

"What bullshit!" Clarence howled, shooting Clay the finger.

Dell laughed and asked, "Did you happen to run across a northbound couple with trail names of Fly Swatter and Train?"

"Yeah," Clarence said, "not too long ago, in the Chairback Range. Train had pulled a leg muscle, which was slowing them down."

"Thank God." Hand on heart, Dell closed his eyes. Relieved to hear they were safe and that he and Grace had a chance to catch up to them, he changed the subject. "Of course, you know about the murder?"

"Know about it! Damn straight!" said Clarence, hurling a horseshoe at the iron stake. "We're the ones who came across that woman's body. Gruesome as anything I saw in the war. God-awful odor! Swarms of flies. Clay and I ran the five miles to Route 15 to report it." He spat on the ground.

Clay extracted a tapered, double-edged, nine-inch long, throwing knife from a sheath attached to his belt. He flung it overhand at a spruce tree thirty feet away. The blade sunk into the trunk with a thump. Needles spun to the ground. "Friggin' ravens were pecking at her intestines. I killed one that was gorging on her liver." He walked over to the tree, yanked his knife out of the trunk, and held it up. "With this." Clay stepped into the horseshoe pit, dug his heel into the dirt. "I *want* to meet the SOB who did it. I'll slice his cock off and feed it to the damn birds."

Wouldn't want to cross these guys, Dell thought. Feeling a bit stunned, Dell shook his head, thanked them for the information, then returned to the hostel to retrieve his and Grace's suitcases from the back room where he'd left them. He carried them up the creaky stairs to their room, one of two private quarters with a separate bathroom. The other accommodations were mostly bunk-bed-style rooms that slept four to six people, with common bathrooms at both ends of the second-floor hallway. None of the rooms were ever locked and the walls were thin. But Dell and Grace had a degree of privacy and one of the few double beds, albeit a squeaky one. They were going first class for thirty-five dollars a night.

At 6 p.m. on the dot, just as Grace pulled up in the Jeep, Keith clanged the dinner bell—a steel triangle dangling from a chain on the porch. About twenty hikers poured into the dining room from all directions with the collective energy and sound of a raging whitewater river. Dell knew not to get between hikers and real food. Real food is any grub other than the instant ramen noodles, mac and cheese, and freeze-dried mush they subsist on for days or weeks on the trail.

Dell grabbed a chair next to Stan Schneider at one of the two tables and saved another chair for Grace. She arrived less than two minutes later but was the last one seated. Knowing the routine, Dell got up to help Keith and Patsy carry heavy platters of food to the tables: mounds of fried chicken, mountains of mashed potatoes, and huge bowls of creamed green peas with pearl onions, as well as yeasty biscuits and fresh sliced tomatoes from their garden.

By the time Dell returned to the tables, Grace had taken his seat next to Stan. The two were talking intently. Dell sat across from Clarence and Clay.

"Elise was so nice," Grace said to Stan. "Frail, lonely, hard of hearing, but very welcoming. She served tea."

Elise acknowledged to Grace that Henry was her son. But except for an annual birthday card, which never included a personal message, only his signature, she hadn't seen or heard from him in years.

"Lev Komaroff, on the other hand," Grace said in a loud voice, bobbing her head up and down, "pays Elise a visit once or twice a year. He's the son of one of her deceased cousins." Grace glanced at Dell and smiled. "Henry and Lev were close friends growing up. Lev revealed to Elise that they still see each other, but she doesn't know where they meet, how often, or what they do."

Clarence and Clay were much more interested in their chicken and mashed potatoes than in conversing, but they looked up, waved hello to Grace, and resumed eating.

After dessert, Patsy's buttery crusted wild raspberry pie, the hikers were finally satiated, and they disbursed. Some went to the back room for a beer, others did their laundry or played horseshoes, but many retired to their upstairs sleeping quarters and turned in early. The empty dining room had chairs askew, sticky lemonade pooled on the floor, crumpled napkins littered the floor and table, and errant peas had been mashed under foot. But no leftovers were in sight. All plates and platters were empty.

Dell and Grace helped Keith and Patsy clean up before prying Tara from the kitchen, where she was scouring the floor for bits of food dropped near the stove. Tara, Grace, and Dell then went outside and walked a short distance down Pleasant Street to the rocky shore of Lake Hebron. A fish jumped out of the water, a black spike leaving concentric circles on the glassy surface. Swallows pivoted, kissing in the air above the lake, and from the far shore came the deep bass "Jug-o'-rumm!" of a bullfrog. Dell kissed Grace on the cheek. They kissed again, this time an *I-love-you* kiss.

After a half hour at the lake, they wound their way back to Shaw's on a soggy path by a marsh with a pink and purple sunset at their backs. Tara nuzzled her snout into the dampness of a moose's hoof print. She shut her eyes as if listening, not with her ears but with her nose. "Tara has an entire university library in her nose," Dell said. "Her sense of smell, will serve us well."

"Yes, she's amazing," Grace said.

Back in their room Tara curled up by the door while Dell and Grace showered together. "Great way to conserve water," Grace said, giggling.

The cramped shower stall made it impossible *not* to lather one another, with the predictable result. They dried off in a hurry, fell onto the bed, and made love as Grace hummed a tune sounding vaguely (vague because Dell's mind was elsewhere) like the Beatles' "I Want to Hold Your Hand." The rhythmic squeaking of the bedsprings had to have carried down the hall and reverberated through the bare walls. *Must drive young men crazy. Acceptable collateral damage.* They slept soundly that night.

Dell and Grace were up with the sun to feed and walk Tara before the first call to breakfast at 6 a.m. Several others, including Stan Schneider, were already in the dining room when they got there. Breakfast at Shaw's for under five bucks was an institution. The menu was simple. A guest chose number two, three, four, or five. Dell picked three and got three scrambled eggs, three bacon strips, three sausages, three servings of hash browns, and three buttermilk pancakes. If you cleaned your plate, you could have seconds of the same. After breakfast, when they were packed and about to leave, Keith gave Dell, Tara, and especially Grace, warm hugs. Dell arranged to leave his Jeep at the hostel while they were in the wilderness. Stan drove them three miles north of town on Route 15 to where the A.T. crossed the road. At the trailhead, a Maine state trooper stepped out of his blue squad car when they pulled up. Stan told the officer that Dell and Grace were with the ATC and worked with the Bureau. Warning them to be very cautious, the trooper nodded and tipped his Smokey Bear hat. They hoisted their packs, skirted the yellow tape strung across the trail between two birch trees, and walked past the first white A.T. blaze. A few more steps brought them face-to-face with the stark warning hikers talked about from Maine to Georgia. It was carved into a large wooden sign.

CAUTION

It is 100 miles north to the nearest road. There are no places to obtain supplies or help. Do not attempt this section unless you have a minimum of 10 day's supplies.

Good Luck

MATC

CHAPTER 24
WILDERNESS

The sun was up as Dell and Grace stepped past the caution sign at the trailhead off Route 15. Dell recalled what Clarence and Clay had said about the murdered woman they'd come upon—"ravens pecking at her intestines," "gruesome," "the odor." The danger was far more immediate than the other times he'd hiked the Hundred Mile Wilderness. It was palpable, ominous. He could taste it.

Grace patted his shoulder. "You're concerned. Your eyes are practically popping out of your head."

Dell stopped on the trail and said, "In the past, Patricia and I were confident we could make it through to Katahdin because we'd already overcome numerous challenges during our two-thousand-mile slog north from Georgia. You and I are probably fit enough. That is an issue, but it's not my main concern. There really *is* a psychopathic killer lurking in these woods."

"You're worried about Willow's safety," she said.

"Yes, and yours."

"But not worried about your own?" Grace asked.

Kruck, kruck. Dell froze. Not the spooky one-eyed bird he and Willow had encountered in Pennsylvania, but a raven, nonetheless. It strutted, penguin-like, along the top of a nearby boulder. *Omen?*

Grace tightened her waist belt and turned toward Dell. "You okay?"

"Yeah, let's go."

Sunlight filtered through the trees signaling a hot day, but it was still cool in the early morning. Dew on the grass had a crystalline sparkle. Several black-capped chickadees, fluffed up like feather dusters, skittered for seeds in the dark shade of the trail not yet touched by the rising sun. And they hadn't hiked a hundred yards into Maine's expansive spruce forest before hearing the hyperactive chittering of a red squirrel protesting the intrusion into its turf.

"Watch out for those guys," Dell warned, pointing a finger up at the squirrel. "They'll steal your food in a minute and maybe drop a pine cone on your head."

Grace smiled and said, "Except for a few birch trees and an occasional beech all I see are conifers. Not much diversity."

Dell swept his hiking stick above his head and said, "Wood products companies like Weyerhaeuser have fostered a vast monoculture of same-age spruce and fir which they harvest, primarily for pulpwood to make paper. Most of the A.T. corridor in Maine runs through what timber companies call a 'working forest.' It's ideal for bark beetles and spruce budworms, who enjoy an endless feast—hence many dead trees."

Grace wrinkled her nose as they started up the first of several low, but irregular and sharp-edged black slate ridges. "What kind of protection does the A.T. have in Maine?"

"Seventy-five percent of Maine's A.T. corridor, which can be as narrow as 250 feet, is owned by the National Park Service where timber harvesting is prohibited." Dell stroked Tara, who had dropped back momentarily from her usual lead position. "The remainder is controlled by state parks and agencies where the level of protection varies."

An hour after starting out they walked past Leeman Brook Lean-to, another classic three-sided log structure with a wood floor and corrugated metal roof. Less than an hour later they arrived at marshy, buggy Mud Pond, the recent murder site, where a red-haired man in his late thirties wearing black pants and a green shirt sat on a log writing in a notebook. Tara crouched, her hair rose, and she uttered a low growl.

He looked up, waved, and called to Tara, "Hey baby. Come to papa."

But Tara sat down on the trail thirty feet away from him and looked back at Dell as if to say, *Don't know about this guy.*

The man stood and extended his hand as Dell and Grace approached.

"Tim O'Connor, FBI. You two look like the ATC folks my boss said might show up this morning."

CHAPTER 24: WILDERNESS

"Indeed," Grace said, as she and Dell took turns to shake his hand. Seeing this, Tara eased over to O'Connor and got a pat on the head.

"It happened five hundred feet from here, right on the trail less than forty-eight hours ago," O'Connor said, glancing to his left. "Pretty well cleaned up now. Except for some flies and a lingering odor, you wouldn't guess there'd been a barbaric murder. When Scaperelli arrives later today, I'll take down the yellow tape."

O'Connor said he'd also been at the Pierce Pond murder site. "No male victim here," he said, "but the two incidents are similar in their brutality." He pointed southward down the trail. "Woman decapitated there." He spat on the ground. "Woman gutted here. The guy's a sicko who enjoys, and I do mean enjoys, slicing and dicing women."

If they were to have any chance of catching up with Willow and Train, Dell knew it was imperative to reach the Long Pond Stream Lean-to by early evening. The lean-to was ten miles away, and at 9:30 a.m. his little plastic thermometer read eighty-one degrees.

Dell turned to Grace. "We'd better get going." Then he looked at O'Connor and said, "Tell Tony we expect to see him soon, hopefully sometime later today."

O' Connor wiped beads of sweat off his face with a shirt sleeve. "Will do. One thing, though. Yesterday, three men hiking south told me something you should know. About twenty miles north of White Cap Mountain, near Lower Jo-Mary Lake, they encountered a guy they described as 'a wacko with a rifle.' He had no backpack, not even a day pack."

Dell dropped his pack on the ground and Grace followed suit.

"That's odd," Dell said, "It's not hunting season. Hikers rarely carry guns, and never rifles. Too much weight, and they're unnecessary. Do you think he got on the A.T. from an old timber road?"

O'Connor nodded and pointed his finger to the ground. "Yeah. And that's almost certainly how the SOB who killed this poor woman got to within easy walking distance of here." He sighed. "That's true of Pierce Pond, too. The locals have harvested trees in these woods for decades; they know every rabbit hole and overgrown timber road. These guys negotiate the backwoods with their pickups and four-wheel drives using winches and chainsaws to get through the tough spots."

Grace asked, "What else did the three southbound hikers say about the man with the rifle?"

O'Connor rubbed his chin. "Real strange. When they asked him where he was headed, he scowled, waved the rifle, and brusquely pushed them out of his way. The hikers said they'd never encountered anyone so threatening and brazenly offensive, whether on or off the trail."

"What did he look like?" Grace asked.

"Buzz cut, on the heavy side, late forties or early fifties. Prominent scar along his jaw."

Raising her eyebrow, Grace looked at Dell. "Ring any bells?"

"Sure sounds like it could be Lev Komaroff, but why he'd be on a remote section of the A.T. is beyond me. I doubt he could hike more than a mile or so even on level terrain without huffing and puffing."

"Tony mentioned that guy," O'Connor said, jotting down Komaroff's name in his notebook.

"Thanks for the information," Dell said as he and Grace strapped on their packs. They waved to O'Connor as he called after them, "Tony and another agent should meet up with you later this afternoon. Until then, you two be very alert."

Dell felt a fluttery sensation in his stomach and Grace bit her lower lip.

"Nervous?" she asked.

"Maybe a little."

"Me, too."

Around a bend in the trail they came to the yellow tape. Absent the tape, the enclosed space would've resembled any other fifty-by-thirty-foot patch of ground on the A.T.—leaf litter, spruce needles, stones, and a fallen tree branch. Tara sniffed the ground with a low whine, then dropped on her belly, head between her paws, and whimpered.

Dell and Grace stood in silence, worry on their faces. *It could have been Willow,* Dell thought. He struggled to put a few words together, a prayer perhaps, but words wouldn't come. The silence cried out for another voice to speak, the young woman's. But the only sound was the buzz of a solitary wasp circling Tara's head. She snapped her jaws together and swallowed it. A blue butterfly alighted for a moment on Grace's arm just as they resumed the hike.

CHAPTER 24: WILDERNESS

"Beautiful," she said.

It took off, loping along in aimless flight, rising and falling in a light breeze until it disappeared into the forest.

An hour of hiking in the direct sun over exposed rock ledges brought them to the highest waterfall on the A.T., Little Wilson Falls. They looked down from the trail at a stream that dropped a hundred feet into a canyon longer than three football fields. The massive right-angled blocks of moist gray-black slate and plunging, sharp-edged dark cliffs resembled Cubist Art fit for the collection at the Tate Modern.

Several teenage boys were swimming naked in a pool at the foot of the waterfall. Their tanned bodies and white butts stood out against the black slate. Dell's thermometer registered ninety-three degrees as he nudged Grace.

"Not a bad idea," he said.

She smiled.

From a rock near the waterfall, a tall slender boy with sun-bleached hair shouted, "Woman!" before he leaped into the water.

A thirty-something shirtless guy in shorts sat dangling his feet in the pool. He gazed up and waved.

Dell and Grace descended a short distance to where Little Wilson Stream flowed out of the pool and crossed the A.T. Like many other lower elevation streams and ponds in northern Maine, it had a rusty color and the organic smell of decaying vegetation. They hopped on rocks across to the other side of the stream, using their hiking sticks for stability, and walked up the trail until coming to a long beaver dam constructed from thousands of gnawed saplings.

Dell said, "I'll bet there are a dozen beavers underneath this dam. Too bad we can't see the critters."

After hiking over another sun-exposed slate ridge, they descended to Big Wilson Stream, a more formidable challenge than its little brother. This stream tumbled down and poured over a passage of rocks, swirling its white foam fingers between fern-lined banks to a calmer, deeper stretch of water where silver minnows flashed and the A.T. crossed.

"We'll have to wade," Dell said. "Our shorts will dry quickly. I'm taller, stay here while I check the depth?"

"Sure." Grace took off her pack and sat down on the bank.

Dell removed his boots and waded halfway across the seventy-foot wide stream on smooth river rocks until the cold stream water reached his waist. Convinced the water level wouldn't get any higher, he returned to the streambank where Grace, now standing, was batting away dozens of blackflies circling her head, going for her eyes, and feasting on her bare arms.

After handing her a canister of bug spray for the blackflies, Dell carried her pack and boots across the stream, holding them above the water. When he returned to do the same with his, Grace and Tara entered the water. Tara assumed it was a game and swam back and forth several times. In midstream, Grace dipped under the chilly water and leaped up.

"Yeow!" she yelled as she wiped her hair from her face.

Once the three of them were on the far side, Tara shook off and they put their boots and packs back on.

"You'd win any wet T-shirt contest" Dell said. Grace poked him in the gut.

BLAM! BLAM!

"What's that? Gunshots?" Dell asked. Eyes wide, he turned to Grace waving his hands. "Off the trail. Now," he said in a hushed voice.

BLAM!

"Quick, hide in the woods with Tara. Tell her to stay, but hold onto her collar in case. Don't move or make noise." Dell said he'd check it out and return soon.

Grace did not take kindly to commands, so Dell was relieved when she called Tara and scrambled into the underbrush.

The murderer is a knife guy. Gunfire doesn't make sense. And the "Wacko with a rifle" Tim O'Connor had told them about was sighted fifty miles north of where they were. Dell knew the Canadian Pacific Railroad, the only active rail line intersecting the Maine A.T., was just a third of a mile away. Sometimes on a hot day steel rails make loud popping sounds, but Dell thought he heard gunshots.

He hid his pack behind a rock and quick-stepped cautiously up the trail toward the blasts. As he neared a sunlit opening, he hoped was probably the rail line, Dell stopped and listened. Silence. Crouching down, he edged into the open area until he could see the tracks.

Sun glinted off the rails. No one was in sight.

CHAPTER 24: WILDERNESS

Blam!

Dell dropped to the ground, gripped his hiking stick, and looked down the tracks in both directions. Nothing. He got up, took a few steps, and placed his hand on a rail.

Blam! Vibrations ran all the way up his arm.

Oh! Thank God. Dell exhaled deeply. *Not gunshots—just steel rails expanding in the blazing sun.*

He walked back to where he'd hidden his pack and where Grace and Tara had fled into the forest. They came out from the underbrush when he called. After he explained the sounds, the three of them continued down the trail. It was midafternoon, and they'd made decent time. But shortly after walking past a small waterfall on Wilber Brook, the sun turned a dull yellow. Black clouds swelled on the horizon. A wind blew in from the northeast and a faint rumble began. The sky did not yet say *take cover,* but an unmistakable menace was in the air. Dell and Grace hurried to put on their Gore-Tex rain gear and waterproof pack covers, then picked up their pace.

"We should try to ford Long Pond Stream before the rain," Dell said. "Otherwise, we won't reach the lean-to until late tomorrow at the earliest."

They smelled the sharp, fresh aroma of ozone.

"The stream is normally only knee deep and an easy rock hop across," Dell said, "but it can be a raging torrent after a rainstorm."

Wrinkling her brow and walking even faster, Grace asked, "How far to the river?"

"Less than a mile, I'd guess. We'll make it if we hurry."

Dense rolling booms of thunder came drumming out of the mountains, reverberating over the looming Barren-Chairback Range that was silhouetted in front of them like a crouching Grim Reaper. The wind increased. Lightning streaked through dark clouds, followed by spine-jolting thunderclaps. A spruce tree fifty yards away exploded in a fiery flash, sending showers of sparks and resinous-smelling smoke into the air.

"Too close!" Dell shouted.

They were now running. The clean, metallic smell of ozone was much sharper.

"We should be curled in a ball, behind some boulder and away from trees," Grace said, breathing heavily.

"Yes, you're right," Dell agreed, gasping for air. But they kept running. Spooked by the thunder, Tara pinned her ears back and ran close to Dell. Rain poured down in heavy curtains, shifting in the wind, pounding their rain hoods, and pummeling them with horizontal blasts.

Long Pond Stream was flowing fast and rising rapidly when they arrived. A frayed rope was strung shoulder high across the thirty-foot wide stream and tied around spruce trees on opposite banks. Dell and Grace put on their rubber soled Teva sandals and lashed their boots and hiking sticks so they hung down from the top of their packs.

Several young women who had pitched their tents on the far side of the stream watched intently. One of them waved her arms and shouted over the sound of rushing water—"No. No. Too dangerous! Wait till tomorrow." Another stepped close to the stream and called out, "You could die."

Grace's eyes flitted back and forth between Dell and the swift-flowing stream. She crossed her arms tightly and said, "Maybe we *should* wait."

"No!" Dell said, his face red, wet, and frantic. *We must reach Willow.* Exhausted and breathing hard, he looked into Grace's green eyes and kissed her cheek. "We'll make it across, love. Trust me."

She frowned, shook her head, and stared at the swollen stream.

"Tara. Sit, stay!" Dell said.

Tara tensed but sat, ears erect, eyes locked on Dell.

They fastened their waist belts and shoulder straps. Dell took a single step out from the bank and was instantly over his waist in water and turned horizontal by the rushing current until his feet found a tenuous foothold. If he had not clutched the rope, the stream would have carried him away.

"Grace!" Dell shouted, as he gripped the rope. "Grab the rope with *both* hands *before* getting into the river. Do not let go!"

She did as Dell said and managed to keep upright while clinging to the rope. But in midstream the torrent swept Grace off her feet and the rope slipped from one of her hands. Still holding on with the other, the current swung her toward Dell, who reached over and grabbed her pack strap just as she lost her grip entirely. Tara barked frantically.

One of the women shrieked, "Oh, no! Oh, no!"

CHAPTER 24: WILDERNESS

Dell strained with all his strength to hang onto Grace with his left hand and to keep her head above water. He clung desperately to the rope with his right hand. Dell wedged his foot against an underwater rock and pulled Grace toward him until the force of the current swept them both to the opposite shore. They spat out brown water and crawled onto the rocks. Dell and Grace, on their knees, unstrapped their soggy backpacks and handed the packs to the concerned young women who rushed to help them stand up and then stumble onto the bank.

Thanking the women profusely and shaking his head, Dell said to his trembling partner, "I'm really sorry. That was close."

"That was stupid!" Grace screamed, red-faced.

Dell winced. "Yes. Very stupid."

Tara had not abandoned her spot on the other side of the stream, but she was standing. She pawed the dirt and howled.

Grace pointed at Tara, then turned to Dell. She narrowed her eyes and asked with a pinched expression, "Do you expect her to fly across?"

Dell looked around and spotted a possible crossing for Tara.

A moss-covered slab of rock about one hundred feet downstream extended halfway across the stream. The rock was still a few inches above the water level, but to reach it Tara would have to jump five feet over swift-moving water. If she succeeded, and navigated along the slippery stone slab to its far end, she'd still have an even longer jump across the stream to reach the bank where Dell and Grace now stood.

"She can do it," Dell said, running down the stream bank and calling out, "Come, Tara." Tara sprinted to where the rock slab was being lapped by the water, opposite of where Dell stopped on the other side.

"Are you kidding me?" Grace said. She threw her arms in the air.

"Come, Tara!" screamed a bone-tired, hyperventilating Dell.

Tara whirled around twice, braced herself, and leaped, easily clearing the five-foot distance to the rock. The moss was slick, but she hunched down and scrambled to the far end of the rock. Only ten feet of whitewater separated her from Dell. She jumped, fell just short of the bank in the fast-moving current, and was swept around a bend and out of sight.

Grace screamed, fell to her knees, and sobbed. "Dell, Dell . . ."

Dell dashed down a barely discernible path to follow downstream until it closed over with tangled bushes and fallen branches. He kept running but couldn't save his legs from the nettles and thorns. Scratched and drenched, the mosquitos found him. They wheeled, whined, and dive-bombed, but Dell didn't stop running until he spotted Tara flailing in the water clambering to get up a steep embankment of smooth black slate. He flopped onto his belly, hooked an ankle around an exposed tree root, reached down, and grabbed her collar. Stream water splashed into his face as Dell yanked on her collar. She squealed as he hauled her onto the bank to safety.

Tara shook off, spun around three times, and knocked Dell to the ground. She smelled like spunk-water and was covered in grit and muck, but he wrapped his arms around his smelly best friend and was rewarded with multiple dog licks. *Stupid, stupid me.*

Grace had followed him down the stream bank, and stood a few feet away, hands on her hips. When Dell spotted her, she turned, shook her head, and walked away.

CHAPTER 25

MOUNTAINS

Dell sheepishly followed an irked Grace and a buoyant, tail-wagging Tara through dense brush and up the streambank toward where they'd left the packs. Uncertain about how to initiate a reconciliation, he said, "Soon we'll be hiking through the most rugged mountains in the wilderness, the Barren-Chairbacks and White Cap Mountain."

She stopped and turned to him, hands on hips. "That's great. Because of your idiotic insistence on crossing the stream, our sopping wet boots, clothes, and packs are much heavier. More weight to carry, and more blisters."

She's right, thought Dell to himself. But he also knew the sun would gradually dry things out, blisters could be managed with moleskins, and above all, that he'd better keep his mouth shut and not try to defend his decision to cross the flooded stream.

They continued to walk up the bank of the rushing stream when Grace asked, "On top of that, how much danger are we in without Scaperelli and his agents?"

"I'd estimate the threat of violence over the next thirty miles to be low, but not zero."

"Good, I guess. Why do you think it'll be low?"

Dell pushed wet hair out of his eyes and said, "For two reasons. None of the murders in Maine, Pennsylvania, or Virginia occurred at high elevations. Neither Henry Dubois nor Lev Komaroff have the physical stamina for strenuous mountain hiking. Also, only two abandoned tote roads once used to haul supplies to timber camps are anywhere near this section of the trail. Both afford easy access to the A.T. for day hikers, photographers, fishermen, law enforcement officers, and MATC trail crews. Therefore, these popular, well-known entry points, really side trails, are very risky for the likes of a Dubois or Komaroff, neither of whom want any visibility."

Grace nodded but said, "Of course, if we'd used common sense and waited for Scaperelli instead of almost losing our lives, we'd now have FBI protection."

"Uh-huh," Dell muttered.

They walked up to the young women who'd helped them out of the flooded stream. The women told them they were Canadian students, *Quebecois* from McGill University.

"Thank you, again," Dell said, placing a hand on his heart. He pointed up the trail in the direction of the Long Pond Stream Lean-to and asked, "Why aren't you staying in the lean-to? It was just built this year." Smiling, he added, "It's raining *chats* and *chiens*."

A freckle-faced blonde shouted out, "*Chats* and *chiens*," and the students dissolved in laughter.

After they'd settled down, one of them said, "Yes, the lean-to is nice—but it only holds eight people, and some old man is taking up at least three spaces. We wanted to stay together."

Grace smiled and said, "Well, we're grateful you decided to camp here by the stream."

With that, Dell and Grace hoisted their wet packs, called Tara, who was playing chase-the-stick with one of the students, and waved goodbye to the group.

One mile of struggling up a steep, rocky, rain-slickened trail in boots that squished with every step brought them to the Long Pond Stream Lean-to. All vegetation in front of the shelter had been scoured away, leaving just mud and rocks. Scraggly saplings and stunted birch trees clung to life around the lean-to's other three sides, a sure sign the area had been clear-cut years ago and never recovered.

Leaning against an inside wall of the shelter was a white-bearded guy whose red suspenders held up his camouflage pants. He stood spooning peanut butter from a jar into his mouth.

"Welcome," he said holding the spoon above his head.

They threw their packs onto the floor of the shelter and hopped inside with Tara, out of the rain. Tara crouched down on the wood planks, fixing her eyes on the stranger. He scooped some peanut butter onto his finger and held it out to her.

CHAPTER 25: MOUNTAINS

"Here, honey."

Tara trotted over, took a whiff, and licked his finger clean. She was all wags as he stroked her back.

He introduced himself as Grizz and wiped peanut butter off his mustache with the back of his hand. "Well, friends," he said, "How'd you'd get across that angry stream?"

Grace eyed Dell and turned toward Grizz with a not-so-subtle groan. This was followed by another penetrating glance at Dell before she replied, "By the grace of God."

Grizz sat down on the shelter's floor, back against the wall, without loosening his grip on the peanut butter jar. He cast his eyes skyward and said, "The Lord does answer prayer, sometimes."

"Yes," Grace said, again looking at Dell. "The Lord saved our hides today."

In the shelter they removed their sodden boots, wrung tea-colored water out of stinky wool socks, and hung most of their wet clothes on the nails that protruded from the walls.

"After West Point," Grizz said without any prompting, "Uncle Sam sent me straight to Vietnam. Infantry. I had three tours in Nam over nine years. Left the Army after twenty-two years as an O-7, brigadier general."

Dell and Grace slipped off their wet T-shirts. She turned her back to Grizz and removed her damp bra. He paid no attention, went back to his peanut butter, and kept talking. They pulled on their mostly dry polyester sweaters and assessed the water damage. Their other clothes were wet, but because items like food, wallets, watches, matches, and the mini stove were in air-tight containers or sealed plastic bags, they'd fared pretty well. The tent and down sleeping bags were in waterproof stuff sacks and only a little water had seeped in at the cinch cords.

"Other than funky smelling boots," Dell said, holding up a mushy cardboard container of dried milk, "this is the only real casualty. No milk for breakfast."

Grizz dug a toothbrush out of his pack. "I turn in early, but you two do whatever you want. Won't bother me." He walked outside to the rear of the shelter to brush his teeth and pee.

"We've had quite a day, one I'll remember for a long time," Grace said. "Sleep sounds good to me." She gave Dell a quick hug, kissed his cheek, and said, "I *still* love you. Lots."

He kissed her back with a hangdog look, then grabbed the aluminum pot and canteens.

"I'll go locate some potable water," he said. "Could you roll out the mats and sleeping bags, set up the mini stove, and jam our wet socks into the bottoms of the bags so they'll dry out by morning?"

"I'm on it."

When Dell returned from the nearby stream, Grizz was in his sleeping bag, Grace had fed Tara, and she'd placed two pouches of freeze-dried chicken teriyaki next to the stove.

"It's not the Inn at Little Washington," she said, "but it'll do."

They cleaned up after dinner as Dell slipped his hand mischievously under her sweater and hung their packs from an overhead beam to deter mice. They climbed into their bags. Grace slept against the wall, Dell was in the middle, and Tara—head between paws and ears on alert—positioned herself next to Dell, not far from Grizz. Despite the rich mix of odors—wet dog, wet socks and leather boots, sweat, peanut butter, and a mineral smell similar to a dentist drilling teeth—they were soon asleep.

Rain rattled the metal roof until early morning when it turned into annoying, intermittent, tinny drips from overhanging birch boughs. Unable to go back to sleep, Dell nudged Grace.

"You awake?"

"Uh-huh. Let's hit the trail."

General Grizz was snoring like an old pickup truck without a muffler. They dressed, ate, packed up, and headed out, all in under thirty minutes.

A peach-tinged eastern horizon welcomed the two of them as they began what Dell knew would be a brutal three-mile ascent and two-thousand-foot change in elevation to the summit of Barren Mountain. But they'd gone only a short distance up the white-blazed trail, skirting around and scrambling over boulders, when they saw thick bushes drifting up and down the slopes, their branches bent to the ground heavy with raspberries. Hikers and other hungry critters had pressed narrow paths into the dense berry patch. Dell and Grace stuffed sweet wild berries into their mouths, staining fingers with bright red juice.

Tara worked her snout into the briars and gingerly plucked off a ripe raspberry. But she soon growled, nose high in the air,

CHAPTER 25: MOUNTAINS

ears at attention. Her nostrils flared and her growls grew louder and more insistent, a warning.

"She hears or smells something," Dell said.

They scanned the slopes as Tara's snarls became sharp, urgent barks and the hair on her back rose.

"Over there!" Grace waved her hiking stick toward the far edge of the raspberry patch. Something was shaking the bushes.

Tara was barking and spinning around, trying to hurl herself into the tangles of the briar patch.

"Stay! Sit!" Dell commanded. She whined but obeyed.

A dark shape rose up from the thicket and grunted. A huge black head peered over the bushes from about 120 feet away. With a sprig of raspberry leaves clinging to one ear, the bear looked in their direction.

"How cute," Grace said, chuckling, "but maybe it's time to leave."

"Stand tall and look big. Don't run." Dell snapped a leash on Tara and took Grace by the hand. "We're out of here, babe. This is Smokey's berry patch." They turned around and retreated back to the trail.

The day was warm and clear as they resumed their ascent, delighted to find steps chipped into the black slate by a thoughtful MATC trail crew. Notches in the stone weren't there years ago when Dell and Patricia slipped on wet moss, and she suffered a nasty fall.

An hour after encountering the bear Dell and Grace came to the Barren Slide, where ages ago tractor trailer-sized boulders had tumbled from the ridge down the mountainside. The A.T. then leveled off on the Barren Ledges, which presented a striking view to the east of Lake Onawa, a modernist's brush stroke of blue on a canvas of spruce green extending as far as the eye could see.

They hiked over the summit of Barren Mountain, with its long-abandoned rusty steel fire tower, and descended a mile to Cloud Pond Lean-to for a water and snack break. Dell applied a moleskin to his blister before it ruptured. It was almost 10 a.m. and a large group of Outward Bound teenagers at the lean-to were adjusting their packs and filling canteens with water from a spring before beginning the descent to Long Pond Stream.

"Dangerous high water. We barely got across," Dell warned their leader, a woman in her late twenties. She thanked him for the information. When he asked her about Willow and Train, she said the group had met them yesterday morning on White Cap Mountain.

"How did they look?" he asked.

"Fly Swatter seemed fine, but he had a noticeable limp."

Dell pumped his fist in the air.

"There's a chance we might catch them by the day after tomorrow," he said to Grace.

She smiled and patted him on the back. Wishing good luck to the group, they headed out along the ridge of the Barren-Chairbacks.

"We'll have a few steep ascents and descents," he said, "but we've already done most of ascending for today. Ten more miles and we will be at one of my favorite spots in Maine, East Chairback Pond. It's off the A.T."

"What makes it special?"

"It's a fifty-foot-deep mountain tarn, a pocket of water formed by glacial scouring. Unlike many of Maine's lakes and ponds at lower elevations, East Chairback's water is cold and clear. It even has native brook trout."

Grace stopped on the trail, turned to face him. She grabbed his waist belt, pulled him toward her, and asked with an impish grin, "Can we skinny dip?"

"Sounds good to me," he said, giving her a hug.

After Dell and Grace had hiked two miles north from Cloud Pond Lean-to they came to a bog near Fourth Mountain where they paused to look at a large patch of pitcher plants. Most of these purple and red insectivorous plants looked like raw meat and, when they put their noses to them, smelled like rotten meat. Each plant had hundreds of downward pointing hairs with dead and dying flies, ants, spiders, and moths trapped in about a half cup of water at the bottom of their fleshy pitcher-shaped leaves. The bog and the pitcher plants triggered a frightening thought in Dell's mind. *Like these insects, Willow could be entrapped by the murderer in the bogs and marshes north of White Cap Mountain around Lower Jo-Mary Lake.*

They hiked up a rise in the trail, away from the bog but Dell couldn't get his fear for Willow's safety out of his head. He checked his thermometer. It read eighty-two degrees. Yet a chill rippled up the back of his neck. As they neared their next stop, he folded a bandanna and wiped sweat from his forehead.

"Willow's in trouble," Dell said. "I *know* it." He kicked a stone off the trail and glanced at his watch. "She and Train are close to where that crackpot with the rifle was sighted. He could still be there. It's the most gnarly and isolated section of the entire A.T."

Grace took Dell's hand. "I was thinking the same thing."

They sat down for a break by a four-foot-high cairn set on a rock outcropping of Third Mountain. A view of miles and miles of spruce forests spread out below them.

Grace kissed Dell's cheek and said, "We'll get to them."

An hour later, before they came to the side trail that descended a quarter mile to the shore of East Chairback Pond, they looked down at the water from a high ridge. Late afternoon sunlight glistened off its surface. Rays of light shot out from the pond's center hexagonally all the way to its shores, as if these brilliant white beams radiated through the body and legs of a giant, water-walking, Jesus Christ bug.

"Wow!" Grace cried out, aiming her hiking stick at the pond. "It looks like either a milky blue sapphire on green velvet or the world's coolest insect."

"The Star of India," Dell replied.

About five hundred feet down the steep side trail to the pond they passed a small bog pocketed against a cliff. Rare, late-blooming yellow lady's slippers peeked out from the moist soil. The flowers gathered themselves in clusters of four, like string quartets about to perform.

Grace spotted the yellow blossoms and yelled, "*Bellissimo!*"

After chasing a chipmunk under a rock, Tara led the way down the trail to the pond where, as Dell had hoped and expected, they had the tenting space to themselves. But they were not alone. A few yards away, at the edge of the water, Tara was sniffing a pile of inch long, oval-shaped pellets. Moose poop.

"Tara. Come," he shouted.

Dell and Grace took off their packs, set up the tent near the pond under a hemlock tree, unrolled the ground mats and sleeping bags, and draped their damp clothes over rocks in the sun.

Dell's watch said 5 p.m. They removed their boots, placed them in the sun, and walked barefooted to the gravelly edge of the tear-shaped pond. Grace dipped her toes in the water.

"Wow, that's what I call cold."

"We could forget about swimming," Dell said.

"No way!" said Grace. Seconds later, she stood before him wearing nothing but a sassy smile.

Dell stripped off his T-shirt and shorts and dropped them next to hers on the gravel. Together, and shivering, they tip-toed gingerly into the pond. Seeing them in the water up to their knees, Tara leaped in and dog paddled out from shore. When the water was at waist level, they plunged in all the way and breast-stroked toward the middle of the pond, which was about a third of a mile across at its widest point. Even in deep water every stone on the bottom was visible. Dell flipped over on his back to look up at where they'd been just a short time ago. The stark, mostly treeless crests of the Chairback and Columbus Mountains were silhouetted against an azure blue sky. He floated, relaxed, thinking of nothing at all, until Grace splashed water in his face.

"Why haven't you kissed me?" she demanded.

"Uh, yes ma'am." He rolled over and they traded wet kisses until interrupted by Tara, who thought that whatever game they were playing looked like great fun. She paddled between them until Dell pushed her away. Tara then swam off in futile pursuit of a duck. Dell and Grace had grown accustomed to the pond's chilly temperature and together treaded water. "This is so nice," Grace said. "I don't think I've ever been happier."

"Then why don't you marry me?"

"Is that a question or proposal?"

"Stop being a damn lawyer, at least for a minute."

"I'd *love* to marry you."

They wrapped their arms around one another, sank below the surface while kissing, and came up simultaneously spluttering, "I love you."

The sun was sinking in the western horizon as they swam back toward the campsite. A few feet in front of them a ten-inch brook trout leaped from the water, all mouth and yellow speckles. A cloud of blood-crazed mosquitos zeroed in on their exposed heads. Swatting and splashing them away, Dell and Grace swam faster. The instant they waded out of the pond the mosquitos were on them—whining, diving, and feasting. Grabbing their clothes from where they'd left them on the gravel, they raced to the tent barefooted and tumbled in, zipped up the nylon bug screen, and zapped the tormentors that made it into the tent. They sprayed

CHAPTER 25: MOUNTAINS

themselves with insect repellant, dressed, and put on hats with mosquito netting before venturing back outside.

"Where's Tara?" Grace asked.

Dell scanned the shoreline until he spotted her on a far bank, tail waggling in the air, nose furiously snuffling the ground like a soldier with a landmine detector. He whistled, and Tara romped along the shore in their general direction, rousting a large raccoon from behind a moss-covered log. The surprised raccoon retreated a few yards but as Tara, head down, ears pinned back, circled the frightened animal, the coon turned to face its adversary with hunched back and bared teeth.

Dell whistled again, not wanting Tara to scuffle with a possibly rabid raccoon. Tara spun around, backed off, and resumed her race around the pond toward them. Her tongue lolled out and, even at a distance, they could make out her German shepherd happy face.

"Tara's innate wildness is heartwarming," Dell said. "Only unleashed dogs display something grand and untamed that they've retained over the millennia. Dogs are devoted to us but also to scents in the soil, sounds in the night, and thrills of the chase."

Touching his arm, Grace said, "Yes, indeed, her love of the wild is joyful, even euphoric."

Panting heavily, Tara had almost reached the campsite when she came to an abrupt stop. She sniffed the ground, then took something into her mouth.

"Tara. Come!" Dell yelled, knowing what she was eating.

Another mouthful, then one more for the road, and she trotted over to them with a satisfied look. Tara had dined on moose poop from one of several deposits near the pond and on the side trail.

"Yuck," Grace said. "No more doggie kisses from you." Grace poured some kibble into a Sierra cup and gave it to Tara. "Here's the *rest* of your dinner, foul one."

When the mini stove had boiled water for their dinner and Grace had poured it into freeze-dried pouches of chili con carne, Tara's eyes locked onto something. She stopped eating and stared in the direction of the pond's outlet stream. From two hundred feet, they watched as a female moose with high, rough-coated shoulders, long neck, and sad face tromped out of the woods to the pond's edge, shaking flies from her shaggy dark hide.

"Stay, Tara," Dell said.

Tara showed no desire to challenge the huge beast. The cow moose waded into the water up to her belly and ducked her head under, lifting fronds of pond weed and water lilies into her gaping mouth. Dell and Grace watched the moose and talked in whispers as they ate.

"Wouldn't an October wedding at St. Columba's be magnificent?" Grace asked.

Dell nodded. *Especially, if Willow was there.*

Tara resumed eating her kibble but never took her eyes off the moose. The sun was setting in an orange and pink glow when the moose trudged back into the forest. Summer bats flew over the darkening pond like dots and dashes. A few feet away in the spruce litter, came the trill of a songbird. Grace spotted the bird.

"What kind is it?" she asked, pointing to a barely visible small brown bird with a reddish tail.

Dell was no ornithologist, but this one he knew. "Hermit thrush. The most common thrush in New England. Little songster, little song, big effect."

"I'd say so," Grace said, pressing against Dell and taking his hand. "Our song."

CHAPTER 26
INTELLIGENCE

Grace shook Dell awake at 5 a.m. in a tent that exuded a dank odor from their harrowing river crossing. "Dell! I hear a baby crying!"

"Baby? What baby?" Dell mumbled, rubbing his eyes. "Must be a bad dream."

"No dream. I swear it was an infant." Grace sat upright in her sleeping bag.

Dell grumbled, rolled over, and peered out of an open tent flap to see a faint pink streak of light peeking over the Chairbacks. Otherwise, it was pitch dark. Tara, who'd slept outside in front of the tent, yawned and stretched her hind legs.

"Tara, stay," Dell said, just as a haunting wail from across the pond shattered the silence. The cry lingered as it ricocheted off the surface of the water. Then another, answering wail came from the opposite bank.

"A loon. Probably calling its mate or chicks."

Grace exhaled. "Chilling. Don't think I'll ever forget that sound."

Wide awake, they crawled out of their sleeping bags, dressed, fed Tara, and boiled water for coffee. Rays of light flitted through the branches of hemlock trees and dappled the ground. After breakfast and a final look at East Chairback Pond, they packed up and were about to ascend the side trail back up to the A.T. when Grace grabbed Dell's arm and pointed to white-blossoming water lilies along the pond's edge.

"Beats Monet's lilies," she said. "You chose such a glorious place to propose."

On top of being bug bitten, they'd been without a hot shower for days and smelled like it. Although Grace's sensuous black hair was imprisoned in a tight French twist and mostly hidden under her baseball cap, her pale green eyes sparkled in the early morning light.

"Well," Dell said, "A glorious woman deserves a glorious setting for her engagement."

They hugged until an impatient Tara emitted a sharp bark—*Enough, let's go!*

Once on the A.T., they descended for a mile on a steep rocky trail that brought them out on a private gravel road where people could drive in from paved Maine Route 11, park, and walk a short distance north on a side trail to the A.T. Most visitors came to see either an almost ethereal stand of 130-foot-tall white pines called the Hermitage or a deep, black slate canyon with swirling river water known as Gulf Hagas that was extolled a bit too effusively by Down Easters as "Maine's Grand Canyon." Dell and Grace skirted around yellow tape strung across the A.T. where the trail crossed the gravel road.

Three people holding cups of coffee glanced their way—a burly white-haired Maine state trooper, the affable but all-business FBI agent Tim O'Connor, and a sturdy but lean woman in her thirties who was wearing shorts and looked like she could hike thirty miles a day with ease. O'Connor waved at them to come off the trail and onto the road where the three were standing.

"Thought you two might appear this morning," he said. "I heard from the grapevine that Long Pond Stream almost washed you away."

As they removed their packs, Dell grimaced and swallowed hard. Grace replied, "Almost."

O'Connor introduced them to state trooper Officer Jim Conklin who doffed his Smokey Bear hat. Conklin appeared to be in his late fifties and was a little chunky but clearly no one to mess with. O'Connor then introduced them to Merilee Lockwood, a Maine Appalachian Trail Club ridge-runner, someone who oversaw the trail and assisted hikers in need.

"Tony Scaperelli, Stan Schneider, and an agent you haven't met, Eric Jacobs, a paramedic, reached Long Pond Stream a couple of hours after you," O'Connor said. "They couldn't get across and returned to Monson the next morning."

"Smart," Grace said, glancing at Dell.

She petted Tara, who'd sat down beside her, as they all stood chatting in the middle of the road.

"Tony wants to catch up to you. I'm here to tell you that," O'Connor said, tilting his head while looking directly at Dell. "Another disturbing report came in about the guy with a rifle who has been threatening hikers near Lower Jo-Mary Lake. And Merilee told us about an additional, much more troubling incident."

"Damn," Dell said. He inhaled deeply and took a step toward Merilee. "Did it involve a teenage girl and a young man with a limp?"

Hearing the concern in Dell's voice, Merilee shook her head. "No. It was a couple, but not Fly Swatter and Train who I met late yesterday afternoon. Real nice. They were headed for Cooper Brook Lean-to. Know them?"

Dell exhaled. "Thank goodness. Yes, I hiked the Pennsylvania A.T. with Willow—I mean Fly Swatter."

Tara cocked her head at the mention of Willow's name.

Merilee's sinewy legs bore an uncanny resemblance to the fluted, muscle-like trunk of the hornbeam, a.k.a., musclewood, tree found in southern Maine. She pushed a strand of hair out of her eyes and said, "The 'troubling incident' Tim just referred to concerned the same guy. Prominent facial scar, heavyset, late forties." Merilee looked at Tara who sat attentively, pressing against Grace. Merilee stepped toward them, ran her fingers through Tara's fur and continued—"A hysterical, teary-eyed young couple I met day before yesterday near Lower Jo-Mary Lake blurted out what had happened to them two hours earlier. Without provocation, the creep with a rifle shot and killed their golden retriever."

"Good God," Grace said, placing one hand over her heart and hugging Tara with the other. "No dog is friendlier than a golden."

According to Merilee, it looked like three shots were fired point-blank, one to the neck, two to the head. "Malice, pure malice," she said, slowly shaking her head. After killing the dog, he aimed his rifle at the couple and said, "You little shits are next. Get your asses out of here or my friend will cut you up." Merilee said she later came across the dead dog. The body of the golden retriever was sprawled smack in the center of the trail, as if to send a message to other hikers.

Grace gasped and Dell shook his head.

"So there are two of them," Dell said. "Likely Lev Komaroff and Henry Dubois. In Pennsylvania three months ago Komaroff told me matter-of-factly that he shot dogs. We know he and Dubois are related and longtime friends, and that they see each other. The words, 'my friend will cut you up' points to . . . . . ."

"Dubois as the murderer," O'Connor said.

Officer Conklin ground his well-polished black shoe into the gravel. "We've also had reports of incidents on this stretch of the trail—hikers threatened by a guy with a rifle."

A grim-faced Tim O'Connor crossed his arms and stepped closer to Dell and Grace. In a tone of voice that sounded more like a demand than a question, he asked, "Where are you camping tonight?"

Dell pointed his hiking stick up the trail. "After fording the West Branch of the Pleasant River, we're going over White Cap Mountain. If we really move along, I hope to pitch our tent fifteen miles from here on the north side of White Cap on the bank of the East Branch of the Pleasant River."

Giving a thumbs-up, O'Connor turned toward Merilee and said, "That'll work, won't it? Scaperelli said he and the other two agents would get on the A.T. later today just north of White Cap from West Branch Ponds Road."

Merilee tucked her hair behind her ears, pulled a Maine ATC trail map out of her back pocket, and scanned it. "Sure. The three of them will have an easy two-mile downhill walk on the A.T. to meet up with Dell and Grace at the East Branch."

O'Connor thought White Cap Mountain should be safe, but he stressed that Scaperelli did not want Dell and Grace to be unaccompanied after they'd descended off the north side of the mountain and, especially, when they approached the vicinity of Lower Jo-Mary Lake. "The area around the lake is very dangerous," O'Connor said, raising his hand. "We agree with the state police; the killer is probably somewhere in that vicinity. Oh, and a separate FBI team is headed south on the A.T. and should arrive at the lake in a day or two."

"We'll land a floatplane on the lake later this morning," Officer Conklin said. "The pilot and another officer will erect a large tent and tarpaulin on shore. The two of them will be there for several days." Taking out his own topographical map, Conklin pointed to

CHAPTER 26: INTELLIGENCE

the region west of Lower Jo-Mary Lake. "We surveilled this area by air for three days searching for remote timber company cabins. Most of them are on impassable tote roads and haven't been occupied in years. Some are hidden under the forest canopy. We think the guy with a rifle, and maybe the murderer as well, could be holed up in one of these cabins."

O'Connor nodded. "Scaperelli and our people in the Bangor office agree. When we get there, we'll go in by foot and investigate some of the cabins or shacks that are closest to the lake."

Dell grimaced and looked at his watch.

"Your face is flushed," Grace said.

"Let's get going," Dell replied. "Willow and Train are either already in or fast approaching the highest-risk area."

He lifted his pack off the ground and strapped it on. Grace did likewise.

O'Connor said, "I'll drive out to Route 11 where there's connectivity for my mobile phone and tell Scaperelli you'll be tenting by the East Branch tonight."

"Sounds good," Dell said. He and Grace bid everyone goodbye. Dell snapped his fingers, "Tara, come," and they headed north on the A.T. toward White Cap.

CHAPTER 27

WHITE CAP

Shortly after leaving Merilee and the federal and state officers, Dell and Grace walked a short distance to the West Branch of the Pleasant River, removed their boots, and waded across without incident. They then began a ten-mile ascent to the summit of White Cap Mountain. The day was mild with a gentle breeze but, looking up, they saw a heavy gray mist obscuring the high peaks. Within minutes of crossing the river they entered a pine-scented cathedral of towering conifers known as the Heritage.

"Oh, wow!" Grace cried out. "So beautiful and peaceful. Wish we could camp here."

"That would be nice," Dell said, "but to protect Maine's oldest and tallest stand of white pines, the state prohibits camping within the Heritage's thirty-five acres."

They listened as the morning wind whistled through the pines. The air's resinous fragrance was so pervasive they could taste it. After they'd walked out of the pines, Grace grew silent for a while until she stopped on the trail, grabbed Dell's arm, and turned to face him. "I feel we've just left a sacred place, a place where God and nature are one."

"Yes," Dell said, as he touched her hand. "It was uncanny how I sensed a kind of harmony, a kinship among things animate and inanimate, pine trees and squirrels, mountains and moose, rain and ravens, rivers and you and me."

Grace dabbed her eyes with her bandanna.

"Anything wrong?" Dell asked.

"No." She looked at him with pursed lips. "Maybe, sort of." She squinted her eyes. "Scaperelli's crew will likely join us later today. More feds are arriving from the north. Maine state police are probably already at Lower Jo-Mary Lake."

"Uh-huh."

"We won't be alone anymore."

He kissed her cheek. "But we'll always be together." They hugged so tightly that they almost fell over.

For the next four miles Dell and Grace followed the A.T. along Gulf Hagas Brook, although the brook was mostly out of sight below them. They ascended through the lone hardwood holdout in an otherwise monotonous sea of conifers—they hiked past oaks and thickets of bush-like mountain maples and their more illustrious cousins—seventy-foot tall, deeply furrowed sugar maples. On the leather-smooth gray bark of an ancient beech someone long ago had carved a still discernible eternal verity. *Mike loves Sue.* Long-leafed black ash trees outnumbered spruce and they paused to admire a yellow birch's three-foot wide trunk and pendulous spreading branches. A breeze rustled through the birch tree's thousands of ovate leaves, triggering a sound like waves hitting a seashore. Blue-green lichens splotched the bottoms of these trees and mushrooms laddered up their trunks as if on terraced ledges. Dell and Grace stepped with care over the maze of roots that crisscrossed the trail, but their bone-tired feet welcomed the springy leaf litter that covered the ground. Only the distant chatter of a red squirrel disturbed the sanctuary hush of the forest. A sentient, faintly incense-like aroma filled the air.

Tangled vines spilled from the banks of a spring-fed rivulet near a sign to the Gulf Hagas side trail. Tara lapped up the cold spring water.

Dell said, "The five-mile Gulf Hagas loop trail circles around stunning deep slate canyons, but we simply don't have time to do it."

Grace took his hand and replied, "Since we'll always be together, there'll be another time."

The A.T. exited the hardwood forest about halfway to the top of White Cap at the Carl Newhall Lean-to, located at the base of Gulf Hagas Mountain. Grace and Dell sat inside on the floor of this six-person shelter, drank some water, ate Snickers bars, and tossed Tara a dog biscuit.

"From here," Dell said, chomping on a candy bar, "we'll have three short but steep ascents before a final climb to the 3,700-foot summit of White Cap where we should have one of the finest views on the entire A.T., better than from Katahdin. After that, it's a rapid five miles downhill to our tenting site."

"It's strange we haven't seen any southbound hikers since leaving the gravel road," Grace said. "Perhaps word got out about the increased police presence and the crazy guy with a rifle."

"Maybe so," Dell said, stroking Tara's head. "Normally, we would've encountered quite a few hikers on this stretch."

"What's the terrain going to be like tomorrow when we're with the FBI agents?"

"After a couple of hours on open rock ledges, the A.T. levels out and descends to mosquito country with miles of squishy mud trails, decayed corduroy roads—logs placed perpendicular to the direction of the trail over swampy areas—and lots of lakes and ponds." Dell scratched a bug bite on his arm. "The trail passes through bogs and marshes that are only six or seven hundred feet above sea level."

Grace wrinkled her nose. "Well, at least we can swim in the lakes."

Dell shook his head. "Afraid not, love. Too many of those low elevation lakes and ponds are crawling with black leeches, some more than three inches long. I found out the hard way years ago when I pried several of the bloodsuckers off my legs."

Grace flinched. "Yuck!" She feigned vomiting, stood up, and retreated to the back of the lean-to to read the log. "Look at this. Train wrote something yesterday." Grace read aloud—*Constant leg pain. Torn muscle, I think. Can't keep up with Willow.*

Hearing Willow's name, Tara, who was sitting on the ground just feet away, yipped, spun around twice, leaped into the shelter, and vacuumed the wood plank floor so vigorously with her nose that she almost knocked Grace off her feet. Grace steadied herself against a wall and shouted, "Whoa! Down, Tara!" Grace raised her hand. "I forgot not to say W-i-l-l-o-w around Tara."

Tara sat, whined, and pawed the floor.

Dell stepped outside, called Tara, and said, "She knows W-i-l-l-o-w's scent even better than her name."

Grace read out loud the rest of Train's message—*Hope we make*

CHAPTER 27: WHITE CAP

it to Cooper's Brook Lean-to. I love W-i-l-l-o-w, but she sure misses that old guy and his dog.

Dell swallowed hard and hung his head.

Grace hopped out of the shelter, took Dell's hand, and said, "Well, *old guy*, we'd better get going."

They lifted their packs and started to ascend the first of three peaks that preceded the final ascent up White Cap. Views from the rocky summits of Gulf Hagas Mountain and West Peak were partly obstructed by stunted spruce trees, and the top of Hay Mountain (elevation 3,244 feet) was entirely wooded. From the sag between Hay and White Cap they looked up through a dense, fast-moving mist at what, for northbound thru-hikers, would be their last significant ascent before they reached Katahdin.

Most of the final climb to White Cap's summit was a tricky rock scramble. Stumbling and sometimes falling, Grace and Dell scraped their knees and legs on jagged stones but Tara, who went in and out of sight ahead of them, bounded from boulder to boulder, tail wagging. She yelped back at them through the impenetrable haze to hurry up.

The fog drifted across their field of vision but thinned as they gained elevation. It moved against a backdrop of dense stands of spruce. They saw streaks of brightness and hints of blue floating in gray bands through the dark mists in front of them. Dell recalled a passage from the Book of John—*And the light shineth in darkness; and the darkness comprehended it not.*

Tara tensed and dropped to the ground on her belly, front legs stretched wide ready to spring away. Her hair shot up along her back from neck to tail, ears back, eyes locked on something just ahead. She blocked the path and wouldn't budge.

Peering down at them through the mist, no more than fifteen feet away and only a couple of yards from a quivering Tara, was a massive bull moose with the melancholy face of a fatigued scholar who'd grown tired of writing in the dim light. But his prominent nose and five-foot-wide rack of thick horn conveyed the authority and self-confidence of an imperial emperor. The moose stood motionless. He squinted at them in his calm enormity, as if awaiting a gesture of obeisance from unworthy intruders who had entered his realm.

Dell's heart was thumping, and he could feel Grace's racing

pulse when he clutched her wrist. Speechless, their eyes glommed onto the musky smelling creature whose hulk towered above them.

Apparently satisfied that Dell, Grace, and Tara presented no threat, the moose grew weary of them. Ponderous, he turned away on his long bones and trudged off through the brush into the opaqueness of the fog-enshrouded mountainside and disappeared. Dell and Grace stood frozen for a moment until Grace bent over, released a loud breath, and said, "Oh, my God."

Dell—who'd encountered moose on the A.T. before, but never this close—patted her on the back, exhaled, and said, "Wow."

Tara pressed herself between them, demanding both affection and assurance that the great beast was gone.

Soon after their encounter with the moose a breeze picked up and took the mist with it, leaving a baby blue sky. The haze was now a puffy gray blanket spread out below them in all directions as they clambered over sharp-edged rocks to the summit of White Cap. The mountain was above the tree line and on a clear day afforded a spectacular 360-degree view. If not for the distant fog, they could have made out Maine's third highest peak, Old Speck, which the A.T. crossed two hundred miles to the south near the New Hampshire border.

Resting on rocks carpeted with yellow-green lichens, Dell and Grace were buffeted by a sharp wind as they huddled close together for warmth, snacked on gorp, and guzzled water. Forty miles to the northeast as the crow flies, and seventy miles on the A.T., they could see Katahdin looming above the mist in its blue-black, mile-high preeminence—a majestic granite massif, the thru-hikers' Mecca.

Dell touched Grace's hand. "Fewer than twenty percent of aspiring thru-hikers ever complete the trek from the A.T.'s southern terminus to the summit of Maine's highest mountain. Did you know that Henry Thoreau got lost in the fog and failed in his attempt to climb Katahdin?"

"No. *Walden* is all I know about him," a shivering Grace replied.

"His experience was an epiphany. Thoreau later exulted that Katahdin was 'solid earth, terrific, the *actual* world. Contact! Contact!'" Dell whacked his hiking stick against a rock.

"How do you know such things?" Grace asked through chattering teeth.

CHAPTER 27: WHITE CAP

"The same way you know about Rilke. My undergraduate thesis was on Thoreau."

"Impressive, professor."

* * *

The chilly wind hastened their departure from the summit. They hoisted their packs and descended 1,200 feet in the first mile, scrambling down a precipitous rocky trail past an empty shelter. A more gradual descent over the next mile was interrupted when a raven swooped chest-high across the trail, landing in a birch tree a few feet from where they stopped. With a single harsh *kruck,* he demanded attention. Tara sat down on the trail with ears up, head tilted and looked at the bird. Raven was not a big bird, he was huge. More eagle than raven.

"The grandest jet-black member of his tribe I've ever seen," Dell said.

Raven gazed down at them with chunky beak and fathomless dark eyes, head bobbing up and down atop a glossy neck. He puffed up his feathers, dropped to the ground, and toddled to within a few feet of them.

"He wants gorp," Grace said.

"Hope that's all he wants," Dell said. He dug into his pack for treats and told Grace about the odd experience he and Willow had in Pennsylvania with a one-eyed raven.

This raven was picky, he preferred peanuts and raisins to M&Ms. He followed them for more than a mile, gliding from tree to tree, until just before they'd reached the turnoff to West Branch Ponds Road where Tim O'Connor had said Scaperelli's group would access the A.T. sometime that afternoon.

It was close to 6 p.m. when they came to their tenting site near a thick stand of spruce trees by the East Branch of the Pleasant River, the agreed rendezvous point with Scaperelli. But no FBI agents were in sight.

Grace dropped her pack on the ground and wondered aloud, "Why aren't they here?"

Dell shrugged, trying to mask his concern. "Time for dinner. Let's put up the tent and eat. They'll come when they come."

They set up camp, cooked dinner, fed Tara, and, afterward, sat by the riverbank on a rough quartzite boulder. The brown river water moved fast, splashing over boulders, cutting into eroded banks. Dell pointed upstream about fifty yards to where a rope was strung across the river from bank to bank.

"Years ago, a timber company built a four-foot-high dam there," he said. "When the water is low, it's an easy walk across the top."

Frowning, Grace said, "I don't see any dam."

"It's submerged under about two feet of swift water. But if you hang onto the rope, which Patricia and I once did in high water, it would be the safest place for everyone to ford tomorrow."

Recalling the traumatic Long Pond Stream crossing on their first day in the wilderness, Grace gave a hesitant nod and asked, "Are you *sure*?"

"Yes, love. Absolutely."

The sun's last rays faded out over the western horizon. Still no FBI. They walked to the tent, crawled into their sleeping bags and Tara claimed her usual spot outside in front.

"I bet none of Scaperelli's crew has ever been here before," Grace said. "Could they be lost?"

Dell scooched closer to Grace. "Don't worry, they'll get here."

"But maybe they took the wrong trail, or have an outdated map, or one of them was injured, or they encountered someone suspicious, or God knows what."

"Maybe," Dell said.

An hour later, Tara's guttural growls roused Dell from an uneasy sleep. He reached for his flashlight, grabbed his hiking stick, unzipped the tent's bug screen, and peeped out into the dark. Tara was standing at full alert, hair raised, and growling.

"Is it them?" Grace mumbled, half asleep.

Some distance away a single faint light, not three, flickered through the trees as it wound down the trail in their direction.

Tara let loose a sharp bark. The light went out.

"Tara, stay!" Dell said. "Grace! Quick! Get dressed, slip on your Tevas, and get out of the tent." *She mustn't be trapped in the tent.*

Dell stumbled outside in just his pants and sandals, hiking stick in one hand, flashlight in the other.

The light reappeared, darting behind trees as it crept toward them. It halted, then moved again.

"I don't like this," Dell whispered to Grace who was now standing beside him.

CHAPTER 27: WHITE CAP

The approaching beam of light got close enough for them to hear boots on the trail. But the footsteps stopped. Dell tensed, poised to give Tara a command.

"Grace," he said, "hold tight to Tara's collar. Let go of it when I shout A-t-t-a-c-k. Then run like hell."

CHAPTER 28
ATTACKED

"Tara!" A shout came out of the dark from where the light shone. "Remember me? I'm a friend."

"Down Tara. Stay," Dell commanded.

"It's Stan Schneider," said Grace. "From Shaw's. Remember? The FBI guy who drove us to the trailhead." She stood beside Dell holding a flashlight in one hand and Tara's collar in the other. Schneider was close, but out of sight behind some trees.

Dell called out, "Stan?"

"Whew! Yes. Is Grace with you?"

"Yes. She has a hold of Tara; it's safe to show yourself."

Schneider walked out of the forest into their flashlight beams and sidled up to Tara.

"Good girl," he said as he cautiously extended his hand to her. She sniffed it suspiciously.

"It's okay Tara," Grace said, petting her. "He's with us."

Schneider scratched Tara's head; her fur eased back into place and her tail wagged.

"I apologize for being so late," he said, taking off his pack. "Tony sent me ahead to set up our tent. He and another agent, Eric Jacobs, have the ARs and first aid kit. They'll be along soon. Why don't you go back to sleep? We'll talk in the morning."

Grace let go of Tara's collar and said, "ARs. Aren't they semi-automatics?"

"Yes, rifles. Armalite semi-automatics. We always come prepared."

"See you tomorrow morning," Dell said. "We've had a long day."

They brought Tara into the tent with them so she wouldn't mistake Tony Scaperelli and Eric Jacobs for threats and freak them out.

CHAPTER 28: ATTACKED

Grace and Dell had almost fallen asleep when Tara growled.

"They must be here," Dell said. "Yes, I hear Tony's voice."

Shafts of light from headlamps flitted through the tent. Soon the lights went out and Tara's growls morphed into sporadic grumbles. Although exhausted, Dell and Grace tossed and turned throughout the night, partly because of Tara's grumblings, her gurgling stomach and vile farts, partly because of rumbling snores from the other tent.

When the sun's rays edged into the eastern sky the next morning, Dell stuck his head out of the tent and exchanged waves with Schneider who was scratching his belly while he stood stretching in front of a three-person dome tent. Tara brushed past Dell, squatted to pee, then ran over to Schneider and snuffled his boots. She flicked her tail and spun around, wanting to play.

"Here, sweetie," he said, as he picked up a stick and threw it for her to chase.

A sinewy young man with blond hair and blue eyes stepped out of the dome tent and ambled over to Dell and Grace who, by now, were both standing outside their tent.

"Hi, Eric Jacobs. I'm the paramedic. Hope we didn't disturb you too much last night."

Dell and a wide-eyed Grace introduced themselves.

"Tony is quite the snorer," Jacobs said, smiling.

Schneider, who'd walked over, grunted in agreement and stuck his fingers in both ears. Their conversation and laughter roused a disheveled Tony Scaperelli who wobbled out of the tent barefoot in an unbuttoned shirt.

"What the hell is all the commotion about?"

Tara snarled and Grace giggled.

"Tara, sit! Stay!" Dell shouted, winking at Scaperelli. "She's a flawless judge of character."

Tony raised an eyebrow but forced a smile. He looked at Grace, who was standing next to Dell, and asked, "How are you holding up Ms. Lombardi?"

Grace crossed her arms and, with a sardonic smile, said, "It's Grace, Tony. I'm holding up quite nicely."

Schneider, who was boiling water on a stove, began to twist his wedding ring, Jacobs grinned and looked down at his boots.

Dell whispered to Grace, "That's my girl."

"Well," Scaperelli said, standing up straight, scratching his scalp, then buttoning his shirt, "Grace it is."

After a quick breakfast of instant coffee and granola bars everyone walked down to the river. Dell pointed upstream to the submerged dam where a chest-high nylon rope stretched across to the other side.

"That's the place to cross the river. The footing isn't great, but it's doable. Just be sure to cling tightly to the rope."

Dell and Grace changed into Teva sandals and lashed their boots to the upper straps of their backpacks. Schneider and Jacobs did likewise. But Scaperelli looked downstream, rubbing his chin.

"I think I see a shorter way across down there. I'll leave my boots on for better traction. See you on the other bank."

"I wouldn't do that, Tony," Grace said. "Dell has made this crossing before. The river does look narrower down there, but it's also deeper and swifter. Boots won't help much on slick rocks, and they'll take forever to dry out." She grabbed Dell's arm and said, "Don't you agree, sweetheart?"

"She's right Tony. Don't do it."

Scaperelli adjusted his pack, then handed his AR to Schneider and his Glock sidearm to Jacobs. "Here, just in case she's right." Tony walked down the riverbank.

The first to inch into the river and proceed step by cautious step over the submerged dam was Grace. She grasped the rope and took her time wading sideways across thirty feet of fast-moving, waist-deep water.

Schneider shouted, "Watch out!"

A large spruce log swept down the river, narrowly missing her. But she maintained her composure, clung onto the rope with both hands, and made it to the other side. She threw her pack on the ground and sprinted down the bank in her sandals to where Tony had begun to ford the river from the opposite shore, only a dozen feet away from where Grace stood.

Over the roar of the river Grace screamed, "Tony, don't!"

He looked up, raised his chin, and let out a booming laugh. "Just watch me." He took a long step off the riverbank onto a wet, moss-covered rock.

Everyone heard a loud "Shit!" as his boots slipped off the rock and the swift-flowing river caught him and pulled him under. His

CHAPTER 28: ATTACKED

pack straps were soon entangled underwater on a dead tree branch. For several seconds, Tony's flailing hand was the only thing visible above the white foam. Then the powerful current and Tony's panicked thrashing snapped the tree branch, and he was jack-knifed to the far side of the river.

Watching in horror, Grace raced down the riverbank, eyes fixed on Tony. She splashed into a foot of water, bent over, grabbed his pack with two hands as he hurtled by, nearly being swept into the river herself, and, with all her might, hauled him onto a gravel bank.

Gasping for air, Tony struggled to stand up with his drenched pack. He dropped back down to one knee and spat out a bloody front tooth and a stream of brown water.

"Goddamn!" He coughed, and again tried to stand up. "Why did you do that? I could've gotten out by myself."

Grace said nothing but gave him a wry smile and an I-told-you-so look.

Stan and Eric had followed Grace across the dam, and they ran down to where she and Tony were. They took their boss's heavy pack and helped him recline against a birch tree.

Breathing heavily, Tony said, "Peterson knows the trail. I don't."

Patting him on the shoulder, Grace said, "We all make mistakes, even Dell sometimes."

"Thank you, *paesá*."

Surprised to hear gratitude from Tony, Grace nodded.

Dell was the last to cross the dam. He grasped the rope with one hand and Tara's collar with the other. The strain on Dell was eased somewhat by Tara's furious dogpaddling against the current. Once on the other side, they both dashed down the bank to join the others.

Tony was shaking his mobile phone. "Damn," he grumbled, "its water-tight container isn't water-tight." He waved his arm up the riverbank in the direction of Little Boardman Mountain. "Schneider, when we get to the top of that mountain give me your phone."

"Of course," Schneider said.

"Connectivity should be good up there, right Dell?" Tony asked.

Dell assured him it would be excellent. "There are no mountains on the A.T. between Little Boardman and Lower Jo-Mary Lake. And when we're at the lake it'll be easy to call the authorities in Millinocket because the town is only fifteen miles to the east."

"Good," Tony said, dumping water from his boots and wringing out his socks and shirt. "Let's climb up that damn mountain; we need to find out what's going on."

After Tony was ready, they all walked up to the dam, put on their boots and packs, and headed off onto the A.T. A three-mile moderate ascent—Tara in the lead, followed by the feds, then Grace and Dell—brought them to just below the 2,017-foot summit of Little Boardman Mountain where views of Katahdin to the northeast and White Cap to the south were partially obscured by spruce trees. It was a warm day when they sat down on chunks of granite at 10 a.m. for a water break. Tony used Schneider's phone to call the party of FBI agents who'd hiked south to Lower Jo-Mary Lake.

"Good God!" Tony yelled out followed by, "God Almighty!" He stood, shook his head, and paced back and forth. "Has the body been flown out yet?"

Dell and Grace leaped to their feet. She put her hand on Dell's shoulder as he bowed his head.

"Is the young man going to survive?" Tony grimaced, turned his back on the others, and rubbed his neck. "Do we have any idea where she might be?" Tony kicked the ground with his boot. "Helicopter?"

Gritting his teeth, Dell walked away from the group muttering to himself, *Willow. Run, damn it, run! Don't let the bastard catch you.*

Grace followed him and once again rested her hand on his shoulder. He hugged her tightly. In a choked voice, Dell said, "I'm scared, love. Scared."

"I know," she whispered.

Tony glanced at the two of them and continued talking. Schneider and Jacobs moved closer to Tony to better catch what he was saying.

"Let me speak with one of the state troopers," Tony said. He continued pacing back and forth, letting out deep breaths. "Sergeant Conklin, Tony Scaperelli, FBI. I'm so sorry." He shook his head. "Uh-huh, I understand. What do we know about the young woman?" Tony stared down at his feet, chin to chest. "Try not to

CHAPTER 28: ATTACKED

disturb her things. We also have a search-and-rescue dog who will need her scent."

Dell dropped to one knee, nose-to-nose with Tara, and cradled her head between his hands. "We'll find her babe. We'll find her." Tara whimpered and licked his face.

"Okay, sergeant. Thanks. We should be there by midafternoon." Tony handed the phone back to Schneider with a deep sigh and pained expression. Everyone stood in a tight circle around Tony. Dell's heart was pounding.

Tony said, "I'll be brief and leave out some details. We want to get to Antler's Campsite on the lake as soon as possible. But here's the gist of it."

He said that about three this morning two state police officers, who'd flown in yesterday and set up camp by the lake, heard frantic screams from the direction of the Antler's Campsite. The officers dressed and rushed to the campsite where they found a knife-shredded tent and an unconscious, critically injured young man. Blood was splattered everywhere, some as far as twenty feet from the tent. The officers initially assumed he was dead until they heard a faint moan. His Ohio driver's license identified him as Theo Payne.

Chills shot down Dell's spine. He looked into Grace's eyes and said, "Train."

Tony explained that a short distance away from this crime scene, in the shell of a long-abandoned cabin once used by fishermen, the officers found a sleeping bag, backpack and boots of a female, but no body. They didn't know whether she was alive or dead or where she might be. On a piece of paper that was found in the woman's pack were two names and two phone numbers, but the young woman could not be identified. No blood or signs of a struggle were found in the cabin.

"Jesus! Those are our names and phone numbers," Dell said as he turned to Grace.

She wrapped her arms around him.

Dell shouted, "I know the couple! Theo Payne's trail name is Train. The woman is Willow Monroe." Tara cocked her head. "Tara knows her, too."

A teary-eyed Grace put her hand to her mouth.

Dell felt dizzy. He recalled how Willow had ended her phone call to him almost three months earlier from Bear Mountain Inn—*I love you Gramps and miss you.* Dell bit his lower lip. *We're coming, honey. Hang on.* He checked his watch.

Tony said that one officer worked to stanch Mr. Payne's bleeding, while the other rushed with his sidearm and headlamp into the forest after the assailant or assailants. In their haste to get to Antler's the officers had left their body armor back in camp and, less than a minute later, the pursuing officer was shot in the chest. On hearing the shot, the officer attending to Mr. Payne sprinted to the scene. The wounded officer bled profusely and died in the arms of his fellow trooper. Tony's voice cracked and he cleared his throat.

Stan Schneider crossed himself and said, "May God rest his soul."

Tony paused for a moment and they all hung their heads. Dell held Grace's hand when he saw her tears and quivering chin.

When Tony resumed his briefing, he said that the surviving officer phoned the Millinocket police who, in turn, called the state police, and FBI in Bangor.

Tony said, "At dawn this morning two more floatplanes landed on the lake. One flew out with the dead officer and Mr. Payne, who was still breathing. He's been taken to the Millinocket Regional Hospital. The other plane brought in two additional state troopers and a search-and-rescue dog. A third plane will soon land on the lake with Tim O'Connor and another agent. It will bring in more body armor and additional phones. A helicopter with infrared will arrive in Millinocket sometime this afternoon. My four guys who are now at Antler's will fan out with the dog and its handler to see what they can find."

They were all standing close together, anxious to get underway. Dell tightened his waist belt, stood up straight, and gave Grace a long look.

Tony said, "All right, ready or not, let's hotfoot it to the lake."

CHAPTER 29

CLOSING IN

The sky was overcast, the air warm and humid, as Dell and Grace followed the team of FBI agents with Tara in the lead. Tara set a blistering pace as they descended from Little Boardman Mountain for two miles, then crossed an unpaved private road and followed the A.T. along the south shore of Crawford Pond where the trail skirted gravel beaches that were separated from one another by a serpentine ridge of sediment. The A.T. then leveled off to a constant elevation of only six or seven hundred feet above sea level, often taking them along moldering corduroy roads in sparse over-harvested forests and through squishy mosquito-infested bogs.

After four miles, they came to a blue-blazed side trail to Cooper Brook Lean-to. Dell told Scaperelli, Schneider, and Jacobs to go on without them because Grace needed a water break and he wanted to see whether Willow and Train had left a message in the shelter's log.

"Don't linger," Scaperelli warned. "We're approaching an especially dangerous area."

"We'll be right behind you," Dell promised. The three agents sped on down the trail.

Cooper Brook tumbled and splashed down a ravine near the six-person log shelter. Despite its "baseball bat" floor of rounded, knotty, three-inch wide spruce logs, the lean-to's location made it one of Dell's favorites on the entire A.T. The steady sound of falling water spilling over rocks had lulled him to sleep in past years, and its swimming hole was especially appealing since, unlike most of the surrounding ponds, it was free of leeches. Hikers, himself included, often sat buck-naked under the cascading water for a revitalizing massage.

But there was no time for such luxuries. Dell went straight to the log and read aloud what Train had written the day before—*Made it! Throbbing pain. Only eight easy miles to Antler's. We'll stay there tomorrow.*

Dell sat with Grace on a rock by the shelter. Neither of them uttered a word as they drank from their canteens and watched a hermit thrush skitter in the duff. Dell tossed Tara a dog biscuit before they all returned to the A.T.

They followed the agents' boot prints in the mud, crossed a gravel lumber road, balanced on wobbly wood planks placed over mucky sections of the trail, and hopped on rocks to cross small streams. About a mile from Antler's they rounded a turn in the trail and came face-to-face with a Maine state trooper in camouflage and body armor holding an AR rifle. Dell snapped a leash on Tara, then waved and said, "We're friendly" as they approached the officer.

"Dell Peterson and Grace Lombardi, I presume," he said with a smile. Tara strained at the leash and nosed his boots. "And this must be Tara," he added.

"You're well-informed," Dell replied, returning his smile.

The trooper accompanied them on the trail as it swung eastward, to where they stopped briefly for an ice-cold drink of naturally effervescent water bubbling up from what generations of grateful hikers called "Seven-Up Spring." The A.T. then hooked north, close enough to the shoreline of Lower Jo-Mary Lake that they inhaled its fresh piney smell, and soon thereafter the trail brought them to an open area, Antler's Campsite. Several tents had been set up and a hundred yards away from the camp three floatplanes were moored on a Caribbean-like white sandy beach. A tarpaulin was stretched between trees for shade. They could see Tim O'Connor on the beach standing by the floatplanes; his red hair gave him away. He thrust both arms in the air and ran up to them, a bead of sweat running down his face. This caught the attention of Eric Jacobs, who waved. Jacobs jogged over to Dell and Grace. In a low but urgent voice he said, "Tony wants to see you right away. He's trying to contact the helicopter."

Scaperelli was slouched in a canvas folding chair under the tarp with his back to them, talking on the phone. Jacobs and O'Connor confirmed that a total of nine FBI agents and three state troopers were now on-site. The four agents who'd hiked in

CHAPTER 29: CLOSING IN

from the north were still out searching the area with a state trooper and his dog, a yellow lab.

"They've called in a couple of times," O'Connor said. "No sign of the missing woman or suspects."

When Tony noticed Dell and Grace, he abruptly ended his phone conversation. He jumped up from his chair, waved, and yelled, "Hey, you two! Come with me to the remnants of the old cabin. Bring Tara."

They walked with Tony through a majestic grove of eighty-foot-tall red pines that emitted tides of sharp woodsy sweetness. A blue butterfly, identical to the one they'd seen at the murder site on their first day in the wilderness, flitted in front of them for almost fifty yards as if guiding them. The air soon buzzed with the sound of blood-crazed flies. Yellow tape marked off a wide perimeter around a bloody, slashed-up tent.

"Tara, come!" Dell snapped a leash on Tara and dropped down on one knee. Lightheaded, his heart pounded. Grace cupped her hands to her mouth to hold back a scream, then made a sign of the cross, and knelt beside Dell. They couldn't look away from the hideous sight before them.

An FBI agent wearing a mask and latex gloves glanced at them and a state trooper waved his gloved hand. Neither man said a word. They returned to their grim task of investigating the crime scene. Train's blood-splattered clothes were strewn across the ground; his sleeping bag appeared to be sliced almost in half. Blood-spotted boots and hiking equipment, red badges of courage, lay scattered haphazardly within the taped perimeter. Signs of a ferocious struggle were unmistakable—a freshly snapped sapling and deep gouges in the dirt pooled with globs of congealed blood. An aluminum tent stake clotted with blood had been placed in a clear plastic evidence bag.

Train might have grabbed the stake in a desperate attempt to defend himself. Thank God Willow wasn't in the tent.

Dell squeezed his eyes shut and tried to recreate the scene in his mind—a razor-edged steel blade, so accustomed to killing, plunged down through the tent, again and again. Train woke in panic, screamed as the first downward thrust pierced his thigh to the bone. Frantic, he scrambled to the front of the tent. Train knew instantly that this was no nightmare. The blade slashed his arm, chest. Pain. Train cried out, "Willow! Run away, AWAY!" Roll, roll out. Punch the sonofabitch. Pain, awful pain.

Dell's throat tightened. He felt the sting of tears in his eyes. A smell of decay and the metallic odor of blood filled his nostrils. Dell breathed slowly and deliberately, trying to fend off nausea. He rubbed his arms, goosebumps. "Forgive me Train," he mumbled to himself, profoundly regretting his initial negative impression of him.

"Excuse me," Grace said with an ashen face as she leaped past Dell, doubled over, and vomited on the ground. "Sorry." She kicked leaves and dirt to cover the vomit and wiped her chin on her shirtsleeve.

"It's okay, *paesá*," Tony said. "That's a perfectly understandable human reaction."

Scaperelli sighed and handed her a canteen of water. Dell gently massaged her back and shoulders and said in a soft voice, "That's fine, love. I might be next."

Rubbing his forehead with his fingertips, Dell turned to Tony. "Well, ah . . . This is . . . What's next?"

"Come with me," Tony said.

They continued on for about forty yards through a pine grove to what remained of an old cabin, a warped, weathered wood platform with its entire back wall missing, no roof, no door, and no glass in the windows. Standing outside, looking in from the open backside of the cabin, they saw Willow's scuffed boots, Gregory backpack, sleeping bag, pink sweater, and Sierra cup laying on the least warped portion of the floor. They also saw, and smelled, her wool socks.

"They're hers," Dell said, choking back tears. "We got it all in Pennsylvania."

Grace wrapped her arm around his waist. "No blood. At least she was able to escape."

"Let's hope. She could well have heard Train's screams and fled the cabin. But we don't know anything for sure"

"That's right," said Tony, who was standing next to Grace. "She might have been with the young man during the attack, was gravely injured, ran or crawled away, and died in the woods. All we know is that we haven't found her." Tony glanced at Tara, then Dell, and said, "We've combed this shack for evidence. No sign of

CHAPTER 29: CLOSING IN

the murder or murderers was found here. Feel free to let the dog do her thing."

Slapping his hand twice on the cabin floor, Dell said, "Okay!" Tara jumped onto the platform and let out a shrill whine. She spun around and around before burrowing her nose into the boots and socks, sweater, and everything else of Willow's. Hyperventilating, she gave out a high-pitched, plaintive howl that Dell had never heard before. She leaped off the floor, bolted into the woods, and vanished from sight.

"Tara!" Grace screamed.

"Tara come!" Dell shouted, but Tara was gone. "Normally I wouldn't be too concerned, but this is very unusual behavior."

A full four minutes passed before Tara slinked back to the cabin, tail dragging, head hangdog low, and fur matted with mud, spruce needles, and briars. She edged closer to Dell, her mournful eyes avoiding his. He clicked on the leash, sat down on the ground, and cradled Tara's head in both hands. Looking into her eyes, they nosed one another.

Dell vowed, "We'll find her, girl."

When he stood up, Grace took his hand and said, "I'm really worried. Willow can't go far without her boots."

"Tony," Dell said, "I have to get into Willow's pack. It's important."

Tony nodded and handed Dell latex gloves.

Dell dug through everything in her pack, including her grungy clothes and musty smelling rain gear, before exhaling deeply. Grace, Tony, and even Tara were watching Dell intently. "Thank God!" Dell said. "The gray sneakers I bought Willow in Port Clinton are *not* here. After I got her a pair of boots, she decided to use the sneakers as camp shoes. Willow's wearing them, I'm pretty sure."

The sneakers were missing, but Dell found something else tucked under a nylon fold at the bottom of her pack, a crumpled school ID with a black-and-white photo of a teenage girl with disheveled long dark hair and an innocent but despondent expression on her face, Willow Monroe. Dell shook his head, showed Grace the photo, and handed it to Tony.

"Willow never told me about this photograph. You'll want it."

"Indeed," Tony said, inserting the photo ID carefully into a small plastic bag which he pulled from his pocket. "Time to get underway."

They walked briskly back to the tarp where Schneider, O'Connor, and Jacobs stood in body armor holding their ARs, waiting for orders.

CHAPTER 30

SWAMP SEARCH

"Get Dell and Grace some vests and phones," Tony told O'Connor. "Tara's hot to hunt for the young woman, Miss Willow Monroe."

In the few minutes that it took O'Connor to walk down to the beach to retrieve phones and vests from a floatplane the whup-whup-whup of a helicopter sounded overhead. Tony got on his phone to the pilot just as the four FBI agents with the state trooper and his Labrador returned to camp after several hours of searching.

The mud-splattered, bug-bitten search party was tired and frustrated. The men sighed, yanked off their gear, and stretched out on the ground. Their dog, who Tara sniffed but then ignored, plopped down in the shade, legs splayed out, panting heavily.

One agent remarked, "The lab dragged us through a slew of mucky bogs." Pointing north, he said, "She then led us around the far end of the lake and down the opposite shore, stopping to sample every damn pile of moose turds." He waved to the east, directly across the lake from where they stood. "We found nothing."

"Listen up," Tony said, getting off the phone and glancing up at the chopper. "The pilot will let us know what his infrared picks up and whether he sees anything with the naked eye. Schneider, O'Connor, Jacobs, Dell, Grace, and especially Tara, come back to the cabin with me. The rest of you stay here for now. The A.T. is supposed to be closed off to hikers, but keep an eye out for anyone you might see on the trail."

Grace and Dell donned their Kevlar vests, which were lighter than Dell had anticipated. They'd taken off their heavy backpacks when they first arrived at Antler's and wisely decided to leave them in camp before heading out to look for Willow. Jacobs, O'Connor, and Dell took daypacks. The two agents carried first aid kits and extra ammunition. Canteens, headlamps, rain gear, phones, snacks, and bug spray were divided among the three of them.

Dell knew this section of the wilderness particularly well and he had tented at Antler's before. Still, he brought his topographical map.

Several years earlier, he'd spent time in the area hiking, fishing, and swatting blackflies with Maine Appalachian Trail Club ridge-runner and fishing guide Charlie Orono, a Native American from the Penobscot Nation. Charlie's people had lived, fished, and hunted for thousands of years along the Penobscot River and throughout the vast expanse south of the tribe's sacred Mt. Katahdin. Charlie and Dell had once slogged through the swamp west of Antler's that encircled Mud Pond to reach a stream teeming with brook trout. He also showed Dell an overgrown, little-known side trail that ran northwest off the A.T. to the top of nearby Potaywadjo Ridge. The ridge was a four-mile-long, mostly bald, more-or-less smooth granite outcropping that rose eight hundred feet above the surrounding area. Charlie said the ridge was named after a tribal chief who could "outrun, outswim, and outspit anyone."

Tony brought everyone back to the cabin. Dell gripped the leash as Tara strained forward. Tara knew Willow's scent and probably didn't need a reminder, but Dell had her sniff Willow's rank-smelling socks again. Dell explained to Tony that Tara's dual set of tracking and air-scenting skills made her a valued search-and-rescue dog. After smelling Willow's personal items, she'd be able to track her. Nose to the ground, she'd know to follow Willow's scent through virtually any terrain, even water. Unlike most tracking dogs, she didn't need to be on a leash because she was trained to stop and wait for Dell to catch up to her. Also, and distinct from almost all other *air-scenting* SAR dogs, she could detect and find a *specific* person (Willow) simply by knowing her scent and sniffing the air. But Dell feared so many hours had elapsed since Willow's disappearance that Tara's air-scenting skills would be sharply diminished.

Tony made a fist, stuck his thumb up in the air, and said, "Let's find her."

"Tara," Dell commanded. *"FIND WILLOW!"*

Tara flew off the cabin floor and plunged into the spruce forest, nose down, heading west across the A.T. toward Mud Pond.

CHAPTER 30: SWAMP SEARCH

She paused periodically to let out a sharp *hurry up* bark to tell the search party where she was. Dell, Grace, and the FBI agents raced after her for several minutes before coming to a swampy area around Mud Pond. Prickly brambles scratched Dell's hands and he heard "ouch" and "damn" from the others when sharp-spiked spruce branches tore through trousers and shirts. Although Tara was out of sight, Dell noticed the head-high swamp grass sway and they heard her *hurry up* bark.

Dell shouted, "Tara, stay!"

He wiped blood-gorged blackflies off the back of his neck and sprayed himself with insect repellent, not that it fazed the blackflies. Dell handed the bug spray to Grace, who was breathing heavily. She and the three agents sprayed it on their exposed skin.

Sweat ran down Tony's face and he scratched his wrists. "Goddamn bugs are shedding more blood than the murderer." O'Connor and Schneider stood behind him and grunted their agreement.

"Tara's impressive," Jacobs said to Dell as he stared at the swaying swamp grass. "I know, I've trained SAR dogs for the Bureau."

Dell smiled. "She's top dog."

Tony got on the phone to the chopper circling overhead. "See anything, Andy?" He squinted up at the helicopter. "Hell, that's not very helpful." He swatted flies away from his eyes. "Keep looking."

"What's going on boss?" Schneider asked, stepping up closer.

Slipping his phone into a side pocket, Tony snapped, "Andy's infrared has picked up several forms but in these heavily wooded areas it's hard to distinguish a human from, say, a deer, bear, moose, or frigging Big Foot." He shook his head. "Looks like Tara's going to be our best bet."

"Okay!" Dell shouted to a still hidden Tara. "Find Willow!"

Two hundred feet in front of them the swamp grass began to shake as Tara headed straight for the shortest distance across the pond, its narrow neck. They watched as she emerged from the grass, plodded through belly-deep mud, waded into the water, and dogpaddled to the other side.

By now, the search party's boots were mired in the ooze of a bog where everything smelled sulfurous, like cooked or rotten cabbage. The closer they came to the pond, the denser the marsh reeds and the deeper they sunk into the muddy quagmire. Dell stopped when the silty mud reached his knees.

"Back! Go back!" Dell said. Nobody objected. They retraced their steps through the muck, gradually retreating to solid ground where they followed Tara from their side of the pond. She wound her way along the opposite shore, alternately smelling the ground and air, until she reached the far end of the pond.

Dell cupped his hands to his mouth and shouted, "Tara, stay!"

When the group caught up to her she was standing on a faint trace, an animal path that led from Mud Pond eastward back toward the A.T. and Lower Jo-Mary Lake. Moose droppings, which Tara apparently hadn't had time to sample, littered the path. She flashed her German shepherd smile and cocked her head as if to say, *Search and rescue is what I do. I do it well, but I'm puzzled.*

"Think the moose pellets confused her?" Grace asked.

"Maybe." Dell pulled one of Willow's stinky socks from his back pocket and rubbed Tara's muzzle with it. "Find Willow!"

Tara let out a muffled woof and began an unhurried stroll down moose poop lane. With a raised nose, she swiveled her head from side to side, breathing in whatever scents she detected on bushes, vines, and branches. After about fifty yards of lateral sniffing she stopped, stuck her nose higher in the air, and inhaled. She caught a whiff of something because her ears shot up, she yipped twice, and sprinted down the path in the direction of the A.T.

CHAPTER 31
FOUND

Tony turned to Dell and gave him a thumbs-up. The two of them and Grace raced after the three FBI agents who were struggling to keep up with Tara on a hot, muggy August day. She led them along the animal path over fallen branches and through thick underbrush with sharp briars and stinging nettles. Gnats flew into their faces and eyes as they dodged moose pellets and maggot-infested scat. Within a half mile, and out of breath, they were relieved to see a white-blazed spruce that signaled the animal path had intersected with the A.T. From this intersection, they could make out the dark blue water and sandy shore of Lower Jo-Mary Lake through a stand of tall pines.

"How'd we get back on the A.T.?" Eric Jacobs asked, scratching his head. "Did we make a wide loop?"

"More like a modified horseshoe," Dell said, pulling the trail map out of his day pack and tracing where they'd been with his finger. "Antler's Campsite is two miles south of here." He pointed to the campsite on the map. "Tara led us west from Antler's, across the A.T., to the marsh around Mud Pond." Dell traced the route on the map with his finger. "After she swam across the pond, we walked northeast along the opposite edge of the pond until we saw Tara sitting on the animal path. From there, she took us due east, back to the A.T. where we're standing."

It was midafternoon as the six of them stood on the A.T. taking swigs from their canteens and sharing a bag of gorp Dell extracted from his daypack. Tara pawed the dirt next to him and started to whine. He leashed her but she tugged so hard he had to hang on with both hands.

"She's zeroed in on Willow's scent. No question about it."

"Better get going," Tony said, swatting a mosquito.

"Okay. Find Willow!" Dell released Tara from the leash and the search party followed her as she ran due north on the A.T., with the lake to their right. Tara paused about every hundred feet or so to look back and make sure she hadn't outrun the group. She gave them impatient *hurry up* barks as they hustled after her on the winding trail around the far north end of the lake. A red-faced Stan Schneider lagged behind the other three agents. He looked over his shoulder at Dell and Grace and huffed, "Didn't the state trooper's yellow Labrador drag that other search team up here?"

"Yeah," Dell said. "But Tara's special. She knows *Willow's* scent, whether on the ground or in the air."

Tara was out of sight, but they heard her yelping, not hurry up barks, but short, sharp, repetitive yelps. About 150 yards after rounding the lake's north shore they came upon Tara. She was wagging her tail and twirling around in a clearing near a brown wooden sign with peeling white letters that read, *Potaywadjo Ridge Trail*. As soon as the search group reached her, she bounded up the ridge trail.

Dell shouted, "Come! Come back here."

Tara trotted back to him, ears erect, head cocked. She gave Dell and Grace a quizzical look before letting out an anxious grumble and pointing her nose back to the ridge trail. She reared up on her hind legs and howled.

"My God!" Dell said, I've been here before."

This was the same trail Charlie Orono and Dell had hiked years ago, but it no longer looked abandoned and overgrown. Brush had been cleared away and it even had its own sign. Looking down on the ground where an excited Tara was nosing and pawing, Dell was startled to see small sneaker prints in the dirt mingled with larger boot prints.

"Those are almost certainly Willow's," Dell said, standing by the sign and eyeing the sneaker prints.

Tony walked over to Dell, looked down at the prints, and nodded. Pointing up the ridge trail, Tony asked, "What's up there?"

"Trail's only a mile long," Dell said. "On top it's mostly bald, with some horizontal and sloping granite ledges. Could be suitable for a helicopter to land. Spruce forest and dense brush soon thin out as the trail gains elevation. Great for infrared."

CHAPTER 31: FOUND

Tony grimaced. "The chopper has returned to Millinocket for refueling, but it will be back before long."

"Boss, we can't wait for the chopper," O'Connor said.

Tony agreed. "Yes. Let's go."

Dell glanced at Tara, and before he could give her a command, she charged up the narrow trail. Running after her, Dell, Grace, and the rest of the search party ascended through an increasingly open, mixed spruce and hardwood forest. As they neared the ridgetop, Tara suddenly sat down on the path. This was unusual for a hard-charging search-and-rescue dog who had not been told to sit.

Dell scanned the terrain. Far below, Lower Jo-Mary Lake wore a silver sheen in the late afternoon sun. Above them, not far from where they were standing, Dell could see an exposed portion of Potaywadjo Ridge. Virtually no trees. They'd left the dense forest behind.

"What's up?" Dell asked Tara, stroking her head. She looked at him, turned away, then stared intently at something in the distance. Everyone's eyes followed hers. Tara raised her nose and sniffed the air.

"I see only rocks, more rocks, and bushes," Tony said. "What's she doing?"

"Pointing to Willow," Dell replied.

It was only then that Dell recalled something Charlie Orono had mentioned when the two of them climbed up to Potaywadjo Ridge.

"Tony, many years ago, I was right here with a Penobscot Indian guide. The guy's name was Charlie Orono."

"Jeez Peterson, you *really do* get around, but what's your point."

"Charlie said his father had told him about a large overhanging ledge on this side of the ridge. Not a cave, exactly, but a cavernous space where, long ago, his people would sometimes take refuge when threatened by other tribes."

"Did Charlie take you there?"

"No. I doubt he'd been there himself."

Tony scratched his chin and raised an eyebrow. "So, where the hell *is* this place?" A whup-whup-whup announced the helicopter's return. Tony got on the phone to the pilot. "Sounds like you're a little northwest of us Andy. We're not far from the top of Potaywadjo Ridge, south side." Tony glanced at the group. "Good."

The search team waved when the chopper popped over the ridge and circled overhead.

"Yes, that's us you see." Tony waved at the helicopter. "Very interesting." He paced back and forth on the path. "Great! I'll tell my Appalachian Trail guy, Dell Peterson. He's got the SAR dog." He looked at Dell, nodded, then paced again. "Okay. Hang around."

Tony stepped over to where Tara was sitting. Everyone else was standing around her on the trail. He leaned down, patted her rump. "I apologize girl. You could be onto something." Tony pointed toward where Tara was staring—a spot off the path about six hundred feet straight ahead at their elevation, horizontal to but well below Potaywadjo Ridge. "Andy is certain he sees a human figure on his screen over there near that large rectangular-shaped rock that's about the size of a railroad boxcar. A short distance from that point, he detected another human figure, but it quickly disappeared from view."

"I see the rectangular rock," Grace said.

Schneider cocked his head. "Me too. The other guy must have heard the chopper and taken cover."

"Who knows," Jacobs said, "maybe into the cave Dell mentioned."

Tony summarized what else the pilot had seen. Not too far beyond where the person had disappeared—possibly into a cave, as Jacobs surmised—the pilot saw a third, smaller figure. The pilot wasn't certain, but he thought it could be a woman crouching behind a boulder. She was just beyond where the cave might be located, at the base of a rocky incline that rose perhaps fifty yards to the top of another ridge. That ridge, which the search party could see in the distance from where they stood, ran roughly parallel to Potaywadjo Ridge. On the far side of that ridge, and out of sight of the search party, was a precipitous drop off.

Grace clutched Dell's arm. "I *know* that's Willow."

"Could be," Tony said. "No time to spare." He wrinkled his forehead and squinted dead ahead at the boxcar-like rectangular rock that Andy and Tara had pinpointed. "Dell, how do you think we should navigate this tilted terrain while working our way toward that rock?"

Dell surveyed the inclined hillside in front of them. Knee-high blueberry bushes and a few stunted birch trees broke up the sloped

CHAPTER 31: FOUND

but uniform landscape of lichen-coated granite boulders and scattered brush that separated them from the rectangular-shaped rock.

Pointing slightly downhill to his left, Dell said, "We'll move more slowly, but if we go this way it'll be less steep and give us better cover." He looked at Tony. "We'll be vulnerable, but the rocks and brush provide some protection."

"Let's proceed single-file, at least ten yards apart from one another," Tony said. "Best marksman is point man." He pulled out his phone and called the agents who were still at Antler's Campsite. "Get your asses up the Potaywadjo Ridge Trail. Pronto! We're three, maybe four miles from you. We'll be just off the trail, close to the top of Potaywadjo Ridge. Be careful. The suspects have probably taken cover up here and the girl, Ms. Monroe, could be close by."

Tony called the pilot to explain Dell's plan. "Andy, do you see any safer approach? We'll be exposed to any screwball with a firearm if we go in from here." Tony sighed. "Damn, that won't help." He stuck the phone into his pocket. "The pilot says there's an old tote road maybe a mile beyond the rectangular rock, but it'll take much too long to find."

"I'll go first. You're a lousy shot Scaperelli." Tim O'Connor winked at Tony, laughed, then took several steps into the bushes and began to weave through boulders toward the target.

"Bullshit," Tony shouted after him.

Tara zipped past O'Connor but Dell called her back and leashed her.

"Grace, Dell." Tony said, "I want you two to hang back, *way* back. We have an eye on these guys now. Keep Tara with you. I'll let you know if we need her."

"Will do," Dell said. Grace nodded.

Scaperelli waded into the bushes behind O'Connor, followed by Schneider and Jacobs. Potaywadjo Ridge rose above them, to their right. They were halfway to the rectangular rock before Grace, Tara, and Dell began to follow.

Edging their way through dense bushes across the angular slope, Dell and Grace tried to stay about three hundred feet behind the agents.

Blam!

Small birds flew into the air. Dell and Grace dove down, slamming their hands and knees onto rocks. *Blam! Blam! Blam! Blam!*

Grace yanked Dell's shirt as she hit the ground. Dell dropped next to her. They flattened their bodies to the ground.

BLAM! BLAM! BLAM! BLAM!

Barely breathing, Dell reached out his hand for Grace. Wide-eyed and shaking, she grabbed it and coughed out, "Good God!"

An unnerving silence followed for what felt like hours but was, in fact, only minutes.

"It's too damn quiet," Dell said. "What the hell just happened?" He wrapped his arm around Grace. "Go back to the path and wait there. It'll be safer, and the agents from Antler's will arrive soon."

Tara whined and tugged at the leash, pulling in the direction of the gun shots.

"No way!" Grace said, looking Dell in the eye and tightening her jaw. "We're in this together."

Still crouching down, they heard Tony's voice. "I hear Schneider," Dell said. "That's Jacob's, too."

Grace said, "I don't hear O'Connor."

They inched their heads up and peered through the brush. Tony was standing about a hundred yards away by the rectangular rock holding his AR rifle in both hands. It was aimed down at something or someone out of their field of vision. He was shouting something undecipherable at Schneider, who was running toward him. Neither O'Connor nor Jacobs was in sight. Sweat ran down Dell's face as he stood up.

"We can't just stay here. Willow's out there."

At the mention of Willow's name, Tara let out a sharp whine.

"Yes, I know," Grace said, standing up.

Tara pulled hard on the leash. Her nostrils twitched, sampling the air. Dell knew Willow's scent was strong. "Let's get going," Dell said. Grace followed Dell as they darted from rock to rock. They both stayed low while making their way toward Scaperelli and the others.

Within minutes they reached the agents. Tim O'Connor was leaning against a boulder, shirt sleeve torn, left arm wrapped in a blood-soaked dressing, blood dripping down his arm and fingers onto the dirt. Jacobs had applied a tourniquet and knelt beside O'Connor crafting what looked like a sling. Stan Schneider stood a hundred feet away from them, AR at the ready, scanning the area beyond the rectangular rock. Tony walked up to O'Connor and Jacobs from that rock and called the pilot.

"Land on the ridge, Andy. O'Connor's down. Needs medical attention. He can walk. Jacobs will help him get to the chopper." He looked up and tried to spot the chopper. "About thirty minutes, I'd guess." He raised his fist in the air. "Good."

"Jacobs!" Tony yelled, pointing up at Potaywadjo Ridge. "Chopper on the ridge right there above us in twenty minutes. Get going." Turning to O'Connor, who was groaning in pain, Tony asked, "You can make it, can't you?"

O'Connor waved his right hand. "Sure."

Then O'Connor hobbled off with his right arm slung over Jacobs's shoulder, Jacobs's arm wrapped around O'Connor.

"Tony turned toward Dell and Grace. "Come with me."

"Look, we've *got* to get to Willow!" Dell said.

"Right. This'll only take a few seconds."

With Tara still leashed, they followed Tony as they negotiated their way across slabs of granite. Tony turned to Grace and said in a low voice, "You may want to wait here with Tara. It's not a pretty sight."

"No, I'm fine."

Tony shrugged and led them around the back side of the rectangular rock where he pointed to a man's body. "Look familiar?"

A heavyset, fifty-something man with a buzz cut and prominent scar along the jawline laid crumpled on his left side at the base of the rock, his neck grotesquely twisted, face staring up at the sky. A gelatinous remnant of an eyeball dangled from its socket. Blood oozed from his open mouth and trickled down his neck. Dell bent over and saw several bullet wounds, at least one to the head. The man's rifle was wedged between a couple of nearby rocks.

"Remington, thirty-ought-six," Tony said, anchoring his hands on his hips. "Is this Lev Komaroff?"

"Yes, that's him." Dell said. "Henry Dubois has to be nearby. Willow, too."

Dell's heart pounded as he glanced at his watch. He looked at Grace whose eyes were wide, eyebrows raised. She tilted her head and squinted at Dell.

"What the HELL are we waiting for?" Dell roared.

He released Tara, who bolted out of sight. Dell sprinted after her.

"Damnit. Wait up!" Grace said as she ran after Dell.

"Hey, hold on," Tony called out. "You two can't be out there alone."

But they kept running. With a tremor in her voice as they ran, Grace said, "Tara knows exactly where to go."

Before Tony hastened after them, they heard him shout to Schneider. "Keep a sharp eye out. Our guys from Angel's will be here soon."

Tara led them up a rise, through a devil's racecourse of rocks where nothing grew except an occasional misshapen spruce tree. On their right was a solid rock face that rose vertically more than one hundred feet to the Potaywadjo ridgeline. Five minutes after leaving Tony and the rectangular rock they came to a large cave-like cavity with a depth of about forty feet under a ledge of protruding granite. Dell and Grace examined the musty cave. No one was inside. Dell saw boot prints on the cave's dirt floor and noted the absence of sneaker prints. Grace picked up recently discarded candy wrappers.

Tara lingered about twenty seconds at the cave's mouth. She smelled the ground and inhaled the air as Dell and Grace inspected the cave. Tara then took off, ears pinned back, bounding forward up the rock-strewn devil's staircase in hot pursuit of Willow. Tara was soon out of sight.

"Quick!" Grace shouted. "Follow her!"

She and Dell ran after Tara, scrambling over rocks, stumbling up the sharp incline until they could see the top of the rise fifty feet above them. That's when they heard a scream.

"That's Willow!" Dell shouted, breathing heavily.

"Oh my God," Grace said, running next to him.

Gasping and wheezing, they were already going flat out. As they struggled up the last few feet to the crest of the rise, clambering over rocks, jagged stones scraped their knuckles and bruised their knees.

Behind them, they heard Tony shout, "Wait! Grace, Dell, wait up!"

But they kept running in the direction of Willow's scream, and Tony fell further behind.

At the top of the rise they saw Willow and Henry Dubois just ninety feet away, down a gentle slope. Willow and Dubois were

CHAPTER 31: FOUND

both standing on a level granite ledge. From the ledge, a treacherously steep gravel bank descended at a sharp angle about fifteen feet to the edge of a sheer precipice. Bits of gravel were rolling down the bank and over the cliff. Between them stood Tara—hair raised, head lowered, and fangs bared in a snarl. Dubois clutched a knife and took a step forward. Even at a distance, Dell recognized the knife as one favored by the military and some hunters—a US Marine Corps fighting knife. Its seven-inch-long blade was pointed at Willow.

A terrified Willow pressed her back against a wall of boulders. Her eyes locked on the paunchy middle-aged man in camouflage and L.L. Bean boots. About fifty feet from Willow, his eyes fixed on Tara, Dubois inched forward, a smirk on his face. Tara growled and hunched lower, poised to lunge. A trembling Willow held her hands high in the air and screamed, "Get the hell away from me, asshole!" Her arms were scratched and bruised, T-shirt torn, pants and sneakers caked with mud.

"Dubois!" Dell shouted, as he ran down the slope toward the two of them. "Drop the knife."

Stunned, Willow quickly glanced over and shouted, "Gramps!"

Startled, Dubois turned to look at Dell. In that instant, Tara pounced. Her jaws clamped down on his forearm and she whipped her head back and forth. Dubois howled, and the knife fell from his hand as he staggered backward.

BLAM!

Dell and Grace flinched from an ear-splitting gunshot as they watched Willow crouch to the ground. Dubois's body jerked to the side, blood spurting from his neck, Tara still latched to his arm. The force of the bullet and Tara's attack thrust both of them off the granite ledge, onto the gravel bank, sliding toward the cliff's edge.

Willow, on her knees with her hands in the air, let out a shrill cry. "Tara! No!"

Tara released Dubois but continued sliding toward the precipice.

"Oh Jesus, Dell!" Grace screamed, as she grabbed Dell's shoulder.

Dell stood with his hands cupped to his mouth and yelled, "Tara! Come! Come!"

CHAPTER 32
THE CLIFF

Still kneeling on the granite ledge, an exhausted Willow watched wide-eyed as Tara's explosive attack and Tony's lethal shot sent Henry Dubois whirling into the air and crashing onto the steep gravel bank. Dubois did a slow slide down the incline, leaving a bloody trail in the gravel before he disappeared over the cliff. His body thudded like a bag of cement hitting pavement when it slammed onto the rocks below.

Dell and Grace stood only yards away from Willow when she staggered to her feet, frantic and screaming—"Tara!"

A panic-stricken Tara scrambled on the sheer gravel downslope, whining and sending up puffs of dust as she fought to avoid going over the edge.

"Willow, don't!" Dell lunged for Willow and caught her arm. He held her tight, sat her down on the level ledge, and yelled, "Listen! Listen to me! Stay right here. Do NOT move. I'll get Tara."

Tara's legs flailed as she skidded on her belly, headfirst and whimpering, down the crumbling bank until she was just a few feet from the cliff's edge. Her front legs were spread wide, claws sunk into loose gravel and scree. She was desperate to break her forward motion but only succeeded in slowing her rate of descent.

Dell gasped. As he turned away from Willow, he saw Grace throw herself headfirst onto the perilous bank, reaching for Tara. "Don't! Don't!" he shouted, but it was too late. Grace slid on her chest behind the frantic dog and grabbed Tara's tail and a hind leg. She managed to curb Tara's downward momentum, but not halt it. Grace and eighty-pound Tara were now bound together in a slow-motion descent, inching toward certain death.

Willow cried out, "Gramps! Do something! Hurry!"

CHAPTER 32: THE CLIFF

Dell sprang forward and flopped flat to his chest on the hard granite ledge from which Grace had leaped. He stretched out both hands and reached Grace's trouser leg with one hand and her ankle with the other. "Gotcha! Don't move."

This further checked their slippage, but the tug of gravity and combined weight of Tara and Grace dragged Dell forward bit-by-bit until much of his upper body dangled precariously off the granite ledge. Scree rolled down the slope, bounced over the cliff, and pinged on the rocks below. Tara's nose was almost at the cliff's edge, all three of them headed for the abyss.

Willow screamed. She took several unsteady steps toward Dell and dropped down behind him on the ledge. She seized his left foot with two hands but was too weak to yank him back. Dell, Grace, and Tara continued edging downward.

"Help! Don't go, Gramps. Help!" she shrieked.

"Goddamn!" Tony shouted as he ran up, gasping and wheezing. He threw his AR to the ground, jumped onto the slab of exposed granite, and clamped his hand on Willow's shoulder. "You're giving me a heart attack," he said. He leaned over, and clutched Dell's belt with both hands. "I've got him, Miss. Get the hell away from this slope. Now!"

Sobbing, Willow let go of Dell's foot and retreated about seventy feet away from the gravel slope.

Steadying himself on the solid rock ledge, Tony shouted, "I've got you Dell. The guys are right behind me. Almost here. Hang on."

"Damn," Dell said, as he tightened his hold on Grace's ankle and trouser leg.

"Grace!" Tony screamed. "Let go of the damn dog!"

"No way," she said, gritting her teeth.

"Holy Mother of God!" Tony hollered as he hauled Dell a couple of inches back onto the rock ledge. Dell tried to pull Grace up the gravel slope, but he had no leverage. Two inches up, one back down; one inch up, two down.

"My arm's cramped, feels like it's going to rip from the socket," Grace said. "Dell, I'm sorry. I can't hold Tara much longer."

Dell looked over his shoulder to see Schneider running his way. "I have *you*," Dell said to Grace. "Help is almost here."

"There they are!" Schneider cried out. Another agent shouted, "Hang on Tony! We're coming!"

A groaning Tony was bent over on the ledge as he strained to maintain his grip on Dell's belt. "Quick!" he shouted. "Get down here."

Schneider and the four other agents scrambled down from the top of the rise to the ledge. One of them grabbed Tony around the waist and the others linked arms to form a chain, just as they heard a low rumble. The slope began to give way. Cascades of gravel and rocks tumbled down the incline and over the cliff. Dust clouds filled the air. No one could see a thing, everyone coughed and choked. Grace struggled to hold onto Tara, and Dell to Grace. Tara moaned.

Willow yelled, "Hold on! Hold on!"

Little-by-little, grunt-by-grunt, Tony and the five other agents muscled Dell, then Grace, who was groaning in pain, up onto the ledge. Then they hoisted a hyperventilating Tara up the deteriorating slope to the ledge.

Willow, who had watched in horror, limped as fast as she could over to a dazed Tara, grabbed the dog's collar, and led her to safer ground. Dell and Grace embraced as tears trickled down their dust-covered faces. FBI agents guided them off the ledge over to where Tara was licking Willow's cheek. After guzzling an entire liter canteen of water, Willow stood and then stumbled over to Dell, almost knocking him off his feet. They wrapped their arms around one another.

"Love you," Willow said. "Somehow, I just knew you'd come."

"Love you, too," Dell said, kissing her cheek.

Grace and Willow had never met, yet they embraced like old friends.

"Thank God," a teary-eyed Dell heard Grace say. Tara wagged her tail and wiggled as she squeezed her nose between the two women. After everyone caught their breath, Schneider, Scaperelli, and Dell climbed onto a nearby stable rock formation where they had a clear view of Dubois, lying more than a hundred feet below.

"Jeez," Schneider said, "Looks as if a barrel of cherry Jello crashed onto that rock."

Dubois was splayed, face down, across a massive, blood-splattered boulder, arms and legs spread wide, blood dribbling from his neck, mouth, and ears.

"Case closed," Tony said.

CHAPTER 32: THE CLIFF

The three men walked back to join the others, all of whom had moved more than a hundred feet away from the cliff. Tony said, "Whatever the ravens, crows, and other critters don't eat, the state police can scrape up tomorrow."

Willow ran over to Dell. "Train?" she asked anxiously, rubbing her wrist. "Is he . . ."

"He's alive. State police told us he's in critical condition. He's at the Millinocket hospital. We'll take you there."

"Omigod!" She covered her face with her hands and sobbed. Dell and Grace wrapped their arms around her.

Tony was on the phone, standing with the other agents a few yards away from Dell, Grace, and Willow. Dell wiped tears from Willow's face as he hugged her. When a bone-tired Willow sat down on the ground, Tara did too. Tara laid on her back in Willow's lap with her German shepherd smile, all four legs in the air, tongue hanging out. Willow folded her arms around Tara and said, "I *really* missed you, sweet girl."

Winking at Grace, Dell said, "Diamonds are *not* a girl's best friend."

"Jealous?" she asked, nudging him.

"I might be if I didn't love you so much."

Grace smiled, bit her lower lip, and whispered in Dell's ear, "What do you think? Should I hug Tony?"

Raising an eyebrow, Dell said, "Good luck."

Dell trailed behind as Grace ambled over to Tony and the other agents. Tony's back was to her as he talked on the phone with a state trooper at Angel's.

"Good," Tony said, scratching his head. "Depending on how the girl does, we should arrive at the camp before dark. I want them all flown out right away." Tony nodded and said "okay" as he slipped the phone into his pocket.

Dell glanced at Willow, grinned, then focused on Grace as she drew near to Tony, her head swinging from side to side with every step. She giggled and gently tapped Tony's shoulder. He stiffened and turned around. She placed her hand on her heart and gave him her sweetest smile as tears welled up in her green eyes.

"Thank you, *paisan*."

Tony's ears turned ruby red, and he took a step back, his eyes pleading for help as he glanced over at Schneider and the others, all of whom were laughing. Grace threw her arms around him, gave him a squeeze, and let go.

"Thank you. You saved us."

Blushing, Tony winced and half-smiled at the same time. He gave Grace a light pat on her arm. This triggered boisterous guffaws from the agents who touched arms and pretended to dry tears from their eyes.

"Okay, okay. Enough of this bullshit," Tony said. "Miss Monroe needs our help getting back to Antler's. Let's get this show on the road!"

CHAPTER 33
DEARLY BELOVED

A setting sun cast a shimmering orange glow on Lower Jo-Mary Lake and outlined Mt. Katahdin to the north as two floatplanes flew east and, twenty minutes after having left Antler's, landed on a nearby lake. From the lakeside dock, a state police van took Willow, Grace, Dell, and Tara to the hospital in Millinocket where Train was being treated.

The admitting physician ordered Willow put on an IV for hydration, but Willow insisted the IV be attached to a wheelchair so she and Grace could go directly to Train's room. While a nurse attended to Willow, Dell found a dog-loving security guard to watch Tara before calling Brad Hornbeck in Harper's Ferry.

"Good to hear your voice, old buddy," Brad said. "So glad you are all safe. FBI headquarters called minutes ago with the good news."

As Dell got off the phone he heard "Code Blue! Code Blue!" on the hospital's intercom. He asked a woman at the front office where he could find Train's room. "Room 212," she said. He walked briskly in that direction.

Grace was pushing Willow's wheelchair down the hall toward Train's room when they heard the code blue emergency call. Two nurses and a doctor rushed by.

"Oh no!" Willow gasped.

The medical team swerved in front of them and entered a room, number 210. Willow let out a huge breath as Grace wheeled her into the next room, 212.

Train's eyes were open, but he was pallid, motionless, and tubes connected him to a beeping monitor. When he saw Willow, he managed a faint smile as his eyes welled up with tears. Weeping, she leaped from her wheelchair, IV attached, leaned over Train's bed, hugged him, and kissed him on the cheek. Dell entered the room and took Grace's hand. When Willow sat back down in the wheelchair, Dell put his arm around her shoulders.

A nurse came in with a furrowed brow. "He's supposed to have only one guest at a time," she said in a sharp voice.

Feigning a pained look, Dell said softly, "We're his friends. I apologize."

"Well, I guess you can stay for a few minutes—no longer."

"What's his prognosis?" Grace asked, laying her hand on Willow's arm.

The nurse smiled as she checked the readings on Train's monitor. "He's finally stable and, as you can see, conscious. He's lost a lot of blood and is still quite weak, but," she winked at Train and touched his hand, "we're confident he'll pull through."

"Whoopy!" shouted a smiling Willow. She stood to hold him again, dampening his pillowcase with her tears.

Dell and Grace spent three days in Millinocket while Willow comforted Train and got a thorough medical checkup. When Willow's IV was removed the next morning, they found her in Train's room, reading to him. Willow was soon throwing a tennis ball to Tara and joining them for dinner. They arranged for Willow to stay at the nearby Down East Bed & Breakfast to be close to Train. On their second day in Millinocket, Dell withdrew cash from an ATM and handed it to Willow.

"Take the money, damn it."

He gave the owner of the bed and breakfast his credit card information and authorized him to charge "whatever Ms. Monroe wants." Finally, he and Grace discussed plans with Willow for her, and hopefully Train, to come to Washington when he was well enough to travel.

Gelpky's Taxi Service drove Dell and Grace from Millinocket to Monson. Tara was wedged between them in the backseat, her front paws on Grace's lap, tail on Dell's. In Monson, they lingered at Shaw's to say thank you and goodbye to Keith, then piled into the Jeep, and headed back home to D.C.

* * *

The trees had turned a waxy red and gold in northwest Washing-

CHAPTER 33: DEARLY BELOVED

ton and late October leaves had begun to float to the ground. Rose colored late-afternoon light filtered through St. Columba's stained-glass windows as Willow, Grace's maid-of-honor, walked down the aisle at the appointed time in hiking boots and a simple peach-colored gown. She held a hiking stick and kept Tara, who sported a white A.T. bandanna around her neck, close to her side.

Along with friends, family, and professional colleagues, many A.T. and law enforcement people were in attendance, including Train, who was still mastering his crutches. Brad Hornbeck, one of Dell's two best men, was there with Cherie Nardone. The substantial FBI contingent was led by Dell's other best man, Tony Scaperelli. Sergeant Clayton Ward of the Pennsylvania state police and Maine state trooper Jim Conklin wore spiffy dress uniforms. Dell was especially touched to see Jamie Doyle, whom Grace had never met, clutching his shillelagh and wearing a traditional Saffron Kilt with shamrocks. And the bride and groom were both delighted that Keith Shaw had made the long trip down from Maine and, to their surprise, he even wore a clean collared shirt.

Rev. Joe Wingate, who'd been such a comfort to Dell after Patricia's death, presided as Celebrant. Dell had introduced Grace to him when the three met in early September to discuss an autumn wedding. It was agreed that, after everyone was seated and immediately before the formal ceremony, Joe would deliver a short homily. The bride and groom were to sit in the front pews and come up to the altar after he had spoken.

At 4:30 p.m. the organist struck up Jeremiah Clarke's "Prince of Denmark's March" as Dell strode down the aisle in his black tuxedo with his daughters, one on each arm, and sat with them in the left front pew. The rest of the wedding party, led by Willow and Tara, followed. Finally, the bride, wearing a floor-length, ivory silk gown and emerald necklace came escorted by both Tony Scaperelli, who looked every bit like a taller version of a tuxedoed Dean Martin, and Brad Hornbeck, who gave Cherie a naughty wink as he walked by. The three glided slowly down the aisle. Grace sat in the right front pew next to Willow and Tara.

In white vestments, Rev. Wingate stood at the altar only slightly elevated above the wedding party and some two hundred guests. Smiling broadly, Joe looked at Grace, then Dell. Without notes, he began to speak.

"I once asked Dell, 'Do you hike the Appalachian Trail because you love it?' He answered, 'Yes, but also *to* love it.'"

Dell nodded and looked across the aisle at Grace, who wiped away a tear with the back of her hand. Willow's arm was around Tara, whose tail went whop, whop on the stone floor.

"Nature, like the love between Grace and Dell, demands reciprocity—a Golden Rule, if you will, to do unto others as you would have them do unto you. The 'others,' of course, are our brothers and sisters, *and* the pristine waters, verdant land, and clean air that sustain us all. Love and respect nature, and mother nature will love and respect us. Love engenders love."

Cherie Nardone cast a furtive glance at Brad.

"For Grace and Dell, the A.T. is a tree-and-mountain-and-creature-filled world. A Creator-filled world."

Head bowed, Jamie Doyle looked down at his rosary beads.

"The trail, as many of you know, was also a trial, a test for Grace and Dell, and for several others who are with us today. It was a testing that fused them together. And let's not forget about one of the Creator's very special creatures—Tara."

Tara's ears perked up. Spontaneous, deafening applause broke out, led by Jamie, Keith Shaw, and the FBI agents, all of whom stood as they clapped, then sat back down.

"Nature is humanity's school, church, park, garden, and concert hall. It is our future—the faint breath of eternity. Ralph Waldo Emerson wrote with certainty that 'Nature' is the 'web of God.' The natural world, and the trail that passes through and intermingles with it, offers countless indications of our divinity, our redemption."

Joe lowered his head. Dell thought to himself, *Patricia is grinning.* Joe looked up. He smiled, fixed his eyes on the bride and groom, and recited a single line from the Thirtieth Psalm—"You have turned for me my mourning into dancing." Then he nodded at Dell and Grace.

They stood and stepped to the altar. Tara wiggled between them and jumped onto the altar. Grace turned and waved for Willow to join them. All four stood together.

"Dearly beloved . . ."

END

ABOUT THE AUTHOR

DUNCAN L. CLARKE is professor emeritus of political science and international relations with a legal background who has published award-winning nonfiction books and dozens of articles. His debut novel, *A Little Rebellion Is a Good Thing* (Brandylane, 2020), told of a student uprising at a public women's college. He has twice hiked the entire 2,200-mile-long Appalachian Trail from Georgia to Maine with his German shepherd. He is a member of the Appalachian Trail Conservancy, Pacific Crest Trail Association, and California's Central Coast Writers.